Praise for **What's Mine**

"Bette Adriaanse is my favorite Dutch writer. No one writes like she does. Her voice— frank, whimsical, philosophical, funny, gorgeously tactless— points a lens at the world that sharpens everything, then she plays with the focus, then resharpens it so the world never looks quite the same. *What's Mine* is a timeless book that deserves a wide readership."
—**Caoilinn Hughes, author of *Orchid & the Wasp*, winner of the Collyer Bristow Prize, the Royal Society of Literature's Encore Award 2021 and the O. Henry award**

"Bette's inimitable voice is always a treat to escape into. I cannot wait for this dark, absurdist tale to go out into the world."
—**Jing-Jing Lee, author of *How We Disappeared*, selected for the British Royal Big Jubilee Read**

"Bette Adriaanse is becoming a major literary novelist in the best European tradition. She has the down-and-out life experiences of the early Orwell, the desperate humor of Flann O'Brien, the prose immediacy of Beckett, and the avalanche of bureaucracy of Kafka. *What's Mine* is a stellar achievement of depicting the absurdist brutality of contemporary urban capitalism where nothing but narcissism and arbitrary outcomes rule."
—**Alan N Shapiro, science fiction theorist**

AN UNNAMED PRESS BOOK

Copyright © 2023 by Bette Adriaanse

Published in North America by the Unnamed Press.

www.unnamedpress.com

Unnamed Press, and the colophon, are registered trademarks of Unnamed Media LLC.

Paperback Original ISBN: 978-1-951213-87-9
EBook ISBN: 978-1-951213-88-6
LCCN: 2023939771

Cover design and typeset by Jaya Nicely

Manufactured in the United States of America

Distributed by Publishers Group West

First Edition

What's Mine

a novel

Bette Adriaanse

The Unnamed Press
Los Angeles, CA

What's Mine

19 August
The Student Hotel, Amsterdam

Today I've seen my street for the first time. It's a long, broad lane in one of the most expensive neighbourhoods in Amsterdam, with stone steps leading up to monumental oak front doors. The lane is framed by tall poplars. There is a small park between the bike lane and the road with wooden benches, just as my mother described in her letter.

I sat down on a bench in front of number 354, and for hours I looked up to the apartment on the second floor—'my house', as I call it in my mind.

The sun went down and lights switched on inside. And after a while I saw him appear in the window, the man who lives there now. He was lifting dumbbells in front of a mirror. There was a colour-changing lamp shining on him, creating a tacky disco effect on his skin and on the leaves of the poplar tree in front of the house.

At ten o'clock in the evening he left the house dressed in white clothes. He came down the stone steps looking about him in a nervous way. I watched him until he turned the corner: he walked fast and close to the walls.

I suspect this man is younger than me, in his early thirties.

Does he know me? Does he know about the history of the apartment? About my father?

I didn't dare approach him yet. All the emotions that surfaced when I saw the apartment caused me to feel too unstable to take action. I did speak with the neighbour who lives directly below him, on the first floor. She came out of her apartment and asked me in that typical direct Dutch way if I planned to sleep on that park bench and whether I knew I could be fined for it. When I introduced myself, explained my reasons for being there, explained the suitcase and the plastic bags, she became a lot more friendly. She said, 'Come back on Saturday, he will be there'.

The Possessions of Luis Sol

It was Saturday. The fridge Luis had ordered was delivered onto the sidewalk in front of his apartment on Rooseveltlaan. It was a warm and humid day, and the back of Luis's neck was turning red. The fridge was in a cardboard box so big it could have been a house for a child, if you cut out a door and window. But Luis did not have a child. He had a one-bedroom apartment on Rooseveltlaan in Amsterdam, a job as a dishwasher at the Bagel Shop on Leidsestraat, a best friend, and a cleaning lady who came by once a week.

Luis's hands slid over the box that held his newest possession. It was a stainless steel fridge with a dark glass door that turned transparent when you knocked on it. Luis had seen the television commercial for the fridge many times: tall green trees were reflected in the dark glass of the fridge, which was standing in a clearing in the woods. A woman in a long dress appeared, the red of her lips contrasting dramatically with the green of the leaves. As she knocked on the fridge door, it became transparent, revealing a small box with a ring in it, lying in the middle of the illuminated fridge shelf. Next to it, a heart-shaped red cake. The woman then looked over her shoulder at the camera—at Luis—and smiled.

Luis put his hands around the slippery box and tried to lift it. Even though he was strong—he could bench-press over three hundred pounds—the box moved only a few inches from the ground before it slid out of his grip. Luis walked around the box.

From the passing tram, people were looking at him and the enormous box.

Luis flexed his biceps. Ever since he moved to Amsterdam, he had worked on what his best friend, Hadi, called "city muscle."

"It's pointless muscle, only for appearances," Hadi said as Luis worked the abductor machine at King's Gym. "But city muscles signify that you are in control of you."

The farm muscles Luis had before he came to Amsterdam, created by carrying hay bales, pushing wheelbarrows, and mucking out stables—those muscles were still there too.

His broad freckled back, his sturdy forearms: that was the old Luis.

The six-pack, the biceps, the spray tan: that was the new Luis.

Often Luis felt like he lived in the space between these two versions of him, as if he floated in a quiet sea between two countries, and he could reach neither one.

Luis shook off these thoughts. He brought his attention back to the box. Normally Hadi helped him with these kinds of things, but he was on Crete with his new girlfriend. He could call Bedas, his boss at the Bagel Shop, but Bedas preferred to keep business and personal separate. That's what he said when Luis went to his house last Christmas to surprise him with the gift of a spa massager foot bath. The only other option was Marina, his cleaner, but her hands were too small.

Luis positioned himself in front of the box, bent his knees, and tried to tip it onto his back. That's how he used to carry the hay bales into Raat's barn back in his hometown of Stompetoren. But it did not work, the box was too slippery. Finally Luis stripped the cardboard from the fridge and put his arms around the appliance. Like a toddler holding his bigger brother for a funny family photo, Luis held on to the fridge and slowly walked it to the stone steps leading up to the front door of number 354.

At the door, Luis looked at the trembling muscles of his forearms and the red lines on his palms where the edges of the heavy fridge had dug into his skin.

"Everything in nature is being pulled down," his mother always said, "and I don't have the energy to resist it."

Gravity was one of his mother's biggest enemies. Luis had never met anyone else who experienced gravity so intensely. Sometimes she stayed in bed for days, complaining about gravity pulling her toward the floor. She was never under a blanket, because a blanket felt like "a house" on top of her. Her body, heavy and short, was covered only by a too-small silk nightgown, since the weight of clothes on her skin was unbearable for her too.

Luis tried to push his mother out of his head as he maneuvered the fridge into the hallway. It was only in these kinds of moments, when he was using all his energy for something, that his mother managed to slip out of the safe in his head and starting walking around his thoughts again.

"You're not going to leave that out on the street, are you?" Luis's downstairs neighbor, Estelle, said, coming out of her apartment. "The street looks like a garbage dump. I have people coming over." She pointed a manicured finger, with a square salmon-colored fingernail, at the cardboard that was lying on the sidewalk at the bottom of the steps.

"No, no," Luis said, trying to wipe the sweat off his forehead with his shoulder. "I will . . . I was . . . A new fridge . . ." His cheeks felt warm. For as long as he could remember, Luis blushed when he talked to people. When he was younger, his face would only light up for a couple of minutes, but now that he was thirty-one, he got lasting red spots on his face that looked like maps of a red world.

"Luis is not a talker," Hadi would tell people when he introduced Luis. "He is a visual person." And it was true. If words were tools to express your feelings, Luis thought they were like gigantic hammers to tick the tiniest nails into the wall. The way Luis came to see it was as follows: In a person's mind, every word is connected to other words. And when someone said a certain word, all these other words would light up. For example, if you said "house," that word could be connected to the word "family" or "enclosed" in the other person's mind, which could be linked to another word like "problems" or "secret." So, according to Luis, the words you said told thousands of extra stories in the minds of the people you were talking to, and you had no control over them.

"This is not some disadvantaged neighborhood where you can just dump your trash on the sidewalk and nobody is bothered by it," Estelle said, putting her hands on her hips.

Luis shook his head. Ever since their first meeting eight years ago—when Estelle called the police when she saw him appear in their shared hallway late at night, only to hang up when she saw him put his key in the lock—she talked about "disadvantaged neighborhoods" when she talked to him. There was something about him that reminded her of disadvantaged neighborhoods, and no matter how expensive his clothes got—he was now wearing an Armani sweater and Versace jeans—it did not change. Hadi said it was because she was what he called a "flat white supremacist." Someone who drank overpriced flat white coffees and felt superior to everyone who did not look and talk like her and her friends.

Luis thought it was because she still hadn't really gotten to know him yet.

"You know, you could get a fine for dumping trash in a public space," Estelle said. "Article Three: Nuisance in the Public Space. It's simply the law in this country."

Luis positioned the fridge in his hallway and started gathering the cardboard, with Estelle looking on from behind her curtain. Estelle was a lawyer for a bank. Every weekday she drove her racing-green Mini to the office district in the South of Amsterdam, her fingers with the salmon-colored nail polish clenching the snakeskin steering wheel. Estelle reminded Luis of his iPhone. Everything about her was smooth, sleek, and shiny.

Luis waved at Estelle when he had finished bringing the cardboard inside. She did not wave back. The red spots were burning on his neck. One day, Luis would invite her up for coffee. If she saw his apartment, he thought, she could see who he really was: someone with taste, someone who had nothing to do with disadvantaged neighborhoods, someone who was not simplistic (he'd heard her call him "simplistic" once, when she was on the phone with a friend in her garden). But he had not found the right moment yet to invite her. She brushed past him when he came across her in the supermarket, and when they met in the hallway, he often just stammered hello and turned red.

It was not like Luis was scared of girls. He'd had girlfriends, and he regularly made out with girls who worked with him at the Bagel Shop. Sometimes they came into the kitchen at the end of Luis's shift on Saturday morning, a white wine smell on their breath, and cornered him. They said they liked his strong arms around their waist, the way he could lift them up and hold them against the wall. For a boyfriend they "looked for another type."

Luis had watched their boyfriends come to the Bagel Shop, these "other types." Sometimes a finance guy in a suit, sometimes a poet in a hat. They were never introduced to Luis. But when those boyfriends cheated on them, the girls did remember Luis. They said, "My friend Luis will mess you up if he hears what you did to me." But Luis did not want to mess anybody up. Despite his intimidating physique, he was not a fighter. He hated conflict and violence, and he was afraid of losing his temper. His tactic in life was to give people what they wanted, so they'd go away.

The sun was setting when Luis finally hoisted the fridge over the threshold of his apartment on the second floor. Putting a piece of cardboard under the appliance, he carefully dragged it over the beige deep-pile carpet that took on different hues as his ambient lighting changed colors. The apartment had only two rooms: a large bedroom that also served as a fitness room, and a living room that also served as the kitchen. In the living room he had introduced a stainless steel theme, combined with glass. All his appliances were stainless steel, and his kitchen table had steel legs with a glass tabletop. His OLED television was on a movable stainless steel cart that a friend of Hadi's had welded for him. The design of the legs was based on the painting *Composition No. IV with Red, Blue and Yellow*, by Mondriaan, of which a print was hanging on the wall.

When Luis moved to Amsterdam, almost eight years ago, he visited a museum every day for the first month. The Rijksmuseum was one of his favorite places. He loved walking through the chambers with the high ceilings; he loved how people started whispering as they entered those spaces and looked up at paintings of aristocrats wearing big white collars. The faces of these aristocrats were often round with bright red cheeks, like Luis's. But their faces took up only a tiny part of the painting. They posed in robes, with hats and chains, with tables full of sea animals, bowls, clocks, mirrors, and skulls. The objects that surrounded them were as much a part of their portrait as their faces. Luis often thought of these aristocrats when he woke up and saw himself in the mirrored doors of the wardrobe next to his bed. The white Gucci sweater draped over the chair, the belt with the Swarovski eagle Hadi had given him for his birthday on top of it, the white leather of his waterbed, the wake-up light, his iPhone, his Egyptian cotton sheets—all these things, Luis noticed, were part of his portrait. The too-close-together dark eyes he'd inherited from his father, the red cheeks his mother had given him—they were only a tiny part of the entire portrait of Luis Sol.

Luis positioned the fridge next to the marble kitchen counter and plugged it in. He had looked forward to the moment when he could knock on the dark glass door and it turned transparent. Luis knocked on the door. The door became transparent. The inside of the fridge became illuminated. The user manual was lying on one of the glass shelves. The blue UV light, which eliminated 99.99 percent of bacteria, shone on the paper. Slowly, the door turned dark again. Luis's reflection looked back at him, the eyes too close together.

For a moment Luis thought of the red-lipped smiling woman in the commercial. Of course he hadn't expected the woman to come with the purchase of the fridge. Or a ring, or a heart-shaped cake. In the bottom drawer of the fridge he found the extra items that were in fact promised with the purchase of the fridge. A double-walled ice bucket. A polished steel wine stopper. Ice tongs. Luis had read about these items when he ordered the fridge. The descriptions of these items felt like a portal to another world, with sentences like "for sensational summer parties," "special wines for special ladies," and "flavors never experienced before." He took the ice bucket from the drawer. It was light and small in his hands.

Luis thought of the woman in the commercial who, in her wide smile kind of way, looked familiar. She looked like the man in the commercial for his Naturell mineral water, who looked like the people on the poster for his King's Gym fitness subscription. These people were all different in their shapes and colors, but in their way of touching, their way of laughing, their way of agreeing with each other, they seemed the same. These were people who never cleaned their father's puke from the floor after Christmas Eve, people who didn't yell at their mother, people who carried no secrets.

Luis drank the mineral water, he went to the fitness center, he bought the fridge. Suddenly he wondered when he, Luis Sol, would go through the portal. When would this clean world of pleasant people open for him? In his mind Luis saw a succession of images: a father's hand slightly squeezing a son's shoulder, a group of friends singing in an open-top sports car, a baby giggling too early in the morning at tired parents who can't help but smile, a wrinkled hand sitting on top of a younger one.

At that moment Luis's doorbell rang. Startled, he bent his head.

The doorbell rang again.

Luis looked up at the clock. It was ten in the evening.

He did not expect anyone. Hadi was in Greece.

The doorbell rang again.

A long time ago, in his childhood home in Stompetoren, his father's friends would sometimes walk into the yard unannounced, invariably carrying a plastic bag filled with cans of beer. They came up behind him when he was sweeping or cleaning the gutter and yelled, "Your dad 'ere?" to his back. Without waiting for a reply, they walked to where they knew his father was: in the shed, supposedly working on carving a wooden chess set but in reality drinking, his legs getting increasingly red from sitting too close to the gas heater. His mother hated these visitors. She hated all visitors. While the neighbors always kept their front doors open, so everyone and their dogs could walk in and out, she kept the front door locked. "Never open the door," she used to say. "Let them write letters."

In the distance, Luis's doorbell rang again, and then another doorbell, Estelle's. Luis heard a door open, Estelle's voice, and then another, deeper voice.

A knock on Luis's door.

"Luis?" sounded from the bottom of his stairs. That was Estelle's voice. She knocked on his door again. "Can you open the door?"

She knocked again, banging on the door this time.

"I know he's home," he heard her say. She knocked again. "Luis?"

Luis stood immobile at the top of the staircase.

"I hope he's all right," he heard a male voice say. "Could there be anything wrong?"

Luis shook his head. Of course he was all right. He was healthy; he could bench-press over three hundred pounds. He had an apartment, a job, a best friend, a cleaner, a new fridge. What would be wrong with him?

The Arrival of William Rose

In the hallway Luis shared with his downstairs neighbor, Estelle, stood a tall man in a long green checkered coat, a scarf tucked into his collar. Rainwater was dripping from his hat onto his shoulders. Estelle stood next to him. The front door was still open, and the streetlamps shone yellow on the wet pavement of Rooseveltlaan.

"How do you do?" the man said, extending his hand.

"I am doing fine," Luis said. He hesitated, then held the man's thin, bony fingers between his for a moment.

"Splendid," the man said. He had a British accent as he spoke Dutch, and his voice was soft, not much more than a whisper. His kept his head low, as if he did not want to be noticed, but Luis thought that people who did not want to be noticed did not ring people's doorbells at night, they did not wear hats or say "splendid."

"My name is William Rose," the man asked. "Pleased to meet you, Mr. . . . ?"

"Luis Sol," Luis said.

"Luis Sol," the man echoed. "Le Roi Soleil. The Sun King."

"What?" Luis said.

"He doesn't understand," Estelle said to the man.

"Louis Quatorze? I am assuming your mother chose your name as a play on the famous French Sun King?"

"My mother did not play," Luis said. He glanced at Estelle. She was wearing a fleece onesie with a bunny print instead of her normal pencil skirt and blazer. Her hair was down and she wore no makeup. He had never seen her without makeup. Her face was pink and shiny, and her eyes seemed to have no eyelashes anymore. It reminded him of when baby rats were born in Raat's shed, back home in Stompetoren, bright pink and unprotected; they would squirm together into a ball. He could feel his neck getting warm, the red spots climbing up from under the collar of his shirt.

"I know it's late," the man said with a smile, "and I do apologize for disturbing you at this hour. The fact is my father and my mother used to live in your apartment, when my mother was pregnant with me. I think I was born here, and I believe I lived here several years as a child." He looked at Luis as if he'd just delivered fantastic news. "And it would mean a lot to me if I could have a look around."

"Oh," Luis said. The word "oh" hung between them for a moment. Luis looked at this man called William Rose. There were three plastic bags filled with folders and papers sitting at his feet. Behind him stood a big suitcase. Water trickled from his coat onto the carpet in the hallway.

Luis rubbed the back of his neck.

"He came all the way from England to see the apartment," Estelle said.

"Oh," Luis said again. He looked at Estelle. She had put a hand on the man's sleeve, apparently unbothered by the wet fabric. She had never touched Luis in the eight years that they'd known each other; she had always stayed at least an arm's length away from him.

"My mother took me to the UK in 1973, when I was three years old," the man said. "She told me I was born in Amsterdam, but she refused to talk about her life then, who my father was. She did not even want to tell me his name. My whole life I have been looking for my origin, my roots. I learned Dutch as a child, just from reading books. I was obsessed with lineages, heritage. It may even be the reason why my academic work is centered on uncovering origins."

"William's a professor at Oxford University," Estelle said.

"Assistant professor," the man clarified with a nod.

"In entomology," Estelle said.

"Etymology," the man said. "Entomology is the study of insects. Etymology is the study of the origin of words. They do bug me sometimes." He laughed.

Estelle laughed too.

Luis did not laugh.

"Last year," the man continued, "my mother died unexpectedly. A car accident. In her estate there was a box, and among the scarves and incense and other hippie nonsense that she collected, I found a letter my mother had written to her sister when she was pregnant with me in 1970. The letter was never sent. It was written on paper with a letterhead from the Hond Foundation in Amsterdam. This address was on the letterhead: Rooseveltlaan 354, second floor."

As he was talking, the man looked past Luis, at the staircase leading up to the apartment on the second floor.

Instinctively, Luis took a step to the side to block his view.

"In the letter my mother described in detail her lover, a Dutch-man named Edward. And when I read that name, it was like putting my finger in the socket. That was my father's name! I suddenly remembered my mother saying it. Shouting it, even! *'Ed-ward! Ed-ward!'* Since then, memories have been catapulting themselves from the depths of my brain to the conscious surface." He looked up toward Luis's apartment. "Fascinating!" he exclaimed. "You should know, I've always had this recurring nightmare in which I am climbing up a long, dark, narrow staircase just like this one. Now I realize this must have been an actual memory. My ex-girlfriend Paulina was a psychiatrist, and she was certain it was Freudian symbolism! The staircase, we all know what that stands for."

"Of course," Estelle agreed, nodding.

Luis looked over his shoulder at his staircase. He had put beige carpet on the steps and painted the walls with three layers of Snow-White Ultra Morning Top Coat.

"Are you sure this is the right apartment?" Luis asked. He gestured toward the street, to illustrate how many similar apart-ments there were on this block, how easily you could mistake one for another.

"You may see all the documentation." The man bent down and started rummaging through the plastic bags with folders. "I have with me the letter from my mother, you will see it says 'Hond Foundation' and has this address, number 354, second floor. My mother also mentions various details about the street in this letter, such as the poplars, the oak front door." The man tried to hand Luis a bundle of yellowed documents.

Luis raised his hand to reject it. "I'm a visual person," he explained.

The man nodded. "Your neighbor told me you moved in eight years ago," he said. "Do you know who lived here before you?"

"It was my mother's place," Luis said. His eyes shot to Estelle. "But she wasn't here very much."

"One of the memories that came back to me is of wooden floorboards," the man said. "Are there wooden floorboards in the apartment?"

"I have put beige deep-pile carpet down in every room," Luis said.

"I am very interested in seeing what it looks like now," William said. "I would love to have a look inside."

"Well, it's painted white," Luis said. He felt the red spots race up to his cheeks, and he rubbed his hands over his face as he added: "And all my furniture is in there. It's mostly design . . . design furniture . . . placed against the walls . . . I believe in placing furniture against the walls . . . instead of . . . you know . . . in the middle of the room."

"This man has been ringing your doorbell for ten minutes," Estelle said. "He came all the way from England for this. All his life he has searched for his father. When he found the letter, he packed everything, leaving behind his students and his teaching, and rushed to Amsterdam. He is a professor."

"Of course everyone does what they want with their furniture," Luis continued, placing his body between the man and his corridor. "But to me, a bed standing in the middle of a room, that isn't right . . . Against the wall is more . . . it is just . . . I don't know."

"And I told him that of course he would be welcome," Estelle said. "I said, 'Luis will understand you deserve to see the apartment.'"

"I'd be forever grateful," the man said. "Tomorrow I have to fly back to the UK and resume my lectures, so this is my only chance." He leaned forward a little, his upper body already crossing the threshold, the wooden line that formed the border between the dusty red hallway Luis shared with Estelle and his own spotless white space.

There was a silence, too long a silence perhaps. Cars drove by along the road. The light in Mrs. Barneveld's living room across the street switched on.

"Luis," Estelle said in a sharp voice, "it's just a look around."

"I . . ." Luis said. He did not want this man in his house with his peering and his wet clothes dripping rainwater on his carpet and his story; he did not want this man's fingerprints on his doorknobs, his memories smeared on the walls, his breath hanging in the rooms. But he could not think of a polite reason for a rejection. For a moment he thought of saying nothing and just closing the door, going back upstairs, and putting his food in the right temperature compartments. Yes, closing the door was an option. And there was the option of saying no, just no. He imagined he did it, saying no, but there was a block somewhere inside of him, and the word was not coming out. Later on he would think of this moment often, and even in his memory he kept saying yes to them.

"Yes," he said. "Just a look around."

And so it happened that the man who called himself William Rose stepped over Luis's threshold, pulling his bags and suitcase up the stairs behind him, knocking chips out of Luis's white paint.

The Philanthropist

The apartment still looks the same as it did when I was here that last time, in 1986. More than twelve years ago now. My key still works. The red curtains were still there. The bed was still the same and even his sheets were left on it. The sweet smell was still hanging in the room. Only the antiques and the artwork were gone.

I spent all of last night cleaning. I have scrubbed the floors with bleach, thrown out all his possessions, cut the mattress up into pieces with a kitchen knife. I put the sheets in a bucket and poured bleach on them. I wanted to burn them, but there is no place where I can make a fire, so I put them in a garbage bag and gave it to the garbagemen when they arrived very early in the street. Then I kicked the bed frame until it broke, slamming the broken parts into smaller parts, until one of the screws scratched my arm. Blood dripped from my arm onto the floorboards, like it did back then. And I remembered his face. I remembered the sound of his voice, the feeling of the fabric, the hole in the curtain and the light that shone through it. I remembered the garden shears, the way the metal shone in the light.

The memories are coming back, and this time I am letting them come back.

I will write down everything from the beginning. I will write it like a story: how it happened, what I did, what I thought, how I felt. All the promises made and all the lies that were told. Not so I can go down in history as a good person—ever since I stole a cigarette from my dad's coat pocket at eleven years old I knew I would be more like a medium to bad kind of person—it's because I feel the memories that I suppressed climbing through other parts of my body, trying to find a way out. They are nestling into corners of my body, in my armpits, my hips, my knees.

I think that if you keep bad memories in your head for too long and never look at them, they come to life. Like a jug of milk going off in the fridge, they start changing and growing, polluting everything.

The Tour

"To the right," Luis said, "is the living room." He squeezed past his visitor into the room. "It also serves as the kitchen."

The man named William Rose walked into Luis's living room and put his wet plastic bags on his glass table. He took off his hat and put it on top of the bags. Rainwater dripped from his coat onto the carpet.

"It's smaller than I expected," William said.

"Small, but good-sized," Luis said. "Fifty-four square meters."

As Luis followed William's gaze around the room, pride rose in his chest. It was nice that someone—a professor—saw how the shapes and colors in the room communicated with each other. He wondered if William noticed how the white of the sofa connected to the white of the marble kitchen counter, while its rounded edges talked to the rounded edges of the glass table, which in turn echoed the glass door of the fridge.

The shape of the new fridge standing in the corner of the room was already starting to feel familiar to Luis, like the silhouette of a broad family member who always stands by the window, looking out over the gardens.

"I have tried to find shapes that go well together," Luis told William. "The space between the shapes needs to stay calm."

"Interior design is an art," William said. "Not everyone can do it."

"Thank you," Luis said. He pushed his flat-screen television on the movable cart away from the sofa. The television was very big, and it always blocked a part of the room. It was an OLED TV that had cost him 3,200 euro. He watched nature documentaries on it with Marina, at the end of her cleaning shift.

As Luis moved it, he noticed his reflection in the dark glass of the television. He turned back around to William, but his guest was no longer standing there. He was kneeling on the floor, his forehead pressed into the carpet.

Is he praying? Luis wondered. Or is he feeling the carpet? Is he ill? Luis had special shampoo to clean the carpet if something happened, but he never had to use it before.

"The pile height of the carpet is three centimeters," Luis said. "It's a polyester-wool blend."

William did not reply. He did not move either.

Luis stared at the back of the head of the man who was visiting his apartment. His greasy hairs were sticking to his scalp; the sharp angles of his shoulder blades were visible under the fabric of his coat. There was a smell coming from him, a strange, sweet smell. It reminded Luis of the smell the apartment had when he first moved in.

Luis opened the kitchen window. The sounds of Saturday night in Amsterdam streamed into the room: distant teenagers yelling, the squealing brakes of a tram, voices coming from the park below, some music from a café.

How long does a visit like this last? Luis wondered. He looked at the clock. "Not long until the last train," he said.

William looked up at Luis. "Excuse me, did you say 'terrain'?"

"What?"

"I thought you said the word 'terrain,'" William said. "Coincidentally, I was just thinking about the word 'terrain,' in the original sense. From *terrain*, in French, finding its roots in the Latin *terranum*."

He looked at Luis as if Luis should reply to this, as if there was anything Luis could say in reply to this.

"A piece of land, ground, a bounded area, territory," William continued. "A geographical location. Do you believe humans can have a physical connection with a geographical location, Luis?"

"Well, who knows, really," Luis said. He always said "well, who knows, really" if he didn't know what someone was going on about. He brushed the fibers of his carpet back into the right direction.

William pulled himself up by the edge of the kitchen counter and brushed off his knees, as if Luis's carpet could have tainted him instead of the other way around.

"Seeing you in this apartment, the word 'territory' arises in my mind," he said. "An area occupied by a single animal, a mating pair, or a group, vigorously defended against intruding conspecifics—organisms of the same species. You being the single animal in this analogy, of course."

William laughed.

Luis noticed William did not look happy when he laughed. It is as if something in him is reversed, Luis thought, like the poles of the Earth will do one day. He had seen that in a documentary he had watched with Marina. It was as if happy and sad were reversed inside this man, who seemed to become happy when he talked about sad things like his lost father, but sad when he laughed.

"Luis, would it be possible to have a look under the carpet?" William asked. "To see the floorboards?"

Luis startled. "The carpets are glued down," he said.

"Do you remember what the floor of the apartment used to look like, before you changed anything?" William asked. "Did your mother change a lot? Do you remember any growing lines on the wall maybe, anything that indicated a child living here?"

Luis shook his head. "It's all so long ago."

"Did your mother ever tell you who she bought it from?"

"It was such a long time ago," Luis said again slowly. "If we want to see the past we need to close our eyes. That is where the past is. But if we open our eyes, we see my new fridge. This is where we are now." He pointed at the fridge, not really sure what he had meant by his speech. He lowered his arm; on his palms he still had red marks from when he carried the fridge inside.

During the next half hour, Luis watched his guest wander around his apartment. He slid his hands over the walls, he stared out the windows, he studied the ceiling, he caressed the window-panes, the thresholds. The long dark coat made him look like an enormous black bat in Luis's white apartment. Luis permitted it all, until William went into his bedroom and closed the door behind him.

"You've seen it all now, I think," Luis said as he opened the door to his bedroom.

William was standing in front of the bed, his arms spread out, his eyes closed. "Seeing is only a small part of the sensory experience," he said. "I'm also feeling it, hearing it, smelling it."

"There should not be any smells," Luis said. "I have an air purifier."

"Oh, the gentle scratching of the branches of the poplar tree against the window," William said, his voice trembling. "I remember it . . . it is coming back . . . And I remember this space." He walked into the hallway. "I remember crawling around down here. I think I may have held on to this banister as I was trying to walk for the first time."

"Well, then you have seen it all, I think," Luis said as he followed William out of the room. He felt that there was something impolite in the way this man held his body, the way he walked in and out of rooms, dangling his arms, closing his eyes, holding his spine so upright. It's impolite to walk so confidently through someone else's home, Luis thought. It's wrong to smear your memories all over someone else's possessions.

In the living room Luis took the bags from his glass table and held them out to his visitor. William had put them there without asking, as though that were normal, as though you could just enter someone else's home and put your toothbrush in the glass on the sink.

William took the bags and turned toward the window, where rain made little streams down the glass. "My mother died on a night like this. A stormy summer night, with heavy rain. Her car collided with a truck." He put the bags down on the floor. "She died instantly, they said."

Luis looked at the bags sitting on the carpet. He thought of the inscription in the wooden clock at his old dentist's office: TIME IS YOUR FRIEND, BECAUSE EVERYTHING ENDS.

"My mother believed in the power of storms," William continued. "She thought they brought out supernatural energy, sometimes positive, sometimes negative. 'Something profound always happens during a storm,' she said. Her irrational ways irritated me. I dutifully called her once a week, I visited her at Christmas and her birthday. But we never truly connected. My scientific mind clashed with her spiritual interests. And I think I have always held it against her that she denied me the opportunity to know my dad." He turned to Luis. "Are your parents still alive, if I may ask?"

Luis cleared his throat.

"I hope you don't mind me being so curious," William said.

"Being curious is a sign of intelligence, my teacher in high school used to say," Luis said slowly. "He always said, 'Luis, why aren't you curious?' But I think if there is something important I need to know, people will tell me themselves. I trust people will tell me what I need to know. I don't want to go around putting question marks on everything."

Luis's voice was raw from all this talking. He never talked so much. And he did not know where to look. His gaze shifted from William to his hands, to the wall behind him, to the clock and the staircase. At the Bagel Shop, when a drunk customer wouldn't leave, they called Luis from the back to escort him out. "DP!" they'd shout, which meant "disruptive person." Luis hated doing it, he hated using force because he was afraid of losing his temper, but he knew it was part of why he was hired. Bedas had said as much. "If a fight breaks out and someone gets hurt, I'll take the responsibility," he'd said. "Never call the police, always call me." But there had never been a fight. Feeling the weight of Luis's hand on their shoulder and seeing the roundness of his biceps and his thick forearms were enough for most DPs to start moving to the door. In the worst cases, a gentle twist of the arm behind the back and a nudge toward the exit did the trick.

Luis looked at William. He put his hand on his shoulder.

"Luis," William said, "it does not escape me that I am overstaying my welcome. And I must tell you how much I appreciate your generosity in allowing me to roam around your personal space. It's just that I was hoping to find a clue here. Something that would prove that I lived here, perhaps a little piece of evidence I could take to court, to prove his paternity. There's so little I know about my father and, therefore, about myself." He swallowed loudly. "Everything I have is this address and his name. His name . . ." William placed his hand on top of Luis's. "May I just ask you one more question, Luis?"

He pronounced Luis's name in the French way; it sounded like a girl's name when he said it.

"My father's name. Are you sure you have never heard that name?" William turned toward Luis. "Think . . . has your mother ever, ever mentioned the name"—he lowered his voice—"Edward Hond?"

At that moment the lights in the apartment went out.

"Right when I said his name . . ." William whispered.

Luis watched his visitor's outline in the faint moonlight. The pale, hollow cheeks. Luis could knock him out with one punch, he was sure of that.

"Timers," Luis explained. "I have timers on my lamps. On Saturday, my day off, I go to bed at eleven thirty."

"Oh . . ." William said. "For a second there I thought . . ."

"That there was a ghost," Luis said. "You thought the ghost of your father switched off the light. But there is no ghost. It is time." He clapped his hands. He remembered his primary school teacher in Stompetoren used to clap his hands when he wanted the children to put on their coats.

William's eyes shone in the yellow light. "I am feeling a bit faint," he said.

"Fresh air," Luis said. "It will help." He tightened his grip on William's shoulder, like he did with the disruptive persons at the Bagel Shop.

"I am not feeling well," William said. "Can I sit down?"

"It's very late," Luis said.

"If you don't mind, if you don't mind," William said, turning toward the sofa, "I will just . . . I need to lie down . . . just for a second now . . ."

"I think it's time to go," Luis said as he slid his hand down William's arm, gently turning it onto his back and directing him out of the room, toward the staircase. "We don't want to make it difficult."

The Fall

It was a gentle push, not forceful.

That's why it was so strange, what happened.

Luis looked at the man lying at the bottom of his stairs.

A memory of his mother emerged in his head.

"Damage is inevitable," she said. She was sitting by the windowsill when she said this, smoking her first cigarette of the morning. "Everything in nature wants to go from whole to broken. Just pay attention. Things start out whole, but then they sag, rot, crumble, break, and die. That's how the forces of nature want it. Look at an egg. There is only one way in which it can be whole, one way in which all the tiny particles together form the egg, but there are a million different ways it can be broken. And if you break something, it can never be completely whole again, because even if you mend it, you'll always remember that it was broken. That's a lesson for you, little Luis. Damage is inevitable."

For a few moments, Luis stood still at the top of the stairs. He looked at William, lying at the bottom of the stairs, his coat spread out like the wings of a crashed bird. Luis did not move. It seemed to him that as long as he stood still, it hadn't really happened yet, and time could still go in reverse. But as soon as he moved forward, time would move forward too, and this situation would become real.

"William?" Luis heard himself say finally.

He walked down the stairs and bent over his visitor. William's eyes were closed. His face was pale. It looked like a mask.

"Are you all right?"

There was no reply. There was a smear of blood on the wall at the end of the hallway where he must have hit his head.

Luis rubbed his hands over his face. His thoughts still felt very far away, as if they were in a different room.

"You fell by accident," Luis whispered in his visitor's ear. "You wanted to leave, and when you took the first step down the stairs you tripped. Your long coat, I think. It's dangerous."

Again, there was no response.

Again, there was the voice of his mother in his head. "Never open the door. Let them write letters."

Luis shook his head. He had to think clearly. He placed two fingers on William's neck, under his ear, like he'd learned in the Bagel Shop's first aid course. But he felt nothing, just like he had felt nothing when he put his fingers on Bedas's neck during the course. He pushed his fingers deeper into William's neck. At the first aid course he'd figured he couldn't feel Bedas's heartbeat because of his thick fingers, but he was afraid to ask because he did not want to draw attention to the calluses on his fingers, created by years of stuffing wet hay into feeding nets for Raat's horses.

If William had tripped on the stone stairs outside the front door, Luis thought, then I would have closed the door and I would never have seen it. And some passerby would have found him and called an ambulance. They would have said, "There is a man here on the pavement, it seems like he tripped, come quick."

As if in a dream, Luis shoved his arms under the limp body, one arm under his back and one under his legs, lifting him up from the floor. With his elbow, Luis opened the door to the hallway he shared with Estelle, where he tried to free one hand to open the front door. He felt it would not be right to throw the body over his shoulder, although that would be easier.

When he heard the sound of keys coming from Estelle's apartment, Luis turned back toward his staircase.

"Luis?" he heard her voice say behind her door. "Is that you? What was that bang?"

A key turned in the lock.

Luis walked back into his hallway and kicked the door closed behind him. "It's nothing," he shouted. With the man cradled as a child in his arms, he walked back up his stairs and into his living room. He lowered the body onto his white leather sofa.

After that, Luis leaned on his kitchen counter and breathed deeply. He heard something that sounded like an alarm and he startled, but then he realized it was himself making the sound. A moan was coming from deep in his throat. He opened the tap and filled a glass of water. His hands trembled. There was blood on his sleeve.

"Here, have some water," he said to William's body.

The body did not respond. There was a scratch on his forehead and a red mark that kept getting bigger.

"William," Luis shouted. "William Rose! Drink some water!" He brought the glass to William's lips and poured some water over his mouth. It streamed from his chin into his collar.

Luis's heart was pounding in his chest; it was almost like there was an animal moving around under his ribs, trying to get out.

"Agh," William said. He opened his eyes.

"You're back," Luis said. "I am so relieved. How are you? Good?"

"Weh?" William mumbled.

"You are in my apartment," Luis said, pressing the glass of water to William's lips. "You are in your father's apartment. In Amsterdam. You were born here."

"Does my father live here?" William said in a soft, dazed voice. He sounded like a child.

"No, I live here. You used to live here, with your father. You came to visit, it was great. Then you tripped. Slipped. That coat."

William's eyes opened a little wider. "Oh," he said. He pushed the glass away. "I fell," he said. "Was I unconscious?"

"Not really," Luis said, putting the glass on the table.

William touched his forehead and looked at the blood on his fingers. "I was unconscious," he said.

"A second," Luis said. "I was thinking, He's fine. He'll come around."

William moaned as he tried to sit upright.

"For a moment I thought, I'll carry him outside," Luis said. He filled another glass with water. "I thought, Fresh air will help."

"My head hurts." William sucked in air between his teeth. "I'm really dizzy."

Luis looked at William's forehead. The spot where his head had hit the wall was slowly getting swollen and purple.

"Don't touch it!" William shouted.

"Yes, no," Luis said, retracting his hand. "But it is good that there is still feeling in it."

William put his hands over his eyes and laid his head back on the armrest of Luis's sofa. For a while he lay like this, letting out a soft moan with every breath.

Luis was standing by the sink, his hands alongside his body. He felt like the room had shrunk or he had grown, like he could stick his arms out the window, his head through the roof. The sweat that had formed on his back and his armpits was cooling down. It smelled of stress. He had not smelled like that in a long time.

"I remember . . ." William said slowly. "I remember telling you I did not feel well. That I had to sit down. And I remember you pushing me toward the stairs. You were twisting my arm onto my back."

"I did not twist your arm," Luis said. "I would not do that."

William rolled up his sleeve and looked at his arm. His wrist was red.

Luis said nothing.

William rolled his sleeve down again.

They were both quiet for some time, Luis standing by the kitchen counter, William lying on the sofa with his eyes closed. He was still wearing his shoes; Luis noticed there was mud on the soles and on the white leather of the sofa. The sofa had cost 3,495 euro. He saved up for a year to buy it. Every three months, he rubbed a special treatment oil into the leather with Marina. Luis looked at the clock above the sofa. It was a quarter to twelve.

"I think the last tram is going at twelve," Luis said.

William let out a loud moan.

"These things always feel worse than it is," Luis said. "The best thing would be to call a family member to pick you up."

William sucked in air through his teeth. "I don't have any family," he said sharply.

"Sorry," Luis said. He was quiet for a moment. "Or a friend..."

William moaned again, louder this time. He sounded like an injured animal.

Luis wondered if Estelle could hear it. Sometimes he could hear her, when she was calling her mother in the bathroom, or when she was watching a television show with the windows open and laughing loud.

"A taxi to the hospital?" Luis asked.

William shook his head. "They will just send me home," he said.

"To your hotel?"

"No," William said. "I cannot go down those stairs like this. Right now I cannot even sit up straight. I must have a serious concussion."

"Well," Luis said, "maybe the shock needs to wear off a bit."

He waited another ten minutes while William lay on his sofa under the ticking clock. For ten minutes he looked at this stranger who was in his house and the clock above him, ticking into the night. There was something Luis should do, he was sure of it, there was a proper step to take, a step that other people would take if they were in this situation.

"I cannot offer you a bed," Luis said. "There is no spare bed in here." It was true what he said. There was no spare bed, no one could say there was a spare bed in the apartment.

Later, when Luis was taking off his socks in his bedroom, sitting on the edge of the bed, he thought, Other people would not have let this happen. They would have said, "No, you are not sleeping on my sofa, absolutely not, we don't even know each other." They would have said no. Luis never said no. He should have said no. But then what? What if William refused to leave? Would they have called the police? What would the police do? What if the police asked how he fell down? No matter how many times Luis played the scenario in his head, he could not think of a way to get this man with his concussion out of the house without having to call the police or forcefully remove him.

Luis wondered what Hadi would have done. He probably would not have let him inside in the first place. Luis thought of how he had said, "Of course you can stay on the sofa," how he had made the sofa like a bed for this stranger called William, how he had wrapped his nice Egyptian cotton sheets over the seat pillows, pillows that had held their shape for years, pillows that did not have one stain. Luis thought of how he had said, "You can use everything you need. There's food on the kitchen counter, I should have put it in the fridge. I have put water on the table. I would let you watch television, but the remote is very complicated." Then he'd taken the remote from the table, put it in his back pocket, and turned the dimmer all the way down until it was dark in his kitchen.

Luis thought of his visitor, how he had sat under the blanket on his sofa before Luis closed the blinds, his eyes shining in the half dark, two glimpses of light following his movements through the room. A memory of his father, who watched Luis from the dark shed on the night that he left, came back to him, but Luis suppressed it.

The Philanthropist

I was nearly seventeen when I met the philanthropist. 1984. I had bleached my hair and wore a blue scarf in it to look like Madonna. I wore thick blue eyeliner and blue nail polish. Inside I was still clear like a glass of water.

In the months before I met him, I had watched my body with distrust and unease. First my period was late. I wasn't really good at keeping track, so I wasn't sure how many weeks. Then a few dots. Relief. It was only a little. But blood is blood! And I cried a lot, so I was definitely on my period. Four weeks later—I had started counting from then on—nothing. My best friend, Anna Beemster, did not have her period for six months when she stopped eating. Maybe I was not eating enough. And I had been throwing up—could it be a stomach bug? My boobs were growing, but they were supposed to finally do that.

I remember I started going to the library during school breaks, pulling books about pregnancy from the shelves and reading them secretly in a corner, scanning the pages for information that would mean I was not pregnant. I did not have increased urination. My nipples were not discolored. During Bible class, while Mr. Schouw wrote the story of the Holy Virgin on the blackboard with a squealing piece of chalk, I negotiated with

God. If I am not pregnant, I will start believing again, I told him, and I will not let Dave put it in me again for sure.

Then, on a Thursday morning after gym class, Hilde pointed at me in the locker room and asked, "Marie, are you pregnant or something?"

Out of nowhere. Out loud. I was standing in my bra and underwear, with my leggings around my ankles. The locker room became quiet. Everyone stared at my belly. My face red like a strawberry, I ran into the bathroom and locked the door. I stayed inside the bathroom for a long time, waiting for my face to turn less red so I could come out and laugh it off. When I finally opened the door all the girls were looking at me. They weren't even laughing or whispering. They looked at me like I was going to die.

And in a way I was dying. We had all seen it when Sonja came back from art academy in Amsterdam, pushing her pram through the village with her Nina Hagen hair and her black nail polish.

"She had to move back in with her parents," we whispered behind her back.

That was death.

With a buzzing sound in my ears, I walked through the quiet dressing room and out of the school. And in that moment, I knew I wasn't going back to school. I remember I did not feel scared. I did not feel sad. All I knew was: I am going to make a plan, get away from my parents, get out of Stompetoren, make a life for myself.

"Can you ask if there's a job for me at the Bijenkorf in Amsterdam?" I asked Anna, who was working behind the counter at her dad's tobacco shop. "Any type of job."

Anna was one year older than me. She was going to do a traineeship at the Bijenkorf department store in Amsterdam with her other best friend, Maureen.

"I was thinking we could get a place to live together, all three of us," I said. "You, me, Maureen. You can borrow my clothes if you want. We can help each other."

"Don't you have another year?" Anna asked.

"I'm done with school," I said.

"They don't take just anyone at Bijenkorf, you know," Anna said. "I had to pass a test in civilized pronunciation and polite services."

"Am I not civilized?" I asked her. "Wasn't it polite of me to change clothes with you when you puked all over yourself on Queen's Day?"

"Shhh," Anna said, looking over her shoulder at her dad, who was in the back of the shop, listening to a soccer match on the radio.

"Anna," I said, "I really need help." I unbuttoned my coat and raised my shirt. "I think I am three months. Maybe four." My voice was shakier than I wanted and my face started to flare up.

"No way!" Anna stared at the roundness of my belly. "What did you do?"

"What do you mean 'what did you do'?" I said as my face became a million degrees Celsius in one second. "What do you and Maureen do when you go behind the mill with Simon and Johan? Have a conversation?"

"Maureen and I only do hand and mouth things," Anna said. She said it with an air, like doing hand and mouth things behind the mill was the most refined thing a girl could do in her free time.

"Oh." I knew I sounded more disappointed than I wanted. They could have told me that.

"I just didn't think you were that kind of girl." Anna stared at my belly. "You know that I told Johan that Dave was lying. I told him you would never do that."

I said nothing.

"You are never gonna get out of Stompetoren now," Anna said. "Never in a million years will the Bijenkorf take you . . . a pregnant sixteen-year-old . . . Your parents are going to kill you. What are you gonna do? Live with Dave?" She looked disgusted. "I mean, I want to help you, but . . ."

"Oh, I don't need your help," I said, buttoning up my coat. "I just thought it would be nice for us to live together since you told me you are always so scared when you are alone at night. Remember, you were crying about it? I don't need help. I have a plan."

"What plan?" Anna leaned over the counter. "Tell me you're not going to get . . . ?" She whispered, "It's an innocent child, Marie."

At that moment I realized what a mistake I had made by telling Anna. I could still deny it at school, say that I just got fat and I was embarrassed, and then spread a juicy rumor about someone else. But now that I told Anna, the whole town was going to know within the hour. And everyone would be watching me.

With hands shaking from anger, I grabbed a newspaper and walked out of the store.

"That's one guilder," Anna dared to shout after me.

Behind the houseboats, I sat down on the ground and rushed through the pages. How hard can it be? I thought. I can do it. I can be a parent. It will be fine. Babies are nice. Here. Board assistant. What is a board? Senior sales engineer. Accountant. Administrative researcher. No, I can't do any of that. Head teacher. No. "Nurses Wanted, Job Guaranteed." Maybe. "Diploma required." No.

I pressed my nails into the palm of my hand to suppress any urge to cry, a trick I discovered in the first year of high school, when I got bullied for always turning red. With my nails dug deep into my skin, I read the ads, until I finally came across one that applied to me. Under the article "Unprecedented Unemployment Numbers," there was a tiny ad that read:

HIGH SCHOOL DROPOUTS DROP IN

GET CAREER ADVICE AT THE JOB CENTER IN AMSTERDAM.

THE TEN THOUSAND JOBS PROGRAM OFFERS

OPPORTUNITIES FOR EVERYONE.

Thirty minutes later I was on the train to Amsterdam, on my own, for the first time. While looking at the flat fields outside my window, I thought of what Anna had said. "An innocent child." I used to be an innocent child once. When did that stop? As a child, I sometimes played in the basement of a flat that had poisoned dead mice in it. I tried to raise them from the dead by laying my hands upon them and saying "*Talitha cumi*" just like Jesus had done with the little girl who could not walk. One of the mice had moved its head, just as I said it.

"You are not holy," my mother had said when I told her. "We are all born in sin."

The Wall between
Dream and Reality

This is what you get when you try to do the good thing, Luis thought. People take advantage of it, they ignore all normal boundaries, and suddenly they're lying on your white leather sofa with their greasy hair.

It was early in the morning, and Luis was sitting on the floor on his knees, using tweezers to try to get tiny glass splinters from the carpet. Small glass shards were stinging Luis's fingertips. Last night he'd dreamed about his mother. She was sitting by his bed, holding his hand, squeezing it, harder and harder. He'd woken up with a scream, pulling his hand back and slamming his phone from the nightstand. It flew across the room and landed on a dumbbell, breaking the screen.

If I did not have a visitor, I would get my Dust Buster 3000 from the kitchen, Luis thought. If I did not have this visitor, if that man hadn't shown up with his muddy feet and his questions about the past, I would not have had a nightmare about my mother in the first place. Then my phone would still be fine, I would still be sleeping, and my alarm would go off at 10:00 A.M. to go to King's Gym.

Luis shook his head. What was it Estelle had said? He "deserves to see the apartment." Why would she say that? Did everyone who ever lived somewhere deserve to see that place until the end of time? Would she have said that if it was Luis at the door and William her neighbor?

Luis wondered what time he could expect his visitor to get up and leave. It was eight o'clock now. He knew that Hadi always got up at six, Estelle at seven. Marina cleaned nightclubs from six o'clock. He also knew that some people did not wake up at a steady hour, people like his mother. Sometimes those people slept the entire morning, sometimes they got up at five to make pancakes and forced everyone out of bed to eat them.

Eight o'clock seemed like a reasonable time to get up and start a new day, although for Luis it did not feel like a new day at all. Yesterday's sweat was still on his skin, and the images of his mother hadn't sunk into the swamp of forgotten dreams, as they normally did, but stayed with him and popped up in his mind from time to time. Because the pain he felt in his nightmare was now connected to the real pain he had in his fingers from the glass, it was as though the wall between dream and reality had been broken in a way that wasn't right at all.

Quietly, Luis opened his living room door a little. The light coming in through the door illuminated the visitor's hair, which was peeking out from under the blanket. It was like some kind of animal had slipped in and curled up on his sofa.

"Good morning," Luis said softly. "It's eight o'clock."

William moved his head. Then he turned around on the sofa, facing his back to Luis.

Luis cleared his throat. He wondered what Hadi would do if William Rose was sleeping on his sofa. He imagined Hadi waking up a guest with a loud hello, opening the blinds, maybe even pulling the blanket off.

"What have other people ever done for me," Hadi liked to ask, "that would make me owe them anything?" Hadi had specific ideas about what people owed each other. "Most people think they are good and nice," he said. "They look in the mirror and they think, Yes, I'm a good person and I say nice things and I recycle all my plastic bottles and I always nod at the homeless person selling the street paper and so on. But they have never been through anything where this niceness was tested. And I can tell you, as soon as something difficult happens, these people quit. As soon as they have to give up one big thing for someone else, they can't do it. And that's only natural. Humans aren't made for being good to everyone. When people shipwreck and there's only one spot left on the life raft, what do people do? Psychologists know it. Historians know it. Biologists know it. Did you know it's not even a crime if you push someone off that raft in that scenario? It's not against the law to kill for your own life."

"I know," Luis would say, because Hadi often told this story.

"But the difference between me and the others is that I'm honest about who I am," Hadi said. "I just come out and say it: I am not nice. Niceness is meaningless to me. I don't owe it to anybody to be nice. I help others when I can. And I am completely loyal to a select few. These few are my mother, Luis, and my future wife. Only with these people I will share, and I will share everything if I have to. For these people I will die. If you can't make relationships with that kind of intensity in this world, you are alone. Going around acting nice, acting polite, it has no value in the end. Like that neighbor you like so much, that Estelle. She thinks she is so good, she never throws trash on the street, she bought a bench of recycled driftwood. But she makes contracts for a bank that trades in weapons and invests in fossil fuels. Her parents helped her buy that apartment. She has never given up anything for anyone. People like that are not honest. I just want to live honestly. If you can't admit who you are to yourself, you are a prisoner of your own self-image."

Usually when Hadi was giving this speech, he was hanging over the counter at the Bagel Shop on Leidsestraat, chewing on a leftover bagel, his eyes a little red. He liked to stop by Luis's work after he'd gone out clubbing. "You and me, we don't question each other," Hadi would say, putting his arm around Luis's shoulder. "We help each other. We trust each other. We wouldn't fight for a spot on the raft, right? We'd go down together."

"Yes," Luis always said. "We'd go down together."

"In our friendship I am all in," Hadi said. "I am selfless. Like a mother is selfless." He patted Luis on the shoulder. "Some mothers at least."

In the living room Luis took a deep breath. Then he said in a firm voice to William, "Good morning. I am opening the blinds."

Before he could reach for the remote for the blinds, William had already raised his head from the pillow and said, "No! No light, please. My concussion."

"Oh," Luis said. "I'm sorry." Why was he apologizing? It was one of the things Luis admired about Hadi: he never apologized.

The closest he ever got to an apology was saying, "Of course I'm not proud of it, but it's in the past now."

"It's eight o'clock," Luis said, his voice a little less firm. "I thought it was a good time to get up."

With a loud moan, William pushed himself upright on the sofa. The blanket slipped from his upper body. He wasn't wearing a shirt, even though he was still wearing his trousers. Luis stared at the man's skinny chest, his pointy spine. He had the body of a child, stretched out. It was impossible not to look at. It reminded Luis of the smaller boys in the locker room in high school, the ones who got pushed around for being too scrawny.

"I have a dreadful headache," William said, sliding his hands over his greasy hair. "And I feel nauseous. Could you hand me the water, please?"

Luis gave William the glass of water. "It stopped raining," he said. "Shall I call you a taxi, for nine o'clock?"

"I am not ready," William said. He pulled the blanket over his upper body and lay down again. "I need a little bit more rest."

Luis could feel the red spots gathering under the collar of his shirt. "Being kind is not the same as being a good person," his mother's voice said to him. "Don't ever let them sell you that crap. Do good and good will come to you, that's all bullshit. If that was true, kind people would be rich. And who are rich? Shit people."

"So," Luis said to his guest, "the thing is . . ." His neck was burning. "The thing is that I have work and we need to get going. You have your plane to catch." He rubbed the back of his neck.

"I thought you worked nights," William said.

"Well," Luis said, "I have an appointment." The red spots burned his cheeks. He hated lying. "At nine o'clock. An important appointment."

"Ah," William said. "Of course. Go ahead and use the kitchen as you normally would. I completely understand."

"What do you understand?" Luis asked.

"That you need to be in here. It's your apartment, for goodness' sake! Go ahead, do not feel burdened."

"I don't feel burdened," Luis said. "We need to go together. You have you plane to catch."

"It's wiser for me to rest some more," William said from under Luis's Egyptian sheets. "My plane isn't leaving until the evening. When I move my head pounds, black spots swarm my vision. If I stand up now, I would throw up."

Again, Luis was struck by how soft and silky this man's voice was.

"We can walk slowly," Luis said. "I will call a taxi, it will take you to your hotel."

"I am in no state," William said, laying his head back down on the pillow. "Every move I make I feel my head pounding and my stomach turning. It would be better to rest some more before I go. Please, just go without me."

"I can help you down the stairs," Luis said.

"Like you did yesterday?" William asked, closing his eyes.

"No, no," Luis said. "We will go slowly. I will call you a taxi. Fresh air, it will help."

"I appreciate that you do not want to leave me alone. And I appreciate your concern. But don't worry about me. I will manage. Go to your appointment. It's nearly a quarter to nine and you have not even showered."

Luis looked down at his body. "Well," he said. Wasn't it a rule that when you leave your house, the guest has to leave your house too? Why were all the rules different from what he thought they were?

"It's not good for people to feel ill in a strange place," he said finally.

William smiled with his eyes closed. "It does not feel strange to me, to be here."

Luis stared at the man on his sofa. He did look strange in the apartment. Everything about him was strange: his voice, his smell, his clothes, his small head sticking out from his blanket. He had to be in his forties, but somehow it seemed to Luis there was a child in his home.

22 August
My father's home, Amsterdam

The man in the house is a simple figure, as I had expected from his appearance when I first saw him through the window. At first glance Luis looks intimidating, but when he starts moving there is something unmistakably innocent and clumsy about him. Even though he's pumped up his body to remarkable proportions—creating an unnatural roundness in his shoulders, his arms, his chest—he often has his head bent, he chooses to stand in the corners of a room and always walks close to the walls.

It's a contradiction I did not understand until I saw his furniture. All those glass surfaces, the glossy paint! All the words with a gl- sound apply here. 'Glam', 'glass', 'glimmer', 'glib', 'glow', 'gloss', 'gleam'. No colour, no texture, no play. Aspirational objects. Objects that signify the desired level of upward social mobility.

This morning I noticed that Luis said 'I am sorry' two times in one hour. He feels a continuing need to apologise for his existence. He is one of those people who have not found a reason for why they have to be alive, why they have to be in people's presence, taking up their time and space. With all my personal sensitivities and shyness, this is a feeling I have never had. Even in my loneliest moments I have always known that I had a purpose, that I belonged somewhere in this world.

Belonging. It's a word I have thought about a lot. 'To be properly placed, situated'.

'William adjusted so easily to the UK', I remember my mother telling Paulina when I first introduced her. 'He did not mind leaving the Netherlands at all and he fit in straight away'.

Of course, the school uniforms were fine by me, I did not care about clothes. And the British way of not expressing your feelings suited me too. But I never felt at home. My books were the closest to a home I would ever know. Those were the worlds I knew; they went with me every time we moved into a new home . . . it must have been at least seven moves. Harry in Exeter with his koi carp business. Paul the dentist in Bideford. Paul Two. Then the Norfolk plumber with the twins I had to share my bedroom with.

I remember how cold I felt towards my mother when I was leaving to study at Oxford. She was hugging me at the Norwich station, making a show of it, as she always did. She saw my admittance to Oxford as evidence that she did well in raising me. 'Another sign that birth fathers are unnecessary', she said proudly.

I still wonder why she hated him so. My mother who liked everyone, who wanted to heal the whole world in her hippie way, who saw something positive in every charlatan who made a move on her. What had my father done? What kind of person was he?

Now, at least, I know the name. And this apartment.

In her letter to her sister, my mother wrote: 'Edward does charity, he trades in antiques, he has seen the whole world! And he knows so much. He is a bit older than me, but that means I am learning a lot from him. The apartment is full of books and art, every wall is covered in paintings. And he has several homes around the world! He says he will take me to countries I have never even heard of before. At the moment, he is busy with work in Amsterdam. Charity work, mostly. He uses the living room as his office, so I go out a lot. There is a beautiful little park that I am helping to improve, framed by poplars. Oh, it's so wonderful. Yes, Edward can be stern sometimes and is easily annoyed, but wouldn't I be too if I did such important work?'

Last night I quietly looked for traces of my existence throughout this apartment. While my host slept, I crawled around on the floor, lifting corners of the deep-pile carpet, tracing the walls with my hands. Though I hoped to find an old nail stuck between the floorboards still suitable for a DNA paternity test, I also would have been happy to find holes in the walls where the nails for the paintings used to be or a trace of old wallpaper. Anything, anything at all, that would be evidence of me living here and Edward being my father. But I have found nothing. It is almost like some forensic team has erased everything.

The Spirit of a Thing

After Luis had allowed his visitor to chase him out of his own home, he stood on the sidewalk in front of his apartment for a while. Cyclists raced down the bike lane, and in one of the apartments down the street a baby was crying. The morning air felt moist on Luis's skin. Luis considered turning around and going back inside and saying, "I never had an appointment, you must go, leave me alone."

There is no need, Luis thought. When he has slept some more and packed his bags, he will go. Luis decided to go to Hadi's store to replace his broken phone. That way, when the visitor left later today, he only had to clean the sofa, shampoo the carpet, and clean the bloodstain from the wall, and he could forget it ever happened.

"So you don't want to replace the screen but trade this in for a completely new one?" Fatma, the girl working behind the counter at Hadi's Phone Centre, asked.

Luis nodded. If Hadi were here, he would have understood that he needed a new one. "The repaired phone will still hold the memory of what happened to it," he liked to say to his customers. "It is contaminated by failure. The new phone is clean. It is a new start. So, in a way, a new phone is a new you. And you deserve it."

Hadi's store was where Luis met him. When he first arrived in Amsterdam he had thrown his old SIM card in the canal and needed a new phone number.

"This isn't a decision to take lightly," Hadi had explained to him, hanging over the counter. "A phone number isn't just a number, it's an opportunity to shine. And I happen to trade in them. Take this one, 0622117712. It's like a song, it will stick in your head. Everyone will remember your number."

"I don't want to be remembered," Luis had said.

"What?" Hadi had called out. "Why? What did you do? No, don't tell me. The past is in the past. Where are you from? Don't say it, let me guess. Chile? No, Brazilian? Red cheeks, black hair, brown eyes, loud voice. You are . . ."

"My father is Spanish," Luis said, "and he had a Moroccan mother. And my mother is Dutch. But I am not Spanish. I am nothing. I am just me, Luis Sol."

Hadi had slammed his fist on the counter. "You are just you! I like that. You know, I am the same. All my life my mother told me, 'Hadi, you were born in the Netherlands, you are Dutch.' But at school they told me, 'You are Iraqi.' My grandfather told me, 'You are a Kurd.' But when I went to Kurdistan, my cousins said I was Dutch. My aunties told me it did not matter, because I was Muslim. But when I prayed, there was no response. And you know what? I am none of that. I am just Hadi, and the planet Earth is where I am from."

At 1:00 A.M. that night, Luis got his first phone call on 0622117712.

"It's Hadi!" Hadi exclaimed. "I remembered your number! Didn't I tell you?"

Luis was pulled out of his memory when Fatma placed a box with a new iPhone on the store counter. "Five hundred euro if you trade in your old phone," she said.

Luis nodded. He had saved up 3,000 euro, which was meant for the refurbishing of the hallway he shared with Estelle. He had an idea for a marble theme, but she had not reacted to any of the brochures he put in her mailbox about it.

"I think it's cool that you know what you want," Fatma said. "That you don't listen to that stuff about the children."

"What children?" Luis asked.

"You know, the children in the mines," she said. "Who have to go into the mines to get the metals, like, the minerals, for these phones."

She placed Luis's new phone on a sheet of pink paper.

"I don't know about the children," Luis said. "And no need to wrap that. It's just for me."

"Just for you!" the girl said. "You are not important? You deserve it." She folded the paper tightly around the box and pulled a ribbon from a spool. One of her pink rectangular fingernails moved a little. She reminded Luis of Nina, a girl Hadi had set him up with. When they were kissing on her bed her eyelashes had come loose. A strip of fake eyelashes sat diagonally across her eyelid like a spider. It had thrown him off-balance. Suddenly he noticed everything: the Christmas lights around her bed, the clothes on the floor, the fake ponytail hanging over the back of her desk chair. He remembered how he had run-walked out of her apartment building in Bos en Lommer, through the dark Vondelpark, just wanting to get home. The relief he felt when he opened his door and saw his own spotless interior was over-whelming.

"Yeah, they say children die to make these phones," Fatma continued, as she pulled another ribbon from a spool. "They say that if you buy one, you are actually complicit. They say these mines, like, collapse sometimes, when the children go in there. And they die. Didn't you read about it?"

"I'm a visual person," Luis said.

"There are also videos of it," she said. "Where you see the children. One kid was six years old. This phone is actually great for videos." Her nail moved away from her finger again as she pulled scissors over the ribbon to curl it.

Involuntarily Luis pushed his thumb against his own nails, pushing them back onto his fingers, even though they were real and it would be impossible for them to come off, as far as he knew at least—maybe they could all fall off and gravity could reverse and you could sit on a chair on the ceiling. Until yester-day, he would have thought it impossible to have a stranger in his apartment uninvited, but still that happened. He thought of William in his apartment. He pictured him walking around the house, leaving mud trails on the carpet, scratching the TV screen with his belt buckle, entangling the window blinds, knocking over the air purifier.

Fatma slowly wound the ribbon around the box. "And what can I do about it? Yes, I look at those videos; yes, they keep me up at night. But I can't quit my job, can I? I have a little girl I need to look after. Hadi says I was born in a fucked-up world, and it is not my job to fix it."

"There is a man in my apartment," Luis said. He felt the red spots burn in his neck.

"It's just so hard to be in this world and like yourself," Fatma said. Her eyes were shiny. "Everything I do, I do for my little girl. But then I am selling these phones that hurt other children! What does that mean? Hadi says I need to care for myself first. Still, I keep thinking about those kids in the mines, I can't sleep because of it." She was holding the box with the phone in her hands, not handing it over to Luis.

"I'm sorry," Luis said. "I can't help you." He put the money on the counter. "There is a man in my house, I should not have left him there."

Without waiting for the receipt, he took the gift-wrapped phone from Fatma's hands and hurried out of the store. Normally he walked home slowly after buying something new, holding his purchase against his chest and looking at his reflection in every shop window. But today Luis sprinted down Van Woustraat, his eyes fixed on his bedroom window in the distance.

"Luis!" Mrs. Barneveld, Luis's neighbor from across the street, called out to him. She was standing in her doorway, on stockinged feet.

"Sorry," Luis called out. "I will stop by later."

"You had a visitor last night," Mrs. Barneveld said, walking out onto the pavement in her stockings and crossing the street. "Who was it?"

Luis turned around. Mrs. Barneveld had lived on Rooseveltlaan longer than anyone else, she was the head of the Roosevelt Park Committee, and she took care of the little park in the middle of the street. Luis sometimes helped her, carrying bags of soil or removing dead branches.

"Did Estelle tell you I had a visitor?" Luis asked.

"No, no, I saw him arrive last night. I was in the park, I'd forgotten my garden shears." She adjusted her hat. "And he looked so much like . . . but no, no, it can't be him, it can't be." She shook her head distractedly.

"His name is William Rose," Luis said.

"Oh," Mrs. Barneveld said, her face clearing up. "Good. For a second I thought . . . good . . . good." Just as abruptly as she'd appeared, she turned around again, her body moving stiffly as she walked to her home.

Traces

William still wasn't dressed when Luis came back into the living room. He was sitting under the sheets on the sofa, eating one of Luis's bagels. Papers had been spread out all over Luis's glass dinner table. The suitcase was lying open on the floor full of canned food: tuna, beans, soup.

"Oh, hello, Luis," William said, as if he was surprised to see Luis enter his own home. "That was a quick appointment. How did it go?"

"It was good," Luis said.

"It looks good," William said. He smiled and nodded at the pink package Luis was holding. "I made myself something to eat, I hope that's all right."

"Have you unpacked your bags?" Luis asked as he looked around. "It is full in here." He noticed fingerprints all over his fridge. Had it been moved?

"Estelle wanted to have a look at some of the documentation about my father," William said, "so I unpacked some of the folders."

"Estelle?" Blood rushed to Luis's cheeks.

"Your neighbor, from yesterday," William said. He put his half-eaten bagel on the armrest of Luis's sofa. "She saw me from the garden when I was looking out the window. Naturally, she wanted to know why I was still here. She asked to come up so she could have a look at my injury. She was very worried. A kind, intelligent woman. A lawyer. She lives on the first floor, just below you."

"I know who Estelle is," Luis said. His heart was pounding in his chest. How often had he imagined her coming up to his apartment, her pin heels disappearing into his deep-pile carpet? He had imagined her seeing the way the light touched the edge of his glass table, the shadows that were multiplied through the different panels of glass making soft squares on the carpet. He had imagined her pink nails sliding over the white marble kitchen counter, he imagined her noticing the lines of the stainless steel cart creating a pattern that was repeated in the Mondriaan print on the wall.

He had wanted to make sure there was music playing from his surround sound speakers, to make coffee for her, to make sure it smelled good. Luis now noticed that his air purifier was unplugged. It smelled different in the room. Sweet. Luis felt an anger drum up in his chest, and his temples started throbbing. "Do not lose control," he heard his father's voice say in his head. "Take a deep breath." He took a cloth from the kitchen counter and scrubbed William's fingerprints from his fridge door.

"Estelle had an interesting suggestion," William said to Luis's back. "She said perhaps I could ring your mother, ask her if she remembers who she bought the apartment from. There's a chance it may have been my father."

Luis shook his head. He turned toward his visitor. He looked like a hallucination, so strange the contrast was between this scruffy man and Luis's clean, carefully crafted white space. "You can't call my mother," he said.

"May I ask why?" William asked.

"My mother is dead."

"Oh," William said. "My deepest condolences."

For a moment, it was quiet. Luis realized it was the first time he had said out loud that his mother was dead. It felt as if some last part of her died when he said it.

William cleared his throat. "Did she ever live here, if I may ask?"

"No," Luis said.

"Did she rent it out?"

"No," Luis said again.

Another silence.

"It strikes me as unusual," William said slowly. "Why did she buy it then?"

"Why do people do the things they do?" Luis said. "Why do they have houses, why do they call each other to talk, why do they want to know everything, why do they take pictures of themselves, why do they make babies, why do they keep secrets, why do they hurt each other? Why are you on my sofa? Why? We don't know why. It is impossible to find out. You shouldn't try it."

"Well, it is a good thing you did not decide to study psychology, Luis," William said, smiling at him. "It would not have been a success."

"I wasn't good at school," Luis said, the red creeping up his cheeks, "but I can read. Just not that fast. It was not that I was stupid. It is just with the books, I cannot . . ."

"It was just a joke," William said.

"I can read," Luis said. "I am just not good at reading very fast, when there is pressure." His voice was rising. He did not know why he was talking so much. It was as if there were a crack somewhere, a little crack in his person, and it leaked. He needed to remain calm, that was the most important.

"I'm just trying to find out more about my past," William said, "but I feel like I am upsetting you when I ask questions about this apartment."

"And I feel you should go back to England," Luis said. "You have seen it all now, there is nothing here to find out. You have slept on my sofa. You ate my food. You used my shower. And that is it."

"It is upsetting to you when people ask questions about your family," William said.

"There is nothing to be upset about," Luis said. "It is just unhealthy to think about your family all the time. You should become your own person."

"I have to disagree with you on this, Luis," William said. "I think where you come from creates who you are, where you belong. We are all from the past. In my view, each person is a palimpsest. Do you know what that is? It comes from the Greek word *palimpsestos*. Do you know that word, Luis?"

"My friend Hadi just went to Greece," Luis said.

"A palimpsest is a page that is used again and again. The old writing is scraped off, a new text is written on it, but if you examine it closely, you can still see traces of the old text underneath the new text, it is part of it. We all carry traces from our past like this. Like the green wallpaper under your white paint, we all have the story of our parents as a layer under our own story."

Luis looked at his white walls. "There is no green wallpaper under it," he said.

"We all carry these traces, whether we like it or not. And it runs deep. Ever since I came here, I feel memories coming back to me. A strong sense of belonging awakening inside of me. I feel very close to my father, now that I am here. I feel his memory coming back to me, but I can't put my finger on it yet."

"Well," Luis said, "maybe your finger will feel better when you're back in England. What time is your plane leaving?"

"Estelle says flying is not a good idea in my state," he said. "She says I have a serious concussion. I had to call the university. Thankfully, they agreed to cover my teaching for a week." He smiled.

Luis stared at him.

"In fact, now that I see you, I meant to ask . . . Estelle suggested that I could spend that week here, actually. She said you wouldn't mind. 'To compensate for the assault and bodily harm,' she said, 'it would be the wisest move for him.'"

Luis said nothing.

William smiled wider now. "I know! Lawyers always talk like that. Assault . . . harm . . . she said that because it happened in your home, and I do have bruises on my arm where you held me, I could press charges. But that is not something I would do. I know you are a good person. You have let me stay on your sofa, in your home."

Luis shook his head.

"I know." William nodded. "Unexpected guests. Nobody likes them. But it would just be a couple of days. I have stacks of articles and documents to plow through: local hospital records, charity registers, bank information, neighborhood history. The chamber of commerce documentation on the foundation. Magazines on philanthropy in the Netherlands. It would be extremely meaningful to me to be able to study these, sitting where my father used to sit, having breakfast where he had breakfast."

"Where I have breakfast," Luis said.

"Did you know the word 'breakfast' comes from 'breaking the fast,'" William said. "*Break-fast*. Not a lot of people know that."

Luis did not know what to say.

They were both quiet for a moment.

The clocked ticked.

Luis tried to find a way to say, "Get out of here," but the words stayed in his throat.

"In any case, I thought my research into my past could be useful for you too," William said. "Estelle has ordered some paperwork from the Land Registry. It will tell us when your mother bought it and who the previous owners were. Who knows, I might find something about the past that tells you something about your mother, what kind of person she was."

"I know what kind of person she was," Luis said. An image of his mother came up in his mind, waiting for him outside his school, standing away from the other mothers, her hands in her coat pockets.

"And I would be grateful to see the notary documents for this apartment," William said. "The deeds or the transfer documents, any ownership documentation you have."

"I have those," Luis said.

"And I would love to see them," William said.

"They are in some box," Luis said.

"It could be useful to have them on hand." William smiled. "Imagine there's a burglar, you call the police, but when they come, the burglar says that he lives here and in fact you are the intruder. The paperwork can prove he is wrong."

"That would never happen," Luis said. "That's just . . ." His heart was thumping irregularly. It felt like there was an animal moving under his ribs. It reminded him of how the rats moved under the straw in old Raat's barn. Luis put his hands on his chest. There was a long silence. Luis heard himself make a noise, a throat noise, as if he was going to say something else. But he did not speak for a while, he did not move, while William sat silently on the sofa, looking at him.

"If it's only for a few days," he said finally. "A week. And then you go back to England." The red spots were burning on his cheeks and his neck. "It's no trouble for me. I am not troubled by it . . . by a visitor."

He made a gesture to the living room, as if the room were much larger than it really was, as if it were almost unnoticeable, a visitor in this room. Without saying anything else, Luis took the brake from his TV cart and rolled the flat screen over the threshold, toward his bedroom.

The Bagel Shop

That night Luis took the plates from the dishwashing machine at the Bagel Shop on Leidsestraat. A cloud of steam hung around him. He worked slower than usual. The presence of his visitor kept taking over his thoughts; it was as though he were sitting on a sofa inside Luis's head. He thought of Estelle's hand on the visitor's arm, the way she had said "William's a professor."

Luis recalled his job interview at the Bagel Store. "Not one diploma?" he remembered his boss, Bedas, asking when Hadi introduced him. "He doesn't even have a swimming diploma?"

"I have a swimming diploma," Luis had said, his face red. "But I don't have it here. It's in some box. And I have been to high school, just not all the way to the end."

Luis remembered sitting at the breakfast table when he was ten, the day he had to do a presentation about bats. An untouched bowl of cereal was in front of him, and his mother was standing behind his chair. "You don't have to do it if you don't want to," she said, hugging him. The nerves clammed up his stomach, his throat. "They should not make you do things you don't want to do. What is it good for anyway? All that wibble wabble they make those little kids do. Bats! Who needs them?

"I'll call the school," she said, kissing his cheek. "You stay with me."

He knew even then it was no good. Too often he stayed at home, too often she came to pick him up early from school.

"Luis is ill," he heard his mother say on the phone in the other room. "He can't come."

He never told her he couldn't understand the sums the teachers wrote on the blackboard. He had missed so many days at school he did not know what they meant by fractions. His day would now be spent helping his mother with chores in the house. In the evening he and his mother had dinner together in the TV room, a small room with cushions on the floor, watching the two channels they had back then, the news, the talk show, the lottery.

During the days he stayed at home, she did not go back to bed in the afternoon. If he did go to school, he sometimes came back to a dark house, the living room empty, no one making dinner. That feeling he had when he knocked on her bedroom door, his coat still on, his backpack on his back, was the feeling he dreaded the most. So he had given up on school. He was never good at it anyway.

At 5:00 A.M. Luis's shift at the Bagel Shop ended. Maya, the Polish girl who worked the counter, offered to mop the floors and close up. Hastily Luis put the chairs on the tables, and without saying goodbye, he walked into the city night. He usually enjoyed this walk home from work. Amsterdam was at its most quiet between five and six in the morning. Most partygoers had gone home, the cafés were closed, the office people weren't up yet. Some night people were still wandering down the sidewalks, looking for something. Only night buses and taxis were sliding down the streets, a solitary cyclist making a gentle noise over the cobblestones, some sleepy tourist with a suitcase.

"Every bad thing that happens pollutes your person," his mother had told Luis on his first day of school, pouring milk over his cornflakes. "You start out completely unpolluted when you come out of the vagina. Inside, your person feels clear like a glass of water. You do exactly what you want to do. But then bad things start to happen to you, and you get polluted. The people, they will mistreat you, they will take advantage of you, they will put you in situations and cause you to do things you wish you hadn't. And you cannot undo it. Regret and guilt and shame build up inside of you, and then one day you wake up and realize that clear water feeling you had inside of you is gone, and it will never come back."

When Luis moved to Amsterdam, he found out his mother was wrong. Every night he came home from work, he let the sounds of his half-sleeping city seep into his ears, and he felt light on the inside again by the time he got into his bed. Clear like a glass of water.

This night Luis walked up his stairs with quick, silent steps. He quietly folded his apron over the banister, stood still by the living room door, and listened. It was completely quiet. In his bedroom, Luis sat down on the edge of his white leather water-bed, turning his house key around in his hand. He thought of the plastic tag that used to be attached to the key. "For Marie," it read in curly letters. "With gratitude. Edward."

The Philanthropist

When I was younger I made decisions as easily as turning a page. The decision to go to the Job Center in Amsterdam I made in a second. Like the time I made the decision to jump from the Chicken Bridge into the canal in February, like the time I made the decision to dye my hair blond with the bleach from under the kitchen sink. Decision-making was my talent. Close your eyes and do it. There was only yes and go.

Now I don't feel like that anymore. There is doubt and hesitation. Even though I am only thirty-one, my body feels like the tree that grew next to the bike rack at school. When the city built a roof over the bike rack, the tree's growth was blocked. It grew on, but in the wrong direction, back into the ground. That's how I feel, like I am growing and aging too, but in the wrong direction. Back into the ground, headfirst.

When I arrived in Amsterdam that day I walked straight from Central Station into the Red Light District—a place I had only heard of when Dave and Simon skipped school to go there and they came back all rowdy. Holding my head up high, I walked past the windows with the red lights and the red curtains, following the canal that would lead me to the Job Center. Women in underwear waved at the men passing by, knocking on the glass and calling at them. The men were old like my father. They walked close to the walls with a strange look in their eyes. Some of them would look at me as if they were in the supermarket and I was a vegetable they could buy. Punkers stared me down as I passed them by, and I was embarrassed by the blue scarf in my orange-blond ponytail. I locked eyes with a junkie who was just sticking a needle in his arm.

I remember I told myself it would all be all right.

I remember NO FUTURE was written in graffiti on the door of the Job Center.

"I think you should try to finish high school," the lady behind the desk at the Job Center told me. She looked at me over the edge of her glasses, her arms folded. The "ten thousand jobs" were nowhere to be seen. "If you insist on dropping out of high school before turning eighteen, you need to register for an employment card in your own town. In Alkmaar."

"But it says here the Job Center offers opportunities for everyone," I said. "Ten thousand jobs. For *everyone*." I waved the ad in front of her face, as if it were evidence in a court case.

"Amsterdam is a big transition for someone your age," the woman said.

"I am not scared," I said. "I might look young, but I am very mature. And I need to make money. Do you know how I could get a house? I heard the social housing program has a long waiting list."

"Since you're underage, you are not able to perform official actions like applying for social housing," the woman said. "Your parents are legally required to house you." She frowned. Then she looked at my open coat and lowered her voice. "You know, there are couples who can't conceive . . . couples who are financially stable . . ."

I got up. The tears that had been building since talking to Anna were starting to sting my eyes. Digging my nails into the skin of my forearms, I walked out of the office and into the streets of Amsterdam. I did not want to cry. I wanted a plan. If only I had money to get my own place, then I could leave my parents. I knew Dave would never have much to offer me and the baby. He was perfectly happy living in that run-down cottage outside of Stompetoren, working in the fields and drinking ten cans of beer each day. His biggest dream was to buy a new tractor.

I wanted more for myself. I had always wanted to leave Stompetoren. I had considered becoming an actress, a weather girl, a presenter. I hadn't really worked it out yet; I was busy getting drunk behind the factory with Anna and Maureen and Dave and Simon. All that was supposed to be a temporary thing. Later would happen later. Plenty of time left.

I tried not to think of how my parents would react. After I had my first kiss, when I was twelve in high school, I made the mistake of telling my mother. I could not sleep and went into my mother's bedroom late in the evening, sat down next to her on the bed, and told her I wasn't sure if I had liked it. The boy had pushed me against a wall and rotated his tongue in my mouth like a windmill. And he squeezed my boob.

My mother had only said, "Never do that again, Marie." Then she turned her back to me in the bed.

I did not understand. Was I supposed to never kiss someone again? Was she ashamed? When I climbed into my own bed I felt so alone, I decided to never tell her anything again. I became really good at being exactly what my parents wanted me to be during the two hours a day I had to spend with them. Be quiet during dinner because we were eating, be quiet during the news because Dad had a hard day, be quiet when he talked because he was always right. When I got my period, I did not ask my mother anything, proud to solve it on my own with the gigantic pads I found in the bottom drawer of my grandmother's bathroom cabinet. I ate mouthfuls of peppermints and parsley after I drank with my friends. My cigarettes I kept in a hollow concrete stone in the bike tunnel.

I was good at secrets.

But this one was going to come out.

After the Job Center visit, I wandered through Amsterdam, peering through shop windows and asking in stores and cafés if they needed to hire someone, only to be sent away or laughed at. I thought of my father's stack of job application letters. I though of the little cards my mother hung in the supermarket: CLEANING LADY FOR HIRE.

"I got this," I said to the baby in my belly as I sat down on a bench in a little park and rolled a cigarette. It wasn't true, but I thought you had to act a little uplifting around people who weren't even born yet. "Something good will happen for us."

And it was at that moment when I noticed the smoke coming from the bushes across from me. There was an old man lying under the branches, his eyes closed, a cigar between his fingers.

His walking stick was lying next to him. The ivory handle was carved in the shape of a dog. I had never seen a walking stick like that before. I looked around. It was a quiet, rich-looking neighborhood with wide lanes and tall poplars.

Gently, I prodded the man with my foot, since bending over was not so easy anymore. "Are you all right, sir?"

The man did not move. I wondered if he had a wallet on him and if God wanted me to look for it.

"Good Lord." A woman carrying garden shears was coming toward me. "Edward?"

"Heart still beating," I said, removing my hand from his chest pocket. "Looks like your husband had one too many. He is just asleep."

"This man is not my husband," the woman said. "This is my neighbor Edward Hond." She nodded at the plaque on the bench. It read MADE POSSIBLE BY EDWARD HOND.

"He makes benches?" I asked.

"He's donated one," the woman said. "He's a philanthropist."

"Aren't they all," I said. "Can't keep it in their pants."

"A philanthropist," she said, "not a philanderer. A philanthropist is someone who has a lot of money and gives it away."

"He gives money away?" I took another look at the man in the bushes. Edward Hond. A man who gives money away.

The woman bent down over Mr. Hond. "Edward! Can you hear me? It's Edna Barneveld, from the Park Committee. Do you need an ambulance?"

I kneeled down too. With my mouth close to his ear I said, "You have to wake up!"

The man opened his eyes a little and looked at me. "Take your shoes off, dear," he mumbled. "You'll ruin the carpet."

"You are not in your house," I said. "You are on the ground and it is wet and cold. That's no place for a tropical person."

"Philanthropic," the lady said.

"Are you an angel?" Edward Hond asked me, clasping my hand.

"No, no, you aren't dead yet," I said. "But you should be in bed. Let me give you a hand."

"How could this have happened?" the man mumbled as I pulled him onto his feet. His gray hair was sticking out on all sides of his head. "I was on my way to the pharmacy. I sat down just for a moment to rest my legs."

I knew how it had happened. The smell of alcohol was coming toward me.

"Edward, you may have had a stroke," the lady said. "Should we call the doctor?" She put her hand on my arm. "I will take care of it. You go on home."

"Doctors just make things worse," I said, pushing the woman's hand away. "Mr. Hond just needs to get to bed."

The old man nodded at the woman as he hung from my arm. "The young lady is very wise. She will take me home. Number 354."

Fathers

The four days following William's arrival, Luis had avoided his living room as much as possible. He ate sitting on the edge of his bed, hoovering the crumbs from his carpet with his Dust Buster 3000. No matter what he was doing—walking home from work, choosing an outfit in the morning, going to the supermarket—Luis thought of William. It was like one of those little games he used to carry around in his pocket, where you had to prevent a little metal ball from getting into a groove and falling through a hole. His thoughts now kept getting stuck in the same groove and falling through the hole over and over again like a bad dream.

In the living room William had spread his documents over the table, his clothes were in small piles on the ground and the windowsill. The documents all had to do with William's father. More and more of these papers were coming in through Estelle. Old phone books for the city of Amsterdam; documentation from the city archives, charity registries, and the Center for Family History; a magazine called *Barons and Baronesses throughout the Centuries*—all aimed at trying to piece together the life of a man who was at the center of all William's thoughts: "my father."

The way William said "my father" irritated Luis, the way his voice got a bit louder when he said that word, as if having a father was something to brag about, as if other people did not have fathers, as if it wasn't the simplest fact that everyone had a father, even animals, except maybe some kind of worm that could invert itself from male to female and have its own children. In any case, Luis had a father, just like William. And no matter what you said about Luis's father, at least Luis didn't have to piece him together from old yellow documents. Luis knew exactly who his father was: David Sol, a man whose eyes were always bleary, a man who never spoke Spanish but still called himself Spanish, a man who went into his barn every night to pretend to work on his wood-carved chess set, a man who accidentally chainsawed his own leg when he was drunk, a man who never stood up for anything but wrote "fuck you" in tiny letters on the back of his wheelchair. But at least he was a man who stayed.

The Philanthropist

The philanthropist walked ahead of me on the stairs toward his apartment on the second floor. I watched him pull himself up by a badly attached banister, and I remember I was afraid that he would fall down on me. I remember thinking I needed to protect my belly if I fell, and I remember realizing I would not be relieved if I miscarried.

The walls of the man's staircase were covered in paintings. They were hanging above and below one another, none of them straight. I had never seen so many paintings in one house. The green wallpaper underneath was barely visible.

Inside the apartment it was dark. I was surprised to see he had only two rooms; I thought a rich man like him would at least have more rooms than my parents in their social housing flat. But still, I could tell he had money. For example there was a crumpled hundred-guilder note hanging from his back pocket, about to fall out, and he did not even notice. There were strange sculptures and antique cabinets and chandeliers everywhere. He had a Miele washing machine and a big color TV. On his desk he had a dagger with an ivory handle to open envelopes with that he said was made for a sultan in Oman. He had a paperweight that looked like it was made of gold. And he had a framed photo of himself on a big boat called *De Hond*.

In his bedroom the philanthropist stepped into his bed without taking his shoes off. He put his cigar on top of a tower of cigar stubs in the ashtray on his nightstand. Then he coughed blood into a handkerchief that he threw on the floor. There was an empty wine bottle standing in the corner of the room, and there was a pile of unopened envelopes addressed to the Edward Hond Foundation for the Needy next to the bed. His dark red velvet curtains were closed; the only light that came in was through tiny moth holes in the fabric.

"I'm a man alone," Mr. Hond said, waving his arm at the mess in his apartment. "An entire life, and all I have to show for it are some houses and some objects. I have no one. I don't even know who to leave my possessions to when I die. 'All great and precious things are lonely.' John Steinbeck. Do you know John Steinbeck?"

"No," I said. "But I used to work with Jan Steenbeek in the tulip fields."

"Blessed are the ignorant," Mr. Hond mumbled, and he patted my hand.

"I suppose," I said, because Jan Steenbeek was very ignorant.

I untied Hond's shoelaces. He watched me as I put them in the corner of the room, next to his walking stick. "You are an angel," he said. "I should give you some reward for helping me. And for saving me from that dreadful Barneveld, who is always after my money."

His breathing made a whistling sound as he pushed himself upright. He started rummaging through a bowl he had on his nightstand, filled with coins, watches, and trinkets. "What do you think of this?" He held up a thick silver ring in the shape of a dog, with tiny sparkling gems as eyes.

"A ring," I said.

"Don't you like diamonds?"

I held the ring in my hands. "Are those real diamonds?"

"I should hope so," he said. "I paid over nine hundred guilders for it." He laughed, which turned into another coughing fit.

While he was doubled over on the bed, coughing, I stared at the ring. The diamond eyes of the dog stared back at me. Nine hundred guilders! That was more than my father's monthly salary at the steel plant.

"The doctors say I should stop smoking," Mr. Hond said, his chest heaving. "But what's the point? I'm not going to be around much longer. Should I go without life's little pleasures? Just so I can live a couple of weeks longer in misery?"

He took the cigar stub from the ashtray.

"I'd rather have one last month with pleasure than a year without."

And in the cloud of cigar smoke the philanthropist blew out, I had a vision. I saw myself opening the heavy oak front door for my parents, guiding them up the stairs to my Amsterdam apartment. I saw the admiration in their eyes as they looked around the baby's room.

I gave the ring back to Mr. Hond. "Thank you, but I really can't accept this," I said to him in my sweetest voice. "You should not have to thank me for a little help. I think a philanthropist like you deserves to be helped; after all, you've helped so many others."

"Did Barneveld tell you that?" Mr. Hond mumbled. "Helping others . . ."

"I just think it is wrong that you are alone, that's all."

"Ach," Mr. Hond coughed. "Who can help me? And don't say I must hire a nurse. I tried, believe me. I nearly married one, for goodness' sake. They just take away your cigars and annoy you."

"I could stop by again next week," I said. "Tidy a little bit. I won't annoy you. I could do the laundry, make you tea, get you those cigars."

"Why would you do that?"

"I could learn from you," I said. "You have seen a lot, you have traveled. And I kind of want to learn about the real world, how it works."

Mr. Hond shook his head slowly. "The real world is a dangerous place. A girl like you might not like how it works."

"Well," I said, sliding my hands over my belly, "knowledge is protection."

Mr. Hond laughed loud. Then he lowered his head onto the pillow. "There are a couple of dirty handkerchiefs under the bed, I believe. If you could pick those up, I'd be forever grateful."

A One-Person Place

"This is Marina," Luis said in a loud voice as he opened the living room door and let his cleaning lady into the space. "Marina, this is William, the man I told you about who sits in my kitchen."

"Oh, hello, Marina," William said, lowering his papers. He took off his glasses and smiled. "Pleased to meet you."

"Hello," Marina said. Then she turned to Luis. "Maybe I can start in the bathroom today?"

"Yes," Luis said, but he did not want her to start yet. He wanted to show William how he lived here, that there were things that happened in this apartment, routines and habits. He wanted him to feel like he was intruding on something.

"Marina speaks Portuguese," Luis said, "but she has learned Dutch in one year." He tried to put his arm around her, but she bent down to get the bucket from under the sink.

"She is a little bit annoyed," Luis said to William. "Because normally there's no one in her way. Normally she starts in the kitchen. We have a routine."

"*Você está gostando daqui Marina?*" he heard William say to Marina suddenly. "*Desta casa?*"

"*Sim,*" Marina answered, shrugging.

"What are you saying?" Luis asked Marina. "What is he saying to you?"

"I speak several foreign languages," William said to Luis. "I am speaking Portuguese with your beautiful cleaning lady. With a PhD in classical languages, one can't help but dabble in a bit of vulgar Latin. But I don't want you to feel excluded."

Suddenly Luis noticed that the paint on the window frame was coming off in some places. He put his hand on the chipped surface. The dull green it was painted in when he first came here had somehow worked itself up to the surface. How was that possible? Three layers of paint. It had to be some kind of humidity problem, probably because William was in here all day, breathing on everything.

"What kind of person is that?" Luis whispered to Marina a little later. "What kind of person stays in someone else's home like that?" He was leaning against the sink while Marina cleaned the bathroom. With his finger he followed the grout between the tiles, the straight lines. His finger trembled. "I would never want to stay in a stranger's house like this, no matter how much pain I had. Would you do that?"

"I am staying with a friend at the moment," Marina said. "My landlord kicked me out because I found a little stray dog and brought it into the house."

"Here we think it's strange," Luis said, "to sit in someone's apartment so unwanted. He even shaves at my sink. This morning I had hairs in my toothbrush. I hear him moving furniture around at night. I have this idea that he pulled up a piece of the carpet to look underneath at the floorboards. He puts everything back in the wrong place. My window blinds are crooked because he does not use the remote properly. And my neighbor brings him groceries." Luis caught his reflection in the mirror. His cheeks looked like someone had slapped him.

"Maybe your friend is lonely too," Marina said as she splashed half a bucket of soapy water into the toilet and flushed it.

"He is not my friend," Luis said.

"Maybe you can help him a little bit," Marina said.

"Should I help everyone?" Luis asked. "Should I give everyone my house and my clothes and my bed?"

"Who is everyone?" Marina asked.

"He said he will go after seven days," he continued. "It's been five now. This apartment is too small for two people. It's a one-person place."

Marina said nothing. She sprayed blue liquid on the mirror.

"When you're here it's different, of course," Luis said. "With you it's fine. You're soft. You are a soft person to have around."

She laughed. It was a hard laugh. He realized he'd never heard her laugh before.

"Luis," she said, rubbing blue liquid over the mirror, "I am not soft."

"Yes," Luis said. "You are soft, you are like a bunny." He liked that comparison. She was a little bit like a bunny, with her big dark eyes and the soft little hairs on her arms.

Marina shook her head. "I am more like a lizard. I wait under a rock, and when it's my time I come out and lie in the sun. And you are a turtle. If there is danger, you hide in your house." She laughed again.

Luis looked at his cleaning lady as she brushed the cloth over the mirror. Her hair was in a tiny ponytail as usual, and she wore jogging trousers and a wide T-shirt. He noticed there was a hole in the fabric under her armpit, so he could see the edge of her salmon-colored bra. Did William call her beautiful? For a moment he wondered whether he really knew Marina at all. He thought of the first time she came to work for him. Together they carried his television up the stairs and put all the channels in the right order. Then they watched a documentary about sea animals. He paid her ten euro per hour, unregistered.

"Luis," Marina said. "Your face."

"I know," Luis said impatiently. "I have red spots. I can't help it. I haven't felt good since he got here. He keeps asking questions. How did this happen, who did what, why? People act like the past has to make sense, like there is some big plan and everything always goes how it should go. But they don't. Most things just happen. Maybe I did accidentally push. Maybe I should have called an ambulance. But they want to ask questions, make documentation, who did what, why did it happen, shine a light on everything. You shouldn't shine a light on a little misunderstanding. A small mistake seems terrible when you shine a light on it. It will seem much more deliberate than it really was at the moment. Most things happen in some kind of mist. No matter how hard you try to make a plan, you still do this and that and you don't know how it works out. One thing leads to another. You should not shine a light on a mistake. Does one little red dot in a black painting make it a red painting? Not until you shine a light on it, until you keep going on about it. People should sweep the mistakes under the carpet and forget about them. Don't you think? Most people just act like they have a plan, but they don't. Most things just happen in some kind of mist. There is no plan." He took a deep breath. It wasn't like him to talk so much.

"I have a plan," Marina said. "When I've made enough money, I'm going to go back to Minas Gerais and finish my master's in biology. Then I am going to set up a communal living space, and together we will build houses and grow food and take care of one another. Also, we will take in stray dogs."

"That is not possible," Luis said. He pushed his finger against his brow. "What I meant to say was some things happen in some kind of mist, no matter how hard you try to make a plan. You panic and you just do something. And later you try to make a story about it. You know what I mean? You just panic."

Marina put her bucket down. She placed her hands on Luis's shoulders. "Don't panic," she said.

Luis wanted to say he was not panicking, but the words stuck in his throat as he felt the warmth of her small, bony fingers wave through his body. His shoulders lowered down under her hands. For a second he had the strange sensation of everything being fine. Pleasant even. Then Marina let go and switched on the vacuum.

Later, when Luis and Marina were watching a documentary in his bedroom, Luis could still feel the memory of her soft hands on his shoulders. Normally they watched the documentaries in the living room, but now that Luis had moved the television to his bedroom, they sat alongside each other on the waterbed. Marina was sitting on one end of the bed, Luis on the other. The documentary was about chimpanzees. Luis could not pay attention to it. The moment between him and Marina brought back a moment from a long time ago, of the yearly horse fair in Stompetoren. He remembered the smell of manure, the trailers from all over the Netherlands coming into the village, the sunburn on his forearms and nose. He was twenty at the time. He was watching the big Friesian horses with their black manes being paraded around from the top of the fence at the edge of the field, when a group of girls approached him. He imagined they were looking for something else or coming to mock him, but instead one of the girls came up to him and said, "My friend Brigitte likes you."

A girl was pushed to the front of the group. She giggled. Luis saw a flash of a smile with braces that shimmered in the sun, hair that had an orange hue to it, like there was a halo of gold around her head. Quickly he lowered his head. Red spots were already swarming his neck, and he was certain this would turn into a joke of some sort. But no one started laughing. Instead, the group left, and the girl, Brigitte, stayed. She sat down next to him on the fence.

Luis remembered he did not dare to look up for a while, knowing his face was bright red like a strawberry, so he just stared at his shoes and at her shoes. She was wearing muddy white sneakers with purple glitter. And she talked: about the horses, about her favorite ones, about his sunburn. She had teasingly pushed her hands on his shoulders, laughing at the white fingerprints that emerged on his red skin.

Why had this memory come back to him so vividly? Of course it was because of Marina holding his shoulders before, but really, it was the presence of the visitor that had caused it. Everything had come loose since he'd arrived.

On the screen, two groups of chimpanzees shouted at each other from the treetops. "When two rival chimpanzees meet on their own, it remains peaceful," the voice-over said. "But when they meet in groups, it's another story."

The chimpanzees on the screen ran screaming through the jungle to attack the other group. When they got hold of one of the others, they took turns jumping on top of him.

"Any body part that sticks out is likely to be pulled off," the commentator said.

Suddenly, Luis switched the TV off. He searched for the words to explain to Marina, but he could not find them.

"I understand," Marina said, even though he hadn't said anything.

They were quiet for a while.

"You know, in biology you learn about survival of the fittest, how brutal it can be. But you also learn about mutual aid among animals. It means that one organism temporarily sacrifices something for another organism to get stronger. People don't talk about that a lot. But animals help each other. Sharing food, showing gratitude, protecting each other . . . the animals do that too. It's in our nature."

She got up from the bed and left the room. In the hallway Luis waited for Marina to get her coat from the living room. He could hear William speaking with her. It sounded like they were speaking Portuguese. He listened to the whispering and the giggling on the other side of the door. When had she started giggling like that?

When Marina came out of the living room, Luis gave her the twenty like he always did.

"See you next time," he said. He wanted to say something, make her laugh too, make her belong to him again, but he could not think of anything. Marina put on her headphones and walked down the stairs, past the brownish blood smear on the wall at the bottom of the staircase. He'd forgotten to ask her to clean it.

The Amsterdam Apartment

That night Luis sat in front of the mirror in his bedroom. His cheeks were red and they seemed fuller. Since William's arrival he'd been eating mostly bagels and doughnuts, and he'd skipped his workouts. Like his mother, he easily gained weight.

Luis thought of the cake his mother had made for his twenty-first birthday. It was a cake made of crustless white bread, with Nutella between the layers. Luis had invented the cake when he was little, and every year she kept making it. Luis remembered looking at it, how it sat on the same old blue plate with the birds on it. He was too old for this. On the screen Tom Cruise was soaring through the sky in a supersonic aircraft. His mother had rented *Top Gun* for him. They were in the TV room, sitting on the pillows on the floor. It used to be his favorite moment of his birthday, eating cake in the TV room, watching a movie. He felt guilty for not enjoying it. In the last few years, it had become unclear if they did these things for him or for her.

Twenty-one. Luis had seen his classmates graduate, he had seen some of them move away, some of them stay, some of them working at their dad's company or café, some of them starting their own thing. Some already had children. He still worked in the fields for Raat and did odd jobs at other farms in the neighborhood. It paid well if he worked hard, but it was all cash money and not something you could call a profession at all.

In the distance, Luis heard the barking of the dogs at the breeder down the dike. A noise he'd heard all his life.

"So, Mum," he said to his mother.

His mother put her arm around him. "Yes."

"The apartment in Amsterdam. That you inherited from this uncle, Edward."

"Yes, the apartment," his mother said slowly.

"What's going on with that?" Luis asked.

"What do you mean 'what's going on with that'?" His mother pulled her arm back.

Luis had taken a deep breath. "Well, it's not rented out, is it?"

"No," his mother said. "Why are you asking me this?" He knew this voice. It meant, "Leave me alone, am I not dealing with enough?" It meant, "If you push further, I will be upset." There could be days of silence, no eye contact. It did not feel right to keep asking about something she did not want to talk about, but Luis pushed on.

"I wondered, why don't we rent it out? I mean, right now it just costs us."

He'd seen the bills come in: city tax, light, water. He knew where she kept the bills, in a coffee tin in her closet in the bedroom. That's also where she kept the key.

"Us?" his mother asked.

"You," Luis said quickly. Red spots were climbing up his cheeks. "It is costing you." He worked up the courage to continue. "I was thinking maybe I could stay there and do up the place.

Get a job in Amsterdam. Brigitte says I need to think about moving out."

"Brigitte?"

Luis and Brigitte had been together for four months by then. She was his first real girlfriend. Brigitte was seventeen. Brigitte wore a bra with yellow bows on the straps that poked out from under her shirt. Brigitte was everything. The day after meeting her at the horse fair, Luis had taken the bus to Alkmaar and waited for her to finish her shift at the supermarket. They wandered around town together and sat by the water, watching a seagull struggle to swallow a fish. She laughed at all his jokes. She made kissing sounds at cats.

She filled him with an energy that made him walk the three hours to Alkmaar when his bike had a flat tire, just to see her during her lunch break. She made him walk into restaurants and request a table and order for them. He went around the farms in Stompetoren to ask for work, so he made more money. Just her asking for something was enough for him to overcome years of shyness. He got his hair cut in a professional salon, instead of in Irma Raat's kitchen, because she said she like the feeling of short hair when she ran her hands over it. When she said she wanted to go to the beach, he worked out the train timetables and he took her to Bergen, and he watched her run into the sea, he untied her bikini strings and rubbed her shoulders with sunscreen. She said she liked the way his face always revealed what he felt, so she never had to guess. She said she felt safe with him because he was strong. She said she liked his eyes.

It was like God (even though he did not believe in God) had suddenly remembered Luis Sol and decided to throw all the luck he'd missed out on during his lifetime his way in one big explosion.

"Do you use condoms?" his mother asked.

"Of course," Luis said hastily. From his tenth birthday on, his mother had given him boxes of condoms, they had been piling up in his drawer. She had given him talks about sex for as long as he could remember, which made him very aware that he himself had been unplanned.

"I have always been open and clear about that," she said. "I have always tried to tell you everything you need to know. Never do anything, let the girl start it."

"Yes," he said. "We are safe. I know . . . I am responsible and . . . we don't do anything she doesn't want, of course, she wants . . . We are just . . . It's not just . . . Brigitte is . . ." He rubbed the back of his neck. "I like her a lot."

"Maybe it's time we meet Brigitte," his mother said.

The Philanthropist

Until I met Mr. Hond, I thought that rich people were tidier than poor people. If I had a stain on my shoe, my mother got mad and said that was "poverty." Putting my feet on the table—poverty. Cursing—poverty. Wrinkled clothes—poverty. When the doctor came to our house, my mother mopped the floors, no matter how sick she was. We always had to be tidy so we did not have the look of poverty, which made me believe the rich didn't have dirty habits at all.

When I got to know Mr. Hond's habits I learned that my mother was wrong. Rich people are filthier than poor people. They just do whatever they want. They have old newspapers lying around, teacups with brown stains, dusty armoires with drawers that have half-eaten biscuits in them. It is "distinguished" to wear old clothes and "eccentric" to not comb your hair. And while my mother was ironing her handkerchiefs and underpants, doing her hair to watch Queen Beatrix get crowned on TV, and making potpourri to freshen up the toilet, Mr. Hond was reading the newspaper half drunk in his bed with his shoes on.

Since that first day I met him, I went to Mr. Hond's apartment every week, spending half the money I made at my new job in the mushroom factory on the train and the bus. Two hours each way. I went on Sundays. While my parents were praying for me in church, or for themselves more likely, I was scrubbing the bloodstains from Mr. Hond's handkerchiefs, ironing his shirts, doing his dishes, clipping his toenails, washing his curtains. My walks from the train station to his apartment on Rooseveltlaan were like a prayer. With every step I prayed: Let—*step*—him—*step*—help—*step*—us.

I always had a cigarette on the stone steps to the front door of number 354 before I went in, my hand on my belly that was growing larger each week. Then I waved at Mrs. Barneveld—the old lady from the park who was always staring suspiciously at me from her window—took a deep breath, and turned around to ring the doorbell.

Inside his apartment it was another world. The old man sat in his bed all day, in gray pajamas with E.H. stitched on the pocket. I got used to the darkness in the house, the sweet, sweaty smell in the bedroom. I got used to the sound of the different clocks ticking, his rasping cough. I got to know all the different paintings, all the sculptures and artworks; I knew how to tell a lithograph from a serigraph and what it means when an Omani dagger has an ivory handle instead of gold. I saw all the photos of his different homes in London and Marrakech and the chalet in Switzerland and the sailing boat.

Even though I had to clean, it was even starting to feel nice to be there. I could dream about my future. Mr. Hond said I was smart and I could be anything I wanted in the world. At home my parents took turns standing at my barricaded bedroom door, hammering on about how I had nothing to offer a baby, how there were procedures and solutions. (A teenage pregnancy, it does not get more "poverty" than that.) At least Hond did not treat me as a problem. He said I could become one of the greatest art dealers in Amsterdam, baby or no baby, if I would stop being so "impossibly naive." While I cleaned around him, he explained how to become a good art dealer, how to make a quick sale, how to bargain with locals, and how to recognize a good war.

"An art dealer knows one thing about wars," Mr. Hond told me. "Where there's war, there's opportunity." He pointed at a black-and-white drawing of a lady in a dress sitting on a horse. "That one, for instance, is a Renoir. Lithograph. It was my first big catch. The owners had to leave the country urgently. Traded it for two boat tickets."

I just nodded. It did not seem very philanthropical to me to scam people out of their art during a war, but ever since I caught our pastor looking up my mother's skirt when we were decorating the chapel, I knew that people can be saints in one area of their lives and sleazy in another.

"And this," Mr. Hond said another time, "is an unknown study by the real Malevich, believe it or not." He pointed at a canvas that was covered in black paint. "It was one of his first tryouts for his famous painting. In Stalin's final years I had a very sharp insight. I had to leave the country for a little while, and I decided to travel to Russia. All art declared 'anti-Soviet' I took off the owners' hands, and I spared many people a trip to the gulag. It helped them, it helped me. And there is another good lesson for you, Marie: economy is like nature, it is about seizing opportunity. If you don't do it, someone else will."

I stared at the completely black canvas. "The painter did not like the painting?" I asked.

"I think he did," Mr. Hond said.

"Then why did he paint over it?"

Mr. Hond started laughing, which always turned into one of his coughing fits because of his lung disease. During these fits he curled up like a child in the bed. This time he stuck his hand out from under the blanket, grabbing hold of my thigh. As he coughed he held on to me, his pointy nails poking into my skin.

"You're delightful," Mr. Hond mumbled as he emerged from under the blanket, his hand still around my leg and his chest still moving up and down very quickly. "So untarnished. A little angel. Standing by me, caring for me. If everyone looked after each other the way you look after me, the world would be a better place. But the world is tough and selfish. It is the animal in men that causes trouble."

"That's true," I said. I thought about the animal in me and Dave when I unbuttoned his jeans behind the mill. I still hadn't talked to him. I wished he would come and see me, but at the same time I avoided him. Anna and I always made jokes about his slow way of speaking, about how all he could talk about was his tractor. But I did not tell her I couldn't keep myself from staring at his brown eyes, his tanned shoulders. He was Spanish, the most exotic thing in Stompetoren.

"Are you sure you don't need any compensation for all the work you do here?" Mr. Hond asked me. "All those train rides, all those Sundays."

"I like spending time with you," I said in my most angelic voice. I sat down on the edge of the bed and put my hand on my belly. "We are like family now. The baby has started to kick."

"I want to feel it," he said. "'The soul is healed by being with children.' Dostoyevsky. Do you know Dostoyevsky?"

"No," I said. "But I can tell he has a nice way of putting things."

"You make my life interesting again, dear Marie," Mr. Hond said. His hand slid under the seam of my sweater and stroked my round belly. "I thought my final days would be joyless. But you bring life back into me. You're a good girl. Obedient. I promise I won't try to take advantage of that. I will take care of you."

Space Law

Luis was stuck in a dream about his mother. She was sitting on his chest; he could not move his body. She said, "Who is listening?" Slowly the voice of his mother became a male voice. The voice was coming from his hallway, in the real world. Luis tried to open his eyes. "Who's there?" he tried to say, but his voice wasn't coming out.

"He is still asleep, our Oblomov," he heard William's voice say in the hallway.

"What are you talking about? Let me in."

Another voice.

Through his eyelashes Luis saw Hadi step into his bedroom. The light coming in through the branches of the poplar tree created a shadow pattern on his white tracksuit. He was back from Crete.

"Luis! Wake up!" Hadi pulled the blanket from Luis's body. "What's the matter with you? I am away for a week and now there's a hobo living on your couch?"

"I have a visitor," Luis said, pushing himself upright.

"I know," Hadi said. "He let me in. Did you get fat?" Hadi took a step back to look at him.

Luis looked down at his belly. "Since William's been here I haven't—"

"William!" Hadi threw his hands in the air. "Why is this guy here?"

"Six days ago he rang my doorbell," Luis explained. "He said he wanted to have a look at the apartment because he was born here. Estelle said he deserved it. But then he got dizzy and fell down the stairs. He has to rest for one week."

"In here? Luis!" Hadi shook his head in disbelief. "Do you understand what is happening here? Do you understand that his injury is fake? That his whole story is fake? Did he even see a doctor?"

"Estelle looked at it," Luis said, rubbing his neck. "And he's a professor."

"A professor!" Hadi laughed. "Why not? Do you know this professor put his name on your letter box? Why are you letting this happen? What's the matter with you?"

"I-I . . ." Luis stammered. He did not know what was the matter with him. He always knew there was something the matter with him, but he did not know what it was.

Hadi turned around. "I will end this for you," he announced.

"Wait." Quickly putting on his jogging bottoms, Luis followed Hadi into the hallway, where he banged open the living room door.

"Oh, hello, Hadi," William said, looking up from his papers. His voice had the same disdainful tone he used with Luis. This time, though, Luis could tell there was something different in his body. Tension.

"Hello," Hadi said. "I thought I'd introduce myself properly. Because I'm Luis's best friend. I have known him for eight years, ever since he moved here. I got him his first job, I found him a cleaner, I even find him girlfriends. We are like brothers, Luis and I, and I keep an eye out for him. He is too kind, Luis, he can't say no. So I make sure that people do not take advantage of him, if you know what I mean."

"It is not very hard to distinguish what you mean," William said. "But I can assure you, I am doing Luis no harm. Au contraire, I was harmed. Did he tell you?"

"He told me about some fake concussion, yes," Hadi said. "Do you want me to bring you to the hospital? My car is outside."

"The concussion is very real, unfortunately," William said. "But it is only rest I need. Luis has allowed me to stay here a little longer, which was very kind of him. I was actually born here, in this apartment."

"Could you speak up a bit?" Hadi said, closing the living room door. "For a man, you have a very soft voice."

"I was born here," William repeated, a bit louder now. Luis noticed him glancing at the door, like he was in a room with a tiger.

"What?" Hadi said. "Louder please."

"I was born here," William said one more time.

"Interesting," Hadi said, not looking away from William. "And now you're fifty and you come out of nowhere, after all these years, just because you were born here? It wouldn't have anything to do with the fact that these houses are worth a fortune? I bet you wouldn't be that interested if you were born in one of the social housing blocks on the other side of Van Woustraat. People only attach meaning to where they were born if they were born someplace nice. Do you think Luis goes around attaching all kinds of meaning to that shithole where he's from?"

"I needed to see my childhood home," William said. "You see, as a child growing up fatherless, I have developed a complex relationship with my identity—"

"It's tragic," Hadi interrupted him. "Now let me tell you my diagnosis. You ring a doorbell, with your soft voice and your professor story. The neighbor likes you because she never trusted Luis and she hates his colored lights and marble name plates, which bring the property prices down. She wants to help you. But your story is fake. I know your type. This is how you get around. You are the kind of person to ring old people's doorbells and tell them you are their long-lost son, and you live like a prince in their house until some relative appears and calls you out on it. Let me tell you, I am that relative."

He put an arm around Luis's shoulders.

"My friend Luis here is a visual person. He is not a communicator. He always feels guilty, even though he's done nothing wrong. That's why he lets everyone walk over him. He does not make friends because he shouts when he thinks he is talking. He scares people. None of the neighbors like him."

Luis did not know that.

"But who has he ever harmed? He might look big, he might shout a little, but shouting is an honest action. Fighting is also honest, when it is a fight man to man. Pretending your father lived here, pretending you were pushed down the stairs, pretending you have a serious injury—that is not honest. Especially if you do it to a harmless person like Luis, who never stands up for himself."

"My injury is very real, unfortunately," William said. "Perhaps you do not see this purple bump on my forehead? I did not do that to myself. Did he tell you he pushed me down the stairs?"

"He fell," Luis said. "I did not push him."

"I don't care if Luis pushed you or not," Hadi said to William. "Luis is my friend, and he can push the whole of Amsterdam down the stairs if he wants to."

"I did not push him," Luis said, standing a little taller. "I think he faked it, I think he planned it. Why else would he bring so much food and clothes with him?"

"I did not jump down your stairs," William said. "I am not suicidal."

"I hear him at night, dragging furniture around, even though he says he can't walk or do things," Luis said.

"We're packing you up, my friend," Hadi said to William. He started throwing documents into William's suitcase. "Everything that's still here in two minutes will go out via the window."

"Careful, careful . . ." William said. His eyes shot toward Luis. "Luis, I told you, all I have of my father . . ." His voice was high. He started taking the documents out of the suitcase again, pushing Hadi's hands away.

"Is everything all right? The door was open and I heard shouting."

Luis turned around. Estelle was standing in the doorway of the living room.

"What is going on?"

"Nothing," Hadi said.

"He attacked me," William said.

Estelle looked at Hadi. "I'm going to call the police. William, you have a witness. He was violent."

"When was I violent?" Hadi asked.

"You were threatening me," William said. "You were damaging my property."

"Do you know what is threatening?" Hadi asked. "Invading someone's home, acting like you own the place, deceiving someone. Maybe we should be the ones to call the police, Luis. Say there is an intruder in your apartment."

"Whose apartment?" Estelle asked. She waved a piece of paper in the air. "I have just received the paperwork from the Land Registry, and this apartment is registered in the name of Edward Hond, William's father, since 1941 to his day."

"Hadi," Luis said, "can I talk to you downstairs?"

The stone steps were cold under Luis's bare feet as he walked Hadi down the stairs toward the street. He noticed a piece of tape was pasted over his marble name plate, above his letter box. The tape had "Prof. Dr. William Rose" written on it, in Estelle's handwriting.

"Why didn't you call me?" Hadi asked. "You could have told me about this guy before."

"Because he would have left," Luis said. "He is leaving today."

"He is not going anywhere!" Hadi said. "What is that nonsense about his father's name in the Land Registry? Do you know anything about that? Didn't your mother inherit this place from some rich uncle or something? What was his name?"

Luis rubbed his hands over his face. "I always wanted to ask. And I did ask. But she never wanted to explain any of it."

"What are you talking about?" Hadi said.

"I mean, who knows how she got it?" Luis said. "How it all went, the details . . . Do you know everything about your parents?"

"You should know, Luis." Hadi shook his head. He put his hands on Luis's shoulders. "I've told you before, you need to get your head out of the sand. What is yours? What do you owe? What are you entitled to? You need to know your rights, your obligations. Not dealing with things, that's for other people"— he nodded at Estelle's apartment—"for people who have an escape hatch, a trust fund, a second home. Okay?"

"Okay," Luis said.

"Okay," Hadi said. He kissed Luis on his cheek. "Call this woman." He handed Luis a business card. "She's the lawyer who gave the 'Resist Preventive Frisk' course in the community center I organized last month."

Luis looked at the card. "Jet Adelman, International Waters and Space Law" it said on one side. On the other side was a picture of two colliding spaceships.

"She takes any kind of case," Hadi said. "And she's affordable, because there's not much work in her field."

This is the fifth day in my father's apartment in Amsterdam. There are things happening I never expected. Most importantly, Estelle requested documents from the Land Registry, and they show that the ownership is still registered in my father's name! I have it here in front of me: Edward Hond, registered in the name of. They did not see any other name in the system. Luis says he has proof of his mother owning this place since the eighties, but so far I have not seen it. He can't explain how she bought it, why she never lived here. How would they ever have gotten such an expensive apartment? From what I found out, they lived in a small home in the countryside in the north of Holland. They sound working class, if they worked at all.

I find myself thinking more and more that something criminal might have taken place here. In the year 1987, the bank account of my father's foundation was completely emptied. Estelle found the end-of-year statements in the chamber of commerce for me. Donations made to charities in Morocco and Switzerland, obscure bank accounts that are now impossible to trace. Who made those donations?

When I first heard of this address, I assumed it would be the starting place of my quest. I imagined there would be traces of my father here; I kind of hoped there would perhaps be family members, a lineage, perhaps even aristocratic! My deepest wish, of course, was to find him. But otherwise his properties, maybe those vacation homes my mother mentioned in the letter. But there is no trace of any family, no other homes. It begins and ends in this apartment.

It's just that I can't imagine Luis being capable of crime. He seems too nervous for it, too transparent. All his thoughts and desires seem to be completely on the surface. Today I heard him talk to himself while he ironed his apron. 'First the seams, then the edges, finally the centre', he was repeating to himself.

We could not be more different as people. I feel like I have found my seat in the theatre of the world, but someone is already in it. I felt this from the moment I stepped through that front door. I can see my origin here, despite all the glass and white and marble Luis has littered this apartment with. 'The space between the shapes needs to be calm', he said that first day I came here. I am guessing my shape is the most disturbing element he could ever have imagined appearing in his apartment.

The Philanthropist

A hometown has tentacles. It grabs hold of you and pulls you in. After five months of working at the Bijenkorf in Amsterdam, Anna Beemster was back in Stompetoren. She had left the nest like a bird, but her parents had wound a string around her leg. And when her mother fell over in the supermarket with a blood clot in her brain, Anna's father started pulling at the string. She had to quit the Bijenkorf and help out in her dad's tobacco store with her civilized way of speaking, though nobody cared for it. It made me very happy to see her behind the counter again. The jealousy that I felt when I saw other girls getting on with their lives scared me sometimes. I felt so angry at anyone who was able to leave Stompetoren and explore the world, while I was growing more heavy and more stuck with each month.

My body was expanding in a terrible way. My belly was round with stretch marks, my ankles were fat. The only clothes that fit me were my mother's wide sixties sweaters, and when I saw myself in the mirrored doors of the mushroom factory canteen, I could not breathe because I felt like I'd become her.

Only when I got on the train to Amsterdam I felt free. Going to Mr. Hond's place was evidence that my hometown hadn't grabbed hold of me yet. In the apartment, I ignored my heavy body as much as I could and scrubbed the toilet, washed his sheets, tidied the house while he watched me from the bed. Every day there were letters coming in for the Hond Foundation, from people asking for money. Mr. Hond just threw them on a pile next to the bed. And whenever I had the chance, I shoved all the letters from the needy in the bin. Why should they get money, while I was here taking care of him? When the old man keeled over, I was going to be sitting front row.

Sometimes the doorbell rang, but I always advised him not to open it. "Let them write letters," I said. "You need your rest."

"You're an angel," Mr. Hond would tell me. "Always looking out for me."

After two months, he asked me to sit down on the edge of the bed. He wanted to talk about something, he said.

"How long until the child comes, dear Marie?" Hond asked. "How are you doing?"

"Only three more months." I started the story I had practiced in my mind so many times. "I know I should be happy, but . . ." My voice broke. I had practiced fake crying in my bedroom mirror many times, but real tears immediately began streaming down my cheeks. It was nice to have someone ask me how I felt without instantly telling me what to do.

"I wish I knew how I'm going to manage," I said. "I have no money, no job, no place to live. My parents are no help. All they talk about is how stupid I am." My parents had called me downstairs the night before. Somewhere inside me there was a hope that they would say, "We forgive you, we will help you, everything will be all right." But it was to give me a list of rules that would apply after I had the baby. Only go out for useful things. Stay home every evening. No jobs. Don't expect them to babysit. Breastfeed for a minimum of twelve months. No alcohol. No boys.

"And the father?" Hond asked.

"The father wants nothing to do with the baby," I said. This wasn't completely true—I had avoided Dave since I found out. But I was sure he must have heard of my changing shape, and he hadn't made any effort to find me. He never showed up at the mushroom factory or at my parents' or anything.

"Does he have money?" Mr. Hond asked.

"No," I said. "He's got a tractor that he rents out, but that's all. And he keeps getting fired everywhere he works."

"Sometimes I feel the poor just aren't worthy of help," Mr. Hond said, shaking his head. "They are so stupid about money, toiling away in some factory, then drinking up the salary. Never investing, never saving. If I was born poor, I would start my own company—something small, like cleaning windows—save up, get employees, live modestly." He folded his skinny arms over the sheets. "I'm afraid I would be rich again very quickly."

"Of course," I said, thinking, You drink wine nonstop and lie in bed all day.

"Of course my family gave me a good start," he continued. "They owned some property, I had good schooling, some money to help me on my way. But my family could give me these things because they earned them, or at least their ancestors did. They worked hard for them, or relatively hard; they were smart people. So of course the kids are smart too. Survival of the fittest. Inequality in wealth is a natural consequence of inequality in strength.

Nature is simply unequal. People refuse to accept that." He nodded at the pile of unopened letters by his bed. "Instead of complaining, those people should try using their brains. Work hard, get on with it."

"But what do you do for the poor then?" I asked. "How, I mean, do you help them?"

"Mostly I let them be," he said. "They won't learn anything if they get everything for free. Everything is provided, good schools, good hospitals. They just need to get themselves together."

"But what do you do with the foundation?" I asked.

"It's always good to have a foundation in your back pocket when the taxman shows up. And, of course, I offer hope. The foundation offers hope. All these people who write letters, the hope motivates them to assess their situation, describe it, make a first step to doing something about it. Visualizing what you need, believing you may have access to it—that is the only way to begin to get out of something."

I thought of my own situation. I visualized Mr. Hond's apartment, redecorated, light blue curtains in the baby's bedroom moving softly in the wind, my name by the doorbell.

"Of course, the foundation does give money away," he said. "The park over there"—he waved at the window with his hand— "I made a donation for the benches. And I bought my boat"—he pointed at the picture frame—"at a charity auction. I have come to believe that charity is as pointless as it is necessary. One needs to do some of it, of course. God forbid the poor get angry at us." He squeezed my hand. "Personally, I think it's better to give everything to someone who deserves it."

"Someone whose life would be changed by it," I agreed.

Holy Base

"Adelman Law, how can I help you?"

"This is Luis Sol," Luis said, pushing his phone against his ear. "I have a question for the lawyer." He was standing in the park in the middle of Rooseveltlaan, still barefoot and without a T-shirt. He did not want to make the phone call in the house where William could hear him.

"I can't hear you," the woman said. "Does this have to do with the Apollo National Park on the moon?"

"The moon?" Luis said, covering the phone with his hand as the sound of a tram's brakes squealed through the street.

"The U.S. planning a national park on the moon? Where their national legislation would apply? I wrote an article about it for my blog."

"I don't care about the moon, there is a man in my house," Luis said.

"That is an absurd statement," the woman said. "The moon matters to all of us. It is important for people to realize this. Outer space qualifies as *res communis*, the property of all, under Article 1 of the Outer Space Treaty. If America did create a national park there, it would mean a part of the moon is ruled by the American government. They would be the first to take possession of a piece of space. All citizens of the world should care about that, because it's their possession that is stolen! Meanwhile China has found a mineral with a potential energy source on the moon. It is an extremely interesting and important phase of extra-terrestrial governing. If we unite as people and we do it differently in space, we could start a whole new system out there. New legislation, new rules, a clean slate. But the people need to do it, not the governments or the companies. We could start an eco-an-archist society, living in equality with animals and technological entities. On paper at first, then in reality. A new world order, Mr. Son."

"My name is Sol," Luis said. "Could I talk to the lawyer, please?"

"I am the lawyer," the woman said. "I am Jet Adelman."

"And I am Hadi's friend," Luis said. "He said you could help me. There is a man in my apartment. He will not leave. It's nothing to do with the moon, it's my life."

"That's a pity," the lawyer said.

Luis heard the sound of papers being moved.

"But a friend of Hadi is a friend of mine. There is a man in your apartment you said? And you are the rightful owner?"

"Yes," Luis said. "I have lived there for years."

"'Rightful' is a confusing term," the lawyer said. "People think it has to do with feeling rightful, but there are no feelings involved. I use the term 'rightful' in the legal sense, which means by law."

"I am a visual person," Luis said. "There is someone in my apartment. I am making this call in the park instead of in my home because I don't want him to hear it."

"The park is a little bit your home," the lawyer said. "*Res publica*. Public property. You own a lot more of this world than you know."

"Can you help me?" Luis asked. "Hadi said you can help."

"I am a licensed space and international waters lawyer," the woman said. "Territory is one of my favorite topics. It's incredibly diverse. For instance, did you know that Iceland once passed a law that stated that the fish swimming in its waters would remain Icelandic fish wherever they went, with Icelandic laws applying to them, and nobody was allowed to catch them aside from the Icelanders? Did you know animals are allowed to cross all borders, unless they are domestic animals? Did you know Russia once placed a titanium flag on the seafloor under the North Pole in an attempt to claim the territory? International territory laws are very interesting because they change. Of course, that is exactly what people have against democracy, deep down. Everything can change all the time, depending on what the majority wants. In the end, the law can turn into anything. This is disturbing to them. It's not like the Bible, no holy base, no deep-rooted foundation that will remain the same whatever happens. I personally find it deeply arousing, how everything can change all the time."

"There is someone in my apartment," Luis said. "He will probably never leave."

"You should come to my office tomorrow at two o'clock. It is on Herengracht 155. Since you are Hadi's friend, I can work for a reduced fee of a hundred fifty euro an hour."

"I make fifteen euro an hour," Luis said.

"We are all standing on someone else in this pyramid, Mr. Sol," the lawyer said. "I am standing on you, and you are most certainly standing on others. Don't you employ someone? Don't you pay them a smaller amount for their time than you're paid for your own time? We are all standing on other people, and it's completely rightful."

"I will be there," Luis said. He hung up the phone and took a deep breath. In the distance he saw Mrs. Barneveld, cutting the hedge with her shears, the blades blinking in the sunlight. She waved at him.

The Philanthropist

"In all honesty," Mr. Hond said, "I have come to depend on you, Marie."

He took my hand between his.

"And as much as I worry about you, I admit my strongest worry is of a selfish nature. I know you say you will come back after the birth, but you would not be the first woman to forget about a man's needs after having a baby. It's an enormous shift in a woman's life. And you need to make a future for yourself."

"I'll come back!" I said. "I can take the baby with me, I'm going to get one of those sling things, I can carry him."

Mr. Hond smiled. "Marie, you are going to change. And I am just a friend to you, something like an uncle perhaps, a mentor, I don't know. But I have my own little selfish needs, and one of those needs is that you keep visiting me. As I deteriorate, I will need you ever more. That's why I want to make you an offer. You like this apartment, don't you?"

I nodded. I remember my heart was pounding against my chest. It was all I needed. A place to live.

"Then I want you to agree to inheriting my apartment," Mr. Hond said. "It will be a way for you to create independence and a way for me to secure your services."

Before I could say anything, Hond raised his hand.

"Stop. What did I teach you? Never say yes to a deal until you know what you are paying for it. My condition is that you keep coming here every Sunday until I go on my final journey, to do your little cleaning and tend to my little needs. Perhaps giggle a little when I make a bad joke. Make this old man feel loved and useful. How about that?"

Inside I felt like jumping on the bed, opening the windows, shouting, "Eat shit, Anna Beemster!" My own life, my own place, my own beginning! I wrapped my hands around the philanthropist's and shook them wildly.

"You won't be able to stop by for a while after the birth," he said. "I understand that. But you are young and elastic, so it won't take long."

"I am so happy," I said. "But it would be awful when you die, of course."

"I completely understand," Mr. Hond said. "You are a very sensitive girl. But you must learn to be practical. Even angels need to live! Even Jesus needed to eat something once in a while."

"He did?"

"Of course," Mr. Hond said. "Not as much as other people, but still, he needed to eat. Butter and honey. Isaiah 7:15. Every earthly creature has needs."

With a wink, he got up from the bed and walked unsteadily to the desk in the corner of the room, which was covered in unopened letters from the needy. His silk pajamas were half buttoned, his gray chest hairs poking out. Suddenly he reminded me of a crocodile, with his narrow eyes and sagging neck.

"Now," he said, "a verbal promise is no good. You need a document." He smiled. "Who knows what kind of distant relatives will suddenly remember old Edward once he keels over?"

"Do you have any family?" I asked. "You said you have no one to leave your estate to."

"I do have some relatives somewhere," he said, "but I'm afraid we've lost track of one another. I confess that family bores me. The nurturing required to maintain a family that comes so naturally to a woman is tedious to me. I grow tired of the caring, the whining, the nagging, the crying. I've always considered myself an *einzelgänger*. A man who lives for beauty. Art."

He sat down in his chair, shoving all the envelopes into the bin next to his desk.

"What is your last name darling?"

"Meeuwisse," I said, hardly able to contain myself as I watched him scribble my name down on the official-looking paper. "I'm Marie Meeuwisse."

"Mary Meeuwisse. Charming alliteration." Mr. Hond cleared his throat and read out loud while he wrote: "'Hereby I declare that I, Edward Hond, leave my apartment on Roosevelt-laan 354, second floor, and everything in it, to Mary Meeuwisse, to be transferred to her when I die, as a reward for her weekly kindness and service during the final days of my life. The taxes will be paid from the estate. Signed: Edward Hond. Amsterdam, November 24, 1984.'"

I heard the pen scratch over the paper.

"And now my signature. Voilà." He put the document in an envelope and placed the Hond seal across it. "When the moment arrives, my notary Petersen will contact you. He will take you through the steps."

I looked about the apartment. This was going to be our place.

"And then, the most important." From a drawer he took a key and handed it to me. On the label was written: "For Marie. With gratitude. Edward." He smiled at me. "Pleased?"

I nodded.

"You are allowed to show some joy, Marie. I know you and the baby need a place to live, and I won't take that smile of yours as if you're dancing on my grave. Remember, I am the one who taught you that protecting self-interest is at the core of human existence."

"Thank you so much," I exclaimed. "I am so grateful."

"Feeling gratitude is a beautiful thing," he said. "Another beautiful thing is to receive it." He leaned forward.

"Of course," I said. I leaned forward and gave him the first of the formal three kisses I gave to my aunts and uncles on birthdays, instinctively holding my breath as I got close to his pink cheek.

"You are special," Mr. Hond said in my ear, as he put an arm around my waist.

"Thank you," I said.

He tugged on the edge of my black sweater. "Did I ever mention that I prefer it when you wear bright colors?" he said. "Black does not suit you."

"It's my mother's sweater," I said. "It's only because I am so fat now. I wear lots of bright colors normally."

"Good girl," he said.

Suddenly, my belly became tight. My stomach had been contracting for the past few days, and now it was painfully tight, but I did my best to not be the first to release the embrace. In my mind I counted, One, two, three. At five he let me go.

In the living room I sat down on a chair. When my belly relaxed again I washed my face and hung out the window for a moment. The leaves of the trees were orange and yellow; the tall buildings in the distance were blue against the gray sky. This will all be ours, I said to the baby in my belly. You will have your own little room with light blue curtains that float in the wind and twinkling stars on the ceiling. I will give you everything you need.

Brigitte

That night Luis couldn't sleep. He looked about his dark bedroom. The cardboard from the fridge was blocking his view of the window; it looked like a little square house inside his room.

Luis thought of the evening when Brigitte came to his house. The sky over the fields was already turning pink when Brigitte's father dropped her off. "Nice to meet you," he said, shaking Luis's hand through the car window. He looked at the barn with its half-collapsed roof. "Call me if you want me to pick you up sooner," he said to his daughter.

Luis took Brigitte's hand and walked her to the front door, unlocking the three different locks.

It was the first time he had brought a girl to the house.

Luis remembered how Brigitte sat at the table, how she had her hands folded in her lap, her shoulders high. He remembered how she moved back when his father greeted her with three kisses. It was only then he realized it: the mistake he made by bringing here to the house. There was too much to be ashamed of. His mother's unfinished projects: the half-demolished kitchen, the half-painted walls. The mess in the kitchen. His mother kept the plates in stacks on the floor under tea towels, their shapes forming towers under the fabric. His mother's body, the way she said, "I suppose your father did not have time to come in?" when she shook Brigitte's hand. The way she talked to him like he was a baby. His dad's shaking hands with brown pointy fingernails, pouring tea.

Brigitte tried to do her best, smiling at his father, giving his mother a compliment about the color of the curtains and saying she liked her dress. She asked if she could help with the tea, and she brought in the saucers with cake from the kitchen. Everything she did seemed to upset his mother. "The curtains look terrible, I know that," she said. "And the dress is too small. Making tea I can still do on my own, thank you." Luis noticed his mother was even using a different voice. It was higher and she pronounced all the words completely, without swallowing the -*n* and turning the *e* into *oi* as she normally did.

"So, Brigitte, Luis says you have been thinking of the future?" his mother asked.

Brigitte smiled, sitting up a bit straighter. "Well, Luis is twenty-one! And I am eighteen. We are going to see if I can study fashion in Amsterdam. My father is in the textile branch, I have always loved textiles. And maybe Luis can get a job in, like, a restaurant. Or something with furniture. He's interested in design. I think he should study design."

"Luis and studying," his mother said.

"I am designing a wooden chess set," Luis's dad said as he turned to Brigitte.

"Then it must be your talent that he inherited!" Brigitte said to Luis's father.

"I also made a crib for him when he was a newborn," his father said. "He was this big when he came out, can you believe it."

Brigitte laughed as his father spread his arms wide.

Luis watched his mother. She sat back in her chair, her arms folded across her body.

"My mother always wanted to live in Amsterdam," Luis said. "She could have been a designer. She made our curtains." He wanted to say something that would make her feel appreciated, so she would not get mad. "She could have lived in Amsterdam, but she stayed here for me and my dad."

"Oh yes," Brigitte said. "Luis said that you have an apartment in Amsterdam! I was so surprised."

"Surprised?" His mother pushed her chair back. "What is surprising about me owning an apartment?"

"That's not what she meant," Luis said quickly.

"Let's have Brigitte tell us what she meant," Luis's mother said.

"I just meant that it's great," Brigitte said. "What you have done as a young mother, raising Luis, which must have been really hard, and then you also found the time to have property and stuff. I was surprised that someone could do that! And Luis is the nicest boy I've ever met. So you did that right." Her voice was shaking a little. "I really feel comfortable with Luis. He knows how to treat a girl."

"It wasn't easy to raise him," Luis's mother said. "And he was so shy. When I was young I was wild, I was curious, I wanted to do everything. But Luis just wanted to sit under the table. If it wasn't for me, he would still be sitting under the table."

"She did a good job," Luis's father said.

Luis saw his mother relax. A smile, even. He squeezed Brigitte's hand under the table.

"But why don't you rent out that apartment?" Brigitte asked Luis's father. "Luis said you could use the money."

Luis squeezed her hand again under the table, harder now.

His father shook his head.

His mother crossed her arms again.

"We could live there, Luis and me," Brigitte continued, switching to Luis's mother. "It's so hard to find a place to live. And we can pay rent and make it look nice. And after a few years we'll leave, and you can rent it all out."

Luis saw his mother squint her eyes.

"How nice that you are willing to help us with our money problems," Luis's mother said.

"I did not say we had money problems," Luis started, but his mother stood up and walked out of the room, into the kitchen.

"You said your parents could use the money," Brigitte said softly to Luis while his mother was in the kitchen. "You told me we would talk to her about it."

"Not now," Luis whispered, his cheeks red. "Not straightaway!"

Under the table, Brigitte let go of Luis's hand.

It was quiet until his mother came back into the living room. Her face was different: the groove between her eyebrows, the hard mouth.

"Brigitte," she said, "do you know where my silver spoon is? I had four on the kitchen counter, and now I have three. Have you seen them?"

Brigitte shook her head.

Luis could see his father's eyes shoot to the door.

"You were the last one who had them," his mother said.

"I don't know," Brigitte said, shaking her head.

"Mum," Luis said.

"Don't look at me like that, Luis," his mother said. "This is between me and Brigitte. I'm simply giving her the chance to tell us something. She may think we are common people, but we have things of value here. Brigitte?"

Luis remembered Brigitte looking at him.

He remembered he looked at the wall, at the shadow his mother's body was making on the wall.

"She is saying I stole them," Brigitte said to Luis.

"I am not sure that's what she meant," Luis said.

"Thank you, Luis," his mother said. "That is not what I meant. I am just saying you are the last one who had them."

Brigitte looked at Luis. And Luis just sat there, watching Brigitte's eyes fill up with tears. She pushed her chair back and walked out of the room.

Eventually he found her at the phone booth down the road. She was calling her dad.

"I am sorry," he said to her. "My mother doesn't mean it like that. It is a sensitive topic for her, the apartment . . . She never lived there. I should have told you . . ."

But Brigitte did not look at him, she walked away.

Luis did not know whether he should follow her. He stood frozen by the side of the road. He wanted to talk to her, but he did not know what to say. He looked at her from a distance, until she turned the corner at the end of the road and the hedges blocked his view.

When Brigitte's father's car passed him by, she did not look up.

At home his mother had already cleared the table.

"If we're not good enough for her, good riddance," she said.

She turned on the TV. His dad was in the barn. Everything was back to normal. All the things that he had imagined would happen for him and Brigitte now came to a standstill. There was no promising tomorrow, no girl's hand in his; there was nothing. Outside his window the birds kept on chirping cheerfully, and they did for the rest of spring and the summer and the next springs and summers, like they wanted to tease Luis, like they wanted to say, "Look, new flowers are pushing their heads from the soil, look, the birds are making nests together, and look, Luis Sol is still alone, he still lives at home with his mother."

The Philanthropist

W hile I was pregnant, I imagined I would have one of those delicate pink baby girls with a tiny nose. She'd have curly hair, or if she was bald, I would put a big bow around her little head. But it was a boy who came out of me, with dark hair not only on his head but also on his shoulders and temples. Square and heavy as a bag of potatoes, he came tearing out of my vagina. He tore me open so badly the doctor brought students with him every time I needed to be examined. I did not care about any of it. Everything changed when I held my baby for the first time. It was an enormous feeling that came over me like a wave when I held his little body against my chest. I just knew that I would do anything to protect him and nothing would be the same ever again.

It was a birth without congratulations, without cards, without gifts. When my parents drove me to Alkmaar Medical Center when the contractions started, I realized I could never allow my child to grow up near my parents. Their silence in the car while I was sitting almost upside down in the car seat, trying not to scream, trying to do breathing exercises that I learned from a book. No one holding my hand. No one telling me it would be all right. The plastic my mother made me sit on. My father's angry nose breathing.

My baby would never feel that way. He would only be loved and protected.

So when my parents came into the hospital room with their funeral faces to look at the baby as if he were their death sentence, I told them they were relieved of their parental obligations. I told them I had found a place in Amsterdam, that a wealthy philanthropist was helping me, that I was going to be a successful art dealer. My father laughed a little, as if he didn't believe me. My mother bent over the crib with my baby. She said something, I don't remember what. Then they left. They left without looking back at me, I remember that.

When the nurse told me two days later I was ready to leave the hospital, I gave her a piece of paper with Dave's phone number and said to tell him his son was born. Dave showed up two hours later with a stroller he found in the waiting room.

"I want to do the right thing," he announced.

"This is only temporary," I said. "I am getting my own place in Amsterdam."

"He looks a bit like my great-granddad," Dave said, ignoring me and staring at his baby. He was talking slowly, like he always did. "My great-granddad Luis. He was used as a human shield in the Spanish Civil War. My father had a picture of him. He was very hairy, just like him."

"We're gonna call him Elton," I informed him.

Dave drove us to his home from the hospital in his tractor. It was getting dark. As we drove out of Alkmaar into the countryside, I held my baby against my chest. Sitting high on the tractor, I could look far into the distance, over the flat land divided into squares and rectangles by dark ditches. Once in a while we drove past a dark farmhouse with one lit window. I felt like I was going deeper and deeper into a cave. I had wanted to leave Stompetoren to go to the big city, not go deeper into the mud.

"Smell that?" Dave asked me. "Raat's burning the muck heap. Not allowed, actually."

We drove into a cloud of white manure smoke and came out on Dave's yard. He did not have a farm, thank God. His house was more like a bungalow with half a field behind it, where the neighbor let his sheep graze. The once white walls of the house were gray, and the barn next to it was half collapsed.

"My father built it with his own hands," Dave said as he helped us down from his tractor.

"I can see that," I said.

"He used to say, 'All I want is a goddamn piece of land with a goddamn fence around it.' And he got it. No mortgage, no benefits. 'The Sols are no servants of the government,' he always said. 'We go our own way.' My parents had to go back to Spain, but I stayed. It's my house now." He looked at me and the baby. "Our house." A blush started spreading out over his face. "Here, I wanna show you something." He took me into the living room of the cottage. In the corner stood a crib built out of scrap wood. It was painted white. "I-I thought . . ." Dave stammered. "It would be nice to . . . for the baby . . . for Elton."

"Let's go with Luis," I said. "He's not the type for a fancy name like Elton, he's going to get bullied for sure." I carefully laid my boy onto the clean blankets Dave had put in the crib. Together we looked at our sleeping strawberry. And I admit that in that moment I was touched by Dave giving in to this change, making room for us. And I still liked his eyes, his slow way of speaking, his hand resting so naturally on my hip. But I knew this was the most dangerous moment. Dave did not want any more out of life than this: a girl, a continuous beer buzz, a tractor. The crib was lovely, but while he had spent a couple of hours playing around with a hammer, I spent nine months creating a baby with my body and then tearing it apart to get him out. I still bled, and my right nipple was inflamed and leaking milk. The baby was squirmy, and sometimes he got so dark red it terrified me. Dave did not know how to caress his little nose so he would fall asleep; he did not know what temperature the bath needed to be. In my pocket I felt the key Mr. Hond had given us.

"Weakness is what brought you here, Marie Meeuwisse," I told myself. "Stop being so impossibly naive."

More Territory

Boats were floating in the canal far below Luis, who was looking out the window of the lawyer's office on the fifth floor of a tall building on Herengracht. The people in the boats below were drinking wine, dancing, and taking pictures of themselves.

When William's gone, I will go and rent one of those boats, Luis thought. Maybe Hadi will come with me. Or Marina. And I will go to Vondelpark and lie down in the sun with all the tourists. I will sit by the monument on Dam Square and watch the street artists. Didn't the lawyer say I own all the public space, a little bit?

During his first weeks in Amsterdam, Luis had done all those things. He went to the markets, the museums; he even swam in the lake when he saw other people do it. But now he was mostly at home, he realized. Why was that?

The lawyer came in and sat down across from him behind a big desk. She had a very straight posture, black curls framing her face. A poster of two colliding spaceships hung on the wall behind her. The words MORE TERRITORY, MORE PROBLEMS were written across it.

"Outer space," the lawyer said when she saw him looking at the poster. "It is the most interesting field in law. The future of law. I studied civil law initially, but I got so tired of all the conflicts. Conflicts, conflicts, conflicts, people seemed to be stuck in endless conflict. In outer space, there is opportunity. At the moment, it is a field in which there is not a lot of work. But we are living in exciting times, Mr. Sol. It's only a matter of time until there is a settlement in outer space. What will the rules be on Mars? Who will make those rules? Who will enforce them?"

Luis said, "Well, who knows, really."

"Ha!" the lawyer said cheerfully. "You are not the only one who doesn't know! The government refuses to pass legislation in advance for these kinds of situations, they prefer to hastily put laws together when things have already gone wrong. Another question for you, Mr. Sol: If big companies make a settlement on Mars, what do you think they would use it for?"

Luis was silent. Apparently, he had to answer questions. He tried picturing life on another planet. He thought of the fantasy world he had in his mind when he was younger. "Flying?" he tried.

"No," she said proudly. "The answer is crime. If there is a lawless place, people will use it for crime: tax evasion, extracting minerals, avoiding punishment, exploitation, you name it. The same has happened with the internet. What do criminals use the internet for? Crime. And the government did not see it coming, they are just about managing to get online. Criminals are having a party on the internet, and the government is still waiting to log on with their modem, *kggwiei-ieie-ggkkk*."

Luis watched her laugh at her own joke with her head thrown back.

"We need a new law for our new extraterrestrial society!" Mrs. Adelman said to Luis, almost standing up from her chair in excitement. "And couldn't this be an incredible opportunity, to start over with a blank slate? On Earth, we can't seem to evolve to equality and peace because there are always old scores to settle, there's already a huge division in wealth and power, people identify very strongly with certain groups. We can't seem to shake history; people die but they let their offspring inherit their wealth and their fears and their issues, and so it goes on. Our history hangs from our backs like a little monkey with its hands over our eyes." She smiled. "I like that sentence. I'm going to put that in my book." She made a note on a piece of paper. "My book will be called *Property in Space*." She smiled at Luis, her eyes beaming. "There will be a lot of interest in this," she said. "A lot of interest."

Luis looked at the clock. He was starting to understand why she was cheaper than other lawyers. He said, "There's a man in my apartment. He won't go away."

"Yes," the lawyer said. She looked a little disappointed. "So this man, is he a tenant? A family member?"

"He is just someone who rang the doorbell," Luis said. "And now he won't go away."

"Is he homeless?"

"He could be," Luis said slowly. "Yes, he could be homeless. Would that help?" He once saw the police remove a sleeping homeless man from a shop window on Kalverstraat. It happened very smoothly, in a matter-of-fact kind of way, none of the people passing by looked up.

"I'm just trying to get a picture of the situation. Did you give him permission to enter?"

"At first, yes," Luis said. "But I did not give him permission to take over my house. He said he was born there and he never knew his father and he just wanted to have a look around . . ." His voice was getting louder as he recalled it. "He fell and then put pressure on me to spend the night. That became a week. And now he's ordered these papers . . . from the Land Registry . . . with some list." Luis took a deep breath. He gave her the papers Estelle had given him a copy of.

The lawyer put on her glasses. "Edward Hond," she said, "is the current rights holder of the property. Registered in 1941."

"Edward Hond is the father of the man who sleeps on my couch," Luis said. "At least that's what he says. I think anyone could be his father. But it does not matter. My mother, Marie Meeuwisse, owned the apartment. She inherited it from some uncle. But she is not on there."

"If she inherited it, it should be registered," the lawyer said. "You are sure it is her property?"

"My mother has had this apartment since I was a child," Luis said. "But she did not like it there. She preferred to be in the house in Stompetoren because of my father and me. When I got older I wanted to leave Stompetoren, so I moved in. I've lived in my apartment for eight years now. I've redecorated it, I've tiled and painted everything."

"Property," the lawyer said, "is a concept, a legal concept. It is also a feeling, a very strong feeling. What it is not is tangible. There is no tangible foundation in nature for property. It is a construct. Do you understand what I am saying?"

"Is it important?" Luis asked.

"Look," Mrs. Adelman said. "I bought this stapler. Since then I've owned this stapler. It is my property. But there is nothing in this stapler that has changed since I bought it. It is the same. The possession is in my head, it is a word, it's a legal concept in a system, it's a feeling I have, but it is not in the stapler. If I want to prove I own it, I can prove it with the receipt, not with the stapler or my feelings."

Luis looked at the stapler. It was a red stapler with a ladybug print. He did not feel it suited a lawyer who cost 150 euro an hour.

"I am trying to make you see," the lawyer said, "that property is a concept agreed upon in our society. It has nothing to do with the feeling you have for the object. It has nothing to do with the object itself." She pointed at her stapler. "If someone changes the law now to say buying something no longer means you own it, that would mean I no longer own this stapler, even though I feel I do. Everything would be the same, but everything would be different. Our rules are just ideas, habits. People hang on these rules very much; they say, 'This is how we do it,' and 'It is not right to do that,' but the fact is everything used to be different and can be different again in the future. This is how we do it now, but we have been doing it like this for not that even long a time. A hundred years? Two hundred years maybe?"

She took a book from the shelf that was called *History of Humanity in a Nutshell*.

"Here, this is my favorite section." Her index finger moved over the sentences, her mouth turning into a smile. "Ha," she mumbled, "it's so funny." She cleared her throat. Another giggle.

Then she read out loud: "'The earliest history of the human race started 2.6 million years ago. The earliest evidence of controlled use of fire stems from 1.2 million years ago.'"

"Ha!" She slammed the book onto her desk and looked at Luis. "It took them more than a million years to make fire! Can you imagine? A million years!"

A high giggle escaped her again. "Imagine them sitting there in the rain!" She closed her eyes and laughed while Luis just sat there and did not laugh, since he could not really see what the funny part was. They seemed to have moved away from the problem of getting the man out of the apartment.

"The funny part," the lawyer said, "is that it took so long." Some last little giggles and a sigh came out of her. "It tickles me," she said. "These things tickle me." She wiped her forehead with a paper towel. "Good. Now, how did we get to this?"

"There is a man in my apartment," Luis said again. "I never wanted him there, and now he won't leave. He acts like it is not my home. And then you talked about your stapler."

"Ah, yes," she said. "I was trying to explain we need to legally prove the apartment is your property if we want to start an eviction procedure. Do you have the deeds? A copy of the notarial transaction? We need to get your mother publicly registered as the current owner."

"My mother is dead," Luis said. He startled himself every time he said it. Yes, she had died. He'd known that for years now. He tried to never think about it. He found out a year after, when Hadi signed him up for an internet class at the community center. The first assignment: type your name and place of birth in the Google search bar. The one result said: "On February 15, 2010, Marie Meeuwisse departed from this world. Her candle went out, but her light will continue to shine. She is leaving behind her devoted partner, David Sol, and her loving son, Luis. We will say goodbye to Marie at the Egmond Cremation Center on Monday, 14:00." He thought of the words "loving son." He could still see how his mother stood in the middle of the living room the day he left, her arms hanging by the sides of her body.

"Mr. Sol?" The lawyer cleared her throat. "Who inherited your mother's estate? Were your parents married?"

"They weren't married," Luis said. "My father would have wanted to, I think. Sometimes I thought he loved her more than she did. Although I'm not sure about it . . . After she had the first heart attack she started to become nicer to him . . . maybe that's why I felt I could leave, that they could do it without me, somehow." He shook his head. Why was he talking about this? He cleared his throat. "She died a few years after I left home. We hadn't spoken for a long time, and I did not go to the funeral. I don't know about the inheritance. I thought it would have gone to my father. Maybe he did not do the paperwork. We are not paperwork people, the Sols. My father always said that the Sols do not need a government. We go our own way. 'The Sols are used for their bodies,' he always said. My great-great-grandad was used as a human shield in the war."

"Your father's family is antigovernment or anarchist," the lawyer said, and nodded. "Barcelona, Zaragoza?"

"His parents were from Zaragoza," Luis said. "My grandparents. How do you know that?"

"And during the eight years you lived in this apartment, you were never contacted by anyone?" the lawyer asked.

Luis nodded. "I pay the city tax, everything."

She shook her head. "If you can't prove ownership, through inheritance or through your mother's purchase of the apartment, it will be impossible to start eviction procedures. You might have squatter's rights, if you go the adverse possession route. If you have lived there and acted as owner for twenty years, you can get possession in court. There is a shortened procedure if you have lived there for ten years uninterruptedly in good faith, which means that you had to believe you were truly the owner."

"I am telling you my mother owned the apartment," Luis said. Red spots started forming under his shirt when he heard the word "squatter." "Why would she lie about that? William is nothing more than a visitor, why should I have to explain it all to him? Why do I need to show all the papers? Can I just come in here and say I'm going to sleep on this sofa until you tell me exactly why this office is yours?"

"It's a rental," the lawyer said. She opened a drawer behind her from which she took a piece of paper that said "Shared Rental Agreement." "I have this office on Wednesday and Friday. The rest of the week it is home to a casting agency for erotic photography."

Luis shifted on the pink velour sofa.

"That sofa is probably cleaner than your sofa at home. The erotic industry takes cleaning very seriously," the lawyer said. "Although it's probably the idea that bothers you. I've noticed that people love the illusion of clean more than actual clean.

Everything must be shiny white, wrapped in plastic. A new phone needs to look sleek and clean, like an alien machine gave birth to it. No matter that people died in unsafe mines harvesting the materials."

Luis pressed his finger against the bridge of his nose. Why the phones again? he thought. Why does everyone keep talking about the phones and the dying people? He said, "I want this visitor to go. Why do I have to go back and show how my mother got it? What did his father ever do to get it? And the person before that?"

"Interesting subject," the lawyer said. "Going all the way back, did our ancestors obtain the land in a fair way? Once upon a time, people could obtain land by conquering and occupation. There was no proper law back then, so to say that was legal is incorrect, and to say that it was illegal is also incorrect. And now that everything has been occupied, and all the new things that are created have an owner before they even come into being, occupying new places isn't possible anymore. One has to legally obtain everything from another. There are only a few things you can obtain without payment, such as babies, animals, air, and plants. Most things have to transfer from one owner to the other. If life were to be truly fair, we should redivide the entire country. But we'd need a good, new system to make sure that from then on, it doesn't get redivided in unfair ways again. Because it would be the savviest people who get in there first, who get the best pieces of land. And they would offer to buy up other people's land, and if *those* people were in need, they would sell it and rent it back, and things would quickly go back to the way it was." She smiled.

"'All animals are equal, but some animals are more equal than others' . . . That does not just apply to Russia. You know what I am saying?"

"No," Luis said.

"Orwell," his lawyer said. "George."

"William Rose," Luis said. The skin of his neck was itching. "The visitor is William Rose, and I came here to ask you what I should do about him. I have to pay you a hundred fifty euro for it."

"Of course," the lawyer said. "As far as I can tell, there are three options. The first option is to find the papers that prove your mother owned the apartment, get the inheritance sorted out, and file for eviction. If, for some reason, it is impossible to prove ownership, the second option is to pursue your rights as holder and occupant. We can apply for adverse possession and transfer the property to you, but that means you need to prove your mother acted as owner and stayed there uninterruptedly."

Luis shook his head. "What is the third option?"

"To kill him," the lawyer said.

"Kill him?"

"It's a joke," she said. "Lawyer humor. I'm sorry. The third option is to wait. Wait for him to make the first move. The man in your apartment has the same problem as you. If he wants to dispute your ownership, he has to go to court to request recognition of paternity. If he has been searching for his father for so long, I don't think his father is on his birth certificate. When he succeeds in proving he is indeed the child of this Edward Hond, he still has to find out if his father is truly deceased, or he has to declare him missing and presumed dead. Then he will have to apply for letters of administration and claim the estate, and you can file your counterclaim. If neither of you can produce sufficient evidence that you should own the apartment, it might be reverted to the state."

"So I do what?" Luis asked.

"Do you have your father's phone number?" the lawyer asked.

Nests

Luis took the tram home from the lawyer's office. The group of boys sitting across from him spoke English; behind him he heard a girl speak German. Luis looked out the window at the people walking down Vijzelgracht. Some people just float all over the world, Luis thought, they only borrow the streets they walk on. Now they are in Amsterdam, tomorrow they are in Tokyo.

The tram was driving slowly, stalled behind a street sweeper.

Luis thought of the sweepers he'd seen in the Efteling theme park, when his mother took him there. It was one of the good weeks, when his mother had energy. Everything was incredible to him there, but the most beautiful thing to Luis was not the fairy-tale figures but the park, how organized it was. He remembered how the cleaning teams spread out over the park near closing time, sweeping and repairing and disinfecting for the next visitors. Maybe that was how cities would be in the future. Everyone coming and going, sitting on the benches, renting little houses, and riding little trains, never staying anywhere long, all their traces cleaned after they left.

Would he ever want to go someplace else? His grandparents from Zaragoza did it, so long ago, and ended up in Stompetoren. Luis imagined himself walking down a strange street in some faraway country. It filled him with horror. Would they be nice to him? He thought of what Hadi had told him about being bullied as a kid, the only foreign family in the little village. People put envelopes with dog shit through their letter box. What if Luis lost his house? Would he go far away? Where would there be a place for him? Who would want to share their street with him?

As the tram turned onto Rooseveltlaan, Luis thought of the day he left Stompetoren and went to Amsterdam. It was two years after the evening Brigitte broke up with him. Two more years of sitting on the sofa with his mother, helping his father, sweeping the yard. Every day he thought, One day I will go. But it was never the right time. First he tried to get Brigitte back, waiting for her outside the supermarket, buying her flowers that he left on her bike seat, until he saw her with a new boyfriend. Then his mother started to have trouble breathing. She had her first heart attack. A small one. Then it was winter, and someone needed to mend the roof that was collapsing under the weight of the snow. In spring his mother had her second heart attack. Lying in the hospital bed after getting three stents placed, she almost seemed happy. Squeezing Luis's hand while the monitor made irregular beeping sounds, she nodded at him as if to say, "You see, everything breaks, and it will never be whole again."

"Your mother will need a lot of rest," the doctor said to Luis. "She will need help."

The doctor did not even look at Luis's dad, who sat in the corner with bloodshot eyes.

They took her home, and Luis carried her from the taxi to the bedroom. Then his father went into the barn, and Luis watched television alone in the TV room. At ten he went to bed, as always, but he could not sleep. He sat up in his bed, his heart pounding. Near midnight Luis walked into his parents' bedroom, woke up his mother, and told her he needed the key to the Amsterdam apartment.

"No," she said, half asleep. "He'll come back."

"Who?" Luis asked.

He opened the closet and pulled the coffee tin from the top shelf.

"Luis," his mother said, more awake then. "Don't touch that." She sat up.

"You're not allowed to get up," Luis said. He put the coffee tin his backpack.

In her blue silk nightgown, his mother walked to the door and blocked it with her arms. "Luis, I am saying no."

He put his hands on her arms, pushing her gently aside. It was not even pushing really—it was more like a touch. He did not say goodbye. He did not kiss her. There was no yelling or crying. She just lowered her arms when he touched them, and then he just walked into his room, where he put the coffee tin in his backpack with some clothes. As he walked into the yard, Luis knew his father was watching him. He saw his eyes as little shimmers of light in the dark shed when he closed the garden gate behind him.

Luis remembered the numb, nauseated feeling that had accompanied him as he walked down the dike, along the dark fields, toward the bus stop. At the Raats' house the sensor lights went on as he walked past their gate. Their dog started barking.

He waved at Mrs. Raat, who looked at him from behind her kitchen window.

"He even waved," he later imagined Mrs. Raat whispering to the neighbors. "How could he have waved?" But it was easy. You raise your arm, like you always do. It is not like you can't raise your arm anymore when you are leaving your ill mother behind. You can easily still wave. Everything could easily still go on: the cows chewed their food, the cars came down the street, the mosquitos swarmed above puddles of water. And Luis took the night train to Amsterdam and never came back.

The city did not even seem to notice the arrival of Luis Sol, who walked into the crowded Amsterdam night in his wellies. Groups of people streamed out of Central Station into the city, young people who were yelling and singing. Cyclists navigated around Luis, yelling at him; taxis honked impatiently when he accidentally blocked them. Luis remembered his first tram ride, the irritated call from the driver when he tried to board through the wrong door. Asking directions to Rooseveltlaan at the tram stop. The key smoothly going into the lock.

For a long time, he had expected his mother to appear at his door, but she did not come. His father didn't come either. Thoughts of them occurred, but he blocked them from his mind: he could not go back into that. He never returned, not even the day when he saw that funeral ad. Aside from hearing his mother's voice in his bedroom late at night, he actually thought of his parents less than he had expected.

Sitting down in the park on Rooseveltlaan, Luis looked at the steel armrests that Estelle had made sure were fitted on the new benches. She had written a neighborhood letter about it, how the presence of the homeless made property prices go down. The solution was called "defensive design." A third armrest was added to these benches so people could not sleep on them.

All the animals can make a nest, Luis thought. All the animals can make their home anywhere, but somehow people have to make it complicated.

He remembered how in Raat's stables swallows had made their nests above the entrance. They were very territorial and swarmed around his head when he went in.

"Mothers trying to protect their young," his father had said. "You don't want to get between that."

Luis took his phone from his pocket and called the landline number that was forever stored in his mind. He imagined the green light on the old gray phone on the dresser in the hallway lighting up. But the phone didn't ring. There was the *tu-du-du* sound that meant invalid number.

The Raats' landline number he still remembered too. It was little Louise-Lotte Raat who picked up, now an adult and sounding just like her mother.

"Hello, I am trying to find David Sol," Luis said.

"David?" There was a moment of silence. "Oh, Dave Sol. The neighbor. No, you're out of luck, he's gone."

"He's gone?" Luis asked, his voice small.

"He went into assisted living after his wife died. Korsakoff he has, I think." She was quiet. "Luis, is that you?" she then asked.

Luis hung up. Korsakoff. He knew what it was. His grandfather, his father's father, had it too. A disease caused by a vitamin

B_1 shortage from lack of nutrition and chronic alcohol abuse. He knew the shaking, falling, mood swings, memory loss. He thought of his father alone in the house, without him, without his mother. He could barely boil an egg.

Luis stood up from the bench. He took a few steps but then stood still on the corner of the street again, for a long time, cars and bikes driving past, some passersby glancing at him.

"Luis?" In front of Luis was a young woman who had stopped on the sidewalk, holding a grocery bag in one hand, a dog on a leash in the other. "Are you okay?"

Only now Luis recognized Marina, who was wearing braids and a long skirt.

"My mother is dead," Luis said. He shook his head. "I already knew that. But my dad . . . I just heard . . . Louise-Lotte said . . ." He couldn't get the words out, they were stuck in his throat. "He is not dead, but now he is . . . and I didn't . . ."

Marina put down her grocery bag. She guided Luis toward the bench and sat down next to him with her arm around his shoulders. Luis noticed the feeling of her hand on his shoulder, so light it was. Familiar and strange. He noticed how Marina's little dog put his brown head on his knee. It was warm too. Luis petted the dog. He noticed he was crying. It was the first time he'd cried since he left.

The Philanthropist

When Luis was four weeks old, I could finally go to the toilet again without having to gently pour warm water over my vagina afterward, because the toilet paper was too painful. The bleeding had stopped. I had cycled around the yard without sitting on the saddle. I felt like I was ready to go back to Amsterdam. Luis was still tiny. I was wearing gigantic pads in my underwear because I peed when I coughed or laughed, and I was so tired I sometimes forgot I existed. But I had to do it. Dave brought us to the station. He said nothing, as always.

While I was pregnant, I had imagined myself walking around Amsterdam with Luis in a baby sling on my back, merry and easy. But now that I was really doing it, I was scared. I was scared he was too cold, too warm; that he was strapped into the stroller wrong; that someone would grab him and run away; that something would fall on his head. I did not want him on my back, I wanted him in front of me, where I could see him. Even when I held him against me, I was always looking down at his face to see if he was breathing well. Dave said I was obsessed, but I sometimes saw him hang over the crib too, his cheek hovering over Luis's little face, to feel his breath on his skin.

On the way to Mr. Hond's place I breastfed little Luis, sitting on the rainy steps in front of a café. I had changed his diaper in the train toilet. My legs were shaking by the time I got to the apartment and put my key in the lock. As I walked up the steep stairs to Mr. Hond's apartment, with Luis close against my chest, the folded-up stroller slipped from my hand. I watched it tumble down the stairs and crash against the front door. It startled me so I almost started crying. Luis started squirming in my arms. All I wanted to do was turn around and go back to the safety of Dave's cottage.

I remember sitting down at the top of the stairs, my whole body trembling. I started talking to Luis really softly to calm myself down. I talked about how pretty the house would be, how we would hang up light blue curtains, how we would watch them dance in a light breeze. How the soft carpet under my bare feet would feel. How we would buy everything we needed. Slowly I started to feel better. Luis had fallen asleep. Holding him close against me, I carried the stroller back up the stairs and went into Mr. Hond's apartment.

"There you are," Hond exclaimed when I came in. "With a little monster!"

I carefully turned my upper body so I did not wake Luis as I showed my baby to Mr. Hond.

Mr. Hond reached out from the bed and squeezed Luis's little leg. "I don't mind this one," he said. "It's quiet."

It was true, Luis was very quiet. He hardly ever cried during the day. When he was upset he just wailed and squirmed a little bit and turned red, like a little strawberry.

"The father doesn't help?" Mr. Hond asked.

"He doesn't even want to touch him," I said. This wasn't true. I would not let Dave touch the baby when he'd been drinking, which turned out to be always. He often cracked open his first beer at 10:00 A.M. He liked to watch me and the baby from the sofa, making comments like "He is crying now" and "Oh, it stopped. You are bathing him," as if he were watching the telly.

"Sometimes a father does not want his life to be disrupted," Mr. Hond said. "Sometimes the child is a disappointment. The weakness, the whining, the repetition." He coughed. "At a certain point in his life, a man can be overtaken by the desire to create progeny. He becomes curious what kind of man would come out of his material. It can happen very late. He will find a woman willing if he is able to make the right promises. But when the baby is there, he realizes the child is not a continuation of his own existence. It's closer to a death, in fact. The woman changes too. Women have a desire to care, but in order to feel alive, a man needs to conquer, fight, create, gather knowledge. I have come to believe a man simply needs to pass on his genes and leave the rest to the mother."

It was clear Mr. Hond never met Dave. He did not seem to have any of these needs, for conquering and gathering knowledge. But I nodded. "You are wise," I said.

Mr. Hond squeezed my arm. "You can put the baby in the living room," he said. "Then come back to me."

After strapping Luis in the stroller in the living room and checking five times nothing could fall on him, I went back into Hond's bedroom.

"You have your old figure back," Hond said. He patted his mattress, which had light brown markings from his sweat. "I like the yellow on you."

I tried to smile. I was wearing a V-neck tulip dress that I'd loved before I got pregnant. I thought it would make me feel like I could still go back to my old self, although inside I didn't feel like anything I was before. My insides were stitched up, I kept peeing accidentally, and having a wall between me and my baby made me feel like I had unscrewed both my arms and put them in another room.

"It's a big adjustment," I started explaining to Mr. Hond. "I have so much to learn. He is an easy baby, he sleeps for six hours uninterrupted, but still—"

"How does it feel to have your own key?" Mr. Hond interrupted me. "This was the first time you came in with your own key, I believe."

"Oh yes," I said. "It went well."

"I thought it would be a little bit more exciting than that," Mr. Hond said.

"Yes, sorry, I mean it was great," I said. "It was truly great." I made my voice go a little higher and smiled. "I am still so happy."

"I am pleased you're happy," Mr. Hond said. He patted my hand. "Your skin is so soft."

"I have to put this cream on Luis a million times a day for his nappy rash," I said. "It's made my hands very soft." I wondered if I would hear Luis if he cried. All I could hear were the ticking clocks and the branches of the tree in front of the house touching the window. It was like time stood still here. Mr. Hond's hand slid from my hand to my stomach that was still round but did not have a baby in there anymore. Was he getting confused?

This would be a good time for him to die, I thought. I immediately felt guilty.

"How has your health been?" I asked him.

"I have pain here," he said as he put my hand on his heaving chest. "The doctors can't do anything for me anymore, but I told them the pain eases where your fingers touch me."

"Thank you," I said. I looked at him. He looked worse than before, his eyes bleary and his skin yellowish. There were new pill bottles on his bedstand. I wondered whether he was getting sicker or if he was just more drunk.

"I feel it in my stomach too." He closed his eyes, moving my hand over his ribs. "For a few weeks I have had pain in the pylorus, the gatekeeper of the stomach."

I watched my hand moving farther down the man's old body, the gray curls of his chest hair flattening under my hand. I tried to listen for my sleeping baby's breathing, but all I could hear were those ticking clocks.

"My chest tightens at night I sometimes, I cannot breathe for minutes," he said. "Then the pain spreads out."

"I'm sorry to hear that," I said.

I want to check on Luis, I thought. Could I say that? I wondered. Will he understand it? Luis had been asleep for about twenty minutes now. He usually slept for at least forty-five minutes. If I spend ten minutes listening to Mr. Hond, I will then go check on him, I decided.

Mr. Hond moved my hand toward his belly.

"Just below my belly button," he said, "there's a stinging feeling. Yes, there."

His hand gripped my hand a little tighter. And I remember the feeling of the elastic band of his pajamas over my hand. That I was trying to understand what was happening and then thinking it was a mistake and he would stop. And I remember I did not say anything. Instead I looked away from my hand. I remember looking at the hole in the red velvet curtain, the light coming in through the hole.

Cleaning

In his bedroom, Luis opened the door to his closet and took his old backpack from the top shelf. He could feel the edges of the coffee tin through the fabric. He quietly stood there for a moment, holding the backpack. The vague smell of cigarettes coming from the backpack brought back the *click-clack* sound of his mother's cigarette maker. Her yellow fingertips. She made her cigarettes in the evening, when he was in bed, but he could hear her in the living room. There was the Beemster tobacco store at the end of the dike, but she refused to go there. It was much cheaper to make them herself, especially with the amount of cigarettes she smoked. She was a chain-smoker, she said. As a child Luis always pictured a chain of cigarettes around her, and he understood it to be a punishment of some sort. When he realized her cranky need to make all the walls and ceilings in the house turn smoky yellow was a sentence she had put on herself, he could not believe it. It was those things, all those little things, that had made his pity dry up.

Taking in a deep breath, Luis took the coffee tin from the backpack.

He remembered when the tin had first appeared. He was thirteen. With his father he had gone to Zaragoza for a week to visit his grandparents. It had been a strange week. His father was different there. He was louder, and Luis saw him cry one night when his grandfather had fallen in the street. Other family members were crying too. Luis remembered he thought it was strange they were crying; he was sure that in the Netherlands it was not allowed for adults to cry on the street. He thought it was like littering, like kissing, like sleeping—none of it was allowed outside the house. Luis remembered he could not ask anyone about it because they did not understand him. He remembered the cold tiles under his feet in every room, the many people who kissed and hugged him, picked him up and carried him, stuffed him with sweets and little cookies. Sharing a bed with three nephews, two sleeping vertically and one horizontally at the foot end. A lot of people who seemed to like him, even though they did not know him. There was no bedtime. And everything was submerged in a language he did not speak.

When they came home three things had changed. His mother had cut her hair, she acted strange, and a coffee tin had emerged in the wardrobe in her room. Luis found it when he was playing. In the coffee tin was a key with a label, a notebook, a sealed envelope, and a map of Amsterdam. When Luis asked about it, she said something about a rich uncle, whom she used to help, who had left her an apartment, and how she was going to do it up and make it beautiful again.

Luis was afraid to ask questions. Afraid none of it was true and she had gone crazy. Afraid that it was true, and they would have to move to Amsterdam where he did not know anyone. Since they came back from Spain his mother was hyperactive, she announced new decisions with an energy that frightened Luis and his father. They were going to do up the cottage. She was going to apply for jobs as a weather girl, because she always like the weather. She was going to be an actress, a journalist. Luis needed a different haircut for once. She threatened to bleach his hair with the detergent from under the sink. Next spring, she announced, they would all jump off the Chicken Bridge together.

Those things never happened. The energy ran out. In the years after, Luis saw this more often after she came back from Amsterdam. Sometimes the energy lasted for a few hours, sometimes for days, but it always ran out again. She threw out all her clothes because they did not suit who she was. Instead of buying any new ones, she wore old eighties outfits that didn't fit her anymore. She painted his bedroom and stopped halfway through. She decided she deserved a new kitchen in the cottage, but when his dad tore out half the kitchen, she gave up on deciding on a new one.

Luis thought she was like his dad's broken tractor: sometimes they got the engine running again, but before it could gain speed and be of use, it died again.

Luis hadn't opened the coffee tin since taking the key out of it, when he was on the night train to Amsterdam. Now he held the tin on his lap in his bedroom and pulled the lid off. There was the map of Amsterdam, the tag that used to be on the key, a sealed envelope, and the notebook that had "Cleaning" written on it. When he opened the notebook, his mother's handwriting jumped at him from the first page: aggressive, square letters he knew from when she used to write his high school sick notes.

The Philanthropist

Of course I could have said no.

Of course I could have said "Stop."

But I let the clock tick forward. I let my hand be moved. I think that I believed that if I did not speak or do anything, I was not really there, and this did not really happen. Maybe I froze because I did not see it coming. When my biology teacher, Mr. Foster, made a move on me when Anna and I ran into him on Queen's Day, I had the same feeling of disbelief. Mr. Foster was always staring at me in class, sometimes standing too close when he explained something. Still, when he pulled me toward him in Café de Pont, pulled me into the coat rack, and pressed his lips onto mine, I did not see it coming. How was I supposed to expect that? He had a beard and he seemed ancient to me. I bent all the way backward, but I did not say anything until Anna pulled me out of there screaming, "Absolutely not happening!"

And Mr. Foster was only thirty. Mr. Hond was like the skeleton in the back of Mr. Foster's classroom.

It was impossible, impossible.

I could at least talk to Anna about Mr. Foster. We said "ew, ew" together every time Mr. Foster walked past in the hallway at school, and I told her exactly how his stuffy breath had smelled and how his mustache had stung like an old broom pushed onto my lips. Anna made him give us an A in biology the next semester.

But Mr. Hond?

It's not like I am the Holy Virgin, I told myself as I looked at my reflection in the train window on my way home. I let Mark do that thing in the alley. Dave, of course. There was some boy at a New Year's Eve party I don't even remember the name of.

Little Luis was lying on my, looking up at me, a tiny river of milk-slime sliding from his mouth into the collar of his shirt. I told him, "It's no big deal. What's the difference with cleaning? What's the difference with scrubbing a stain from a towel, rubbing a sponge over a plate? Dave says the Sols have always been used for their bodies. Picking, carrying, cleaning. Even a human shield. I can be like a human shield for the two of us. It's so unimportant. Who even remembers a touch? It's just a little wibble wabble. I will forget about this like I forgot the name of the New Year's Eve boy. And when Hond dies, there is no one who knows this ever happened except for me. If no one remembers it, it hasn't even happened at all. We will have our new start."

Luis just stared back at me, a little cross-eyed.

And I remember how I suddenly thought about this baby being my child, about how strange it all was, that we used to be two persons in one body. And then I thought of the billion stars twinkling in the sky every night and how I had told my baby, when he was still inside of my vagina, that we were like one of those stars, twinkling all the way up there, and that maybe life was a bit weird now, but it was part of some big, beautiful idea, something too magnificent and too big to even try to understand, and everything would become fantastic for us.

The only thing we had to do was to wait for Mr. Hond to die. Then there would be no more Stompetoren, no more Dave pleading at the bedroom door when he came home drunk, no more muck heaps and fields and dark ditches, no more people whispering behind my back in the supermarket. I imagined the light blue curtains waving in a gentle breeze in the bedroom. I imagined me sitting by the window in sunlight scattered in a thousand directions by a crystal chandelier, watching little Luis playing in the park in the middle of the street. I pictured myself waving at the other mothers in the park, who all waved back to me.

What He Wanted

Luis closed his mother's diary. He sat on the edge of the bed in his bedroom, like his mother used to sit. With the philanthropist. Edward Hond. The branches of the poplar tree scratched over the window, like they did when she was there. Luis did not move. He thought of what she wrote: "If no one remembers it, it hasn't even happened at all." In the mirror he saw himself, the crumpled white Versace shirt, his seven-day beard, the pile of cardboard at his feet. He thought of the look on his mother's face when he asked about the apartment in Amsterdam. The way she crossed her arms over her body.

Luis sat for a long time on the edge of his bed until the sound of William flushing the toilet took him out of it. Edward Hond. William's father. Carefully, he opened the sealed envelope that was in the coffee tin and took out the document. The diary he put back in the tin, which he stuffed in the bottom of the backpack and pushed to the back of the closet.

With the document in his hands, Luis walked into his living room. He placed it on the glass table in front of William without saying anything. The paper was a bit yellow, there were lines where it had been folded.

William looked at Luis for a moment, then took the paper in his hands. The living room was dark. It was 1:00 A.M. The only light came from William's laptop, and it was shining blue on his pale face as he looked at the document for a long time, reading it and rereading it, turning it around in his hands.

"What is this?" William asked finally.

"This is a document written and signed by Edward Hond," Luis said. "Marie Meeuwisse was my mother. She took care of him when he was ill. She cleaned up around him, did the dishes, washed his clothes. He was grateful. He gave her the apartment." Luis clapped his hands. "Now you know."

William was quiet for a long time. He stared at the document. "Is it real?" he asked then.

"Of course it is real," Luis said. "How could it not be real? You are holding it in your hands, aren't you? You are touching it."

"It is the Hond Foundation letterhead," William said. "It looks like the same paper my mother wrote her letter on." He opened one of his folders and took out the letter. The paper and the letterhead were exactly the same.

"You wanted to know what your father wanted," Luis said, "and he wanted to give the apartment to her."

William shook his head. He slowly read, out loud: "'Hereby I declare that I, Edward Hond, leave my apartment on Rooseveltlaan 354, second floor, and everything in it, to Marie Meeuwisse, to be transferred to her when I die, as a reward for her weekly kindness and service during the final days of my life. The taxes will be paid from the estate. Signed: Edward Hond. Amsterdam, November 24, 1984.'"

There was a spasm in Luis's chest. He shook his head. "So there you have it," he said. "Now you know."

William was quiet for a long time.

"I told you it belonged to my mother," Luis said. "But you wanted documents. Now you have it. You said you wanted to know if everything happened the way Edward Hond wanted it. Now you know it did."

"As a reward," William repeated slowly. "Why . . ." He shook his head. "Why would he give an entire apartment to a cleaner?"

"My mother was a very good cleaner. She cleaned with care and precision."

"How do you know about this?" William asked. "Why didn't you tell me before?"

"I did not want to tell you because I did not want you to know your father did not care for you," Luis said. "The truth is that your father never mentioned you. He said children could be disappointing and my mother was all he cared for. I remember him saying, 'Marie, you are the only one I can stand.'"

"This document says 1984," William said. "Weren't you born in 1985? How could you know anything about it?"

"Because you made such a fuss about my history, the memories are coming back now," Luis said. "It's like an avalanche. Since you got here I dream about my mother. I remember new things every day. I don't even want it, the dreams and the memories. I don't want you here. But still you are here. And still I have the memories. And now I remember I was always parked in the stroller in this living room while she cleaned. I remember hearing the sound of your father's breathing in the other room; he was so sick, his breath was like the sound of a car starting. I remember the sound of my mother's cleaning, I remember the splashing of the water in the bucket."

"You were a baby." William shook his head.

"I am a visual person, we have good memories," Luis said.

"Can you also tell me how he died?" William asked. "When?"

"I don't remember it exactly, but it must have been some lung disease," Luis said. His heart pounded, the red spots burned. "I don't know when. I remember more visual things. I remember the ceiling above my mother's bed in the hospital where I was born. I remember how my father's face would appear above my crib when I was little, blocking out the light from the ceiling lamps, as he tried to feel my breath on his cheek. I remember how he drove us home from the hospital when I was just born, I remember the smell of the burning muck heap on that evening. I remember how my mother always pressed me against her chest when she walked up the stairs to this apartment. I remember those kinds of things, not dates and illnesses."

"It's scientifically impossible to have such early memories," William said.

"Didn't you remember all kinds of things about this apartment?" Luis asked, rubbing his neck. "Floorboards and trees and all that? The banister you held when you learned to walk?"

For a while William said nothing. He turned the document around in his hands, read it again and again, took photos of it, and he went through his own papers, comparing the letterhead on the document with the envelope of his mother's letter.

"I don't know what to think of this," William said finally. He looked panicked and a bit lost, sitting under the sheets on the sofa.

"It's the answer you were looking for," Luis said. "Now you can go back to Oxford."

"Don't you think it's strange," William said in a soft voice, "that he would leave it to his cleaner and not to his son? And why didn't she register the property in her name? Where are the notary documents? How did he die? Why wasn't his death registered? How did she know him?"

"Why didn't your father want you?" Luis asked. "Why isn't he on your birth certificate? Some things we will never know."

He watched William stare at the paper. It was not often he was so quiet. He looked like he was going to cry.

"You wanted to know everything about your past," Luis said. "You insisted. You hoped there would be some beautiful story that would make you feel good and important. And then Estelle made you crazy with her law stuff."

William looked at Luis, his eyes shiny.

"Your father did not like weak people," Luis said. "Maybe you cried too much. Maybe you were too demanding. It could be anything. Just being family does not make people like you."

William's face looked paler than it was before.

"And isn't it for the better?" Luis said. "Now you can carry on with your own life." He took the document from the table. On the threshold he turned around. "And it is the fair thing, after all, isn't it? I mean, what have you ever done for him? Maybe you are his son, but you did not even know him. All you did was get born. My mother gave everything to your father, every week, for a really long time." He rubbed his face. "I mean, the cleaning, all of it."

William did not reply. The screen of his laptop went dark, taking away the blue hue from William's face.

"I'm glad it all is cleared up now," Luis said into the dark. "I'll help carry your bags down tomorrow."

That night, when Luis shaved his beard over the sink, letting the cold water run down his face, the hairs in his toothbrush did not bother him anymore, the socks William left on the floor did not bother him, the empty shampoo bottle did not bother him. He looked at his face in the mirror above the sink. Having gained some weight made his jawline softer, and he saw his mother looking back at him. He wondered how long it would take for the apartment to not feel tainted anymore. How long would it take to forget what had happened?

27 August
My father's home, Amsterdam

A terrible night. Could it be true? The letterhead on the document Luis gave me is identical to the letterhead on my mother's letter, the signature an exact copy of the signature on my father's foundation's statutes. The paper and the ink look thirty years old, to my untrained eye. And if it's real, does that make the other things Luis said real as well? That my father never mentioned me, except that children could be disappointing?

Of course, I have wondered why he didn't come for me all those years—why he never called, not even on my birthday; never wrote a card or letter. Why he wasn't there at school performances, when I got my diploma, anything. But I never believed he didn't want me. I always kept believing there was a different reason for it. That he missed me as much as I missed him. That he didn't forget me.

I remember a moment many years ago, when Professor Vergez came up to me after I defended my dissertation. He asked why I kept looking at the door during the ceremony. I said it was a nervous tic. How could I tell this deeply serious, objective, precise professor, 'I was waiting for my father to come in. My father whom I don't know, my father who is now at least eighty, my father who never showed any interest in me. I believe that today, at the defence of my doctoral dissertation, he will show up for me. For this reason, I have included the section on origins of the Middle Dutch word slim(p) *in my dissertation, even though you correctly noted that it seemed irrelevant to the central thesis.*

I managed to get a Dutch newspaper to write a couple of words about it, and I believe that my father has read that article. I believe that he got tears in his eyes when he saw my name. He looked in the mirror for a long time and booked a ticket to Oxford. And now I believe he is late because of a delayed train from Gatwick. I have checked this on my phone several times'.

How could I say this to Professor Vergez? He would, rightfully, think I was crazy. Not only was it pathetic of me, but it was completely unscientific to believe something so statistically unlikely. In our work, we must always gather evidence, everything we propose must be made plausible or we will be scorned and mocked by the academe. In regard to the origin of words it is too easy to see connections and evidence when they aren't there, and in our field we deeply despise those who fall for tempting but unfounded conclusions. 'Believers', we call them.

And still, in relation to my father, I was a secret believer. I never told anyone about my 'faith'. Not even Paulina. I knew she would jump on the opportunity to go through some psychological process with me. She was always aching to help me accept the reality of my cold pointlessness on this earth. I have never met someone who delighted so much in the cold pointlessness of our lives as Paulina, who always got a sparkle in her eye when she talked about it.

The truth is that I do not want to heal from my delusion. I do not want to accept this paternal rejection. I never gave up the implausible idea that I would one day have some interaction with my father that would explain everything. Just yesterday, I imagined him watching this apartment from across the street, proudly observing his son reclaim his property. Of course I knew that wasn't real, but I allowed myself to have these dreams because there is a seed of belief in me.

I don't know what will happen if I let go of this belief. I left everything behind to find the truth about my father. I even gave up my job at the university. I always imagined the truth would be positive. Who goes looking for a treasure chest that has nothing in it?

I keep thinking of what Luis said about my father: 'He did not like weak people'.

Am I weak? Was I some experiment? Did he want a child to see if it would be weak? Is it strange that I think this entire ordeal could be some kind of test, created by him to show my character? That he will appear when I show that I am not weak? Am I losing it?

A Turn for the Better

Luis woke up early. He watched the stripe the sun made on the wall move from the windowsill down toward the radiator and align with the edge of the bed. With his remote he raised the blinds. He opened his bedroom window. Cold air streamed in. A group of pigeons swept over Rooseveltlaan and landed on one of the chimneys on top of the apartment block across the street. Luis looked at them for a moment. The way the pigeons were trying to share the too-small surface of the chimney reminded him of what the lawyer had said about the moon. *Res communis*, property of all. Did that mean that everyone had a little part of it, and the more people were born, the smaller each part got? Or did it mean that everyone had all of it all the time?

Luis opened the door to the hallway. William's suitcase was standing in the corner by the staircase. Next to it were his plastic bags, overstuffed with crumpled papers and yellow folders.

So, he was leaving. Finally, a turn for the better. Finally, the apartment would be the kingdom of Luis Sol again. For so many nights he had longed for the moment when William would be gone. He thought it would give him an immense feeling of happiness, but it was more a sense of regret that he felt. For a second he wondered whether he was really happy before William came, but then he reminded himself that he was building his happiness, he was building his life and his interior design, and as soon as he had the apartment to himself again, he would find his way back to it.

It was reading his mother's diary that gave him this sense of regret. When this man is gone, I am going to clean this place from top to bottom so I can forget it, Luis thought, but then it occurred to him that his mother already tried that.

Luis looked at the old yellow papers sticking out of one of William's bags. It was gray and wet outside. He imagined rainwater seeping into the bag, damaging the letter from William's mother.

Luis shook his head. Why did this man treat himself like this? And his possessions? Why did he wear old, dirty clothes, why didn't he comb his hair?

He thought of what Marina had said when William had just arrived. "Maybe your friend is lonely too." Maybe that was the problem with William, that he'd always been lonely. It seemed that he never had parents to really teach him things, like how you shouldn't sit in other people's apartments uninvited. Luis's mother had always told him, "Never go where you are not wanted." For her, this included all restaurants, museums, hotels, his school, the library, the Farmers Association, the church, the Bijenkorf and other expensive stores, squares and streets. But at least she taught him things. She taught him to always look tidy. To keep your distance from strangers. To believe only what you see. To stay away from charity and social services. To wait for the girl to make the first move so you are sure she wants it. And at least Luis had a father. Not much of a father, not a father you would see on television, but at least he had seen exactly who his father was and where he came from, and he did not spend his whole life dreaming about him.

William just had those stupid documents.

In his bedroom, Luis opened the bottom drawer of his mirrored chest. When he signed up for the internet class at the community center, Hadi had gifted him a silk-lined off-white faux-python laptop bag. He hadn't used it yet, since he did not have a laptop, and it was still in the tissue wrapping paper. He never took the little protective piece of paper from the zipper. It was a good size for folders and documents. Luis used the ribbon from the wrapping of his iPhone box to make it look like a real gift.

Knocking on the living room door, Luis felt strangely excited about giving William the bag. It seemed like the best way to give a tainted memory a more positive ending, so it would not sit in his mind, polluting everything.

Luis knocked again. When the door opened, it was not William standing there, as he'd expected, but Marina, who was holding a pillowcase in her hands. The small brown dog sat at her feet.

"Good morning," Marina said.

"Hello, Luis," William said from the sofa. He looked strange; his eyes were wide and shiny, with dark circles underneath. "I asked Marina to do some cleaning in here and take my laundry to the cleaners. And you know Estelle, of course."

"Good morning, Mr. Sol," Estelle said. She was sitting next to William on the sofa, in her lilac pantsuit. "I am here in my capacity as Mr. Rose's lawyer, he let me in."

Bewildered, Luis looked about the room. How deep had he slept not to hear any of them come in?

Luis decided to turn to Marina, because in the end, she was the one who worked for him. "What are you doing?" Luis said to Marina. "It's not Wednesday. You don't have to do his laundry."

"He pays," Marina said. "I need some extra money because I need a new place to live. I am in a hostel now. I can't stay with my friend anymore because her flatmate came back."

"There's no need to make the bed," Luis said to her, still clenching the parting gift. "The sofa, I mean. William is leaving."

At that moment Luis noticed the papers were spread out over the table again. He noticed the suitcase was back in the living room, as were the plastic bags.

"No," Luis said to William. "You have seen the will. I have told you the story. Your suitcase was in the hallway."

"I had to vacuum in here, so I put them in the hallway," Marina explained.

"Mr. Sol," Estelle said, "allow me to explain. Mr. Rose, my client, has consulted with me this morning about a piece of paper you have produced. I have studied the photos and reassured him that this will, or whatever you want to call it, is not legally binding. Certainly not until a judge says it is so. And I highly doubt you will take this to court."

"Court?" Luis said. "He said the only thing that mattered to him was that it happened how his father really wanted it."

"Mr. Rose disputes the legal validity of the document and is not diverted from his legal course of action. We have submitted a request to the court to acknowledge Edward Hond's paternity.

When paternity is established, we will request to declare Edward Hond missing and intestate, which would mean his possessions will transfer to his next of kin. William is going to inherit the apartment, as we believe is only right."

She pointed at Luis.

"You should start packing up, that's my advice. If you maintain your misguided position that you own this place, you will have to go to court. Even if a judge decided your mother should have inherited the property, instead of his real son, inheritance tax would need to be paid. This apartment is worth about half a million. Your tax-free threshold is next to nothing as a nonrelative, which means you would need to produce 180,000 euro if you inherit it in place of your mother."

Luis shook his head. "You said it was his letterhead, that the letter looked real," he said to William.

"If that document is real," William said in a dry voice, "it still does not mean it was what he wanted. Often, people are manipulated on their deathbed. Often, a son reaches a stage where he must overrule his father. It is a classic moment in a father-son relationship. Expansion at the service of conservation. Each generation builds on the other, improving. Nietzsche."

"What are you talking about?" Luis said. "First you had a story about your father's wishes, now you have a story about father-son relationships and expansion conversations . . . Why do have to make everything sound so . . . so . . . while you just want to take this apartment from me." Luis felt the redness race up to his face. "And then you talk to me about manipulation. The Sols do not manipulate. But you manipulated from the beginning. You said, 'I've come to see the house.' You could not even be honest and say, 'I've come to claim the house. I've come to live in the house. I've come to take over the house and sit in your living room and smear my fingerprints on your fridge and dig in your past and make it uncomfortable to even go into your home.'" Luis held up the laptop bag with the ribbon around it. "I even wanted to give you a gift. Because I felt bad for you."

William looked at the faux-python laptop bag. He cleared his throat. "That is nice, but it is a shallow and misleading gesture. I do not want a gift. I just want what is mine. You are the intruder here. You are the one who should go. Then I will happily give you a gift."

"Why didn't you stay in England?" Luis asked, his voice high. "Why did you come here? Didn't you have everything there, a job, a home?"

"The information about this address came when I was at a crossroads in my life," William said. "My girlfriend had left me, because she said I was not a complete person. I did not know my true self, she said. And she was right. I only knew half myself. And it is a human need to connect to one's true story, one's roots. Just looking at Estelle, for instance, you can tell so much about her. Her style says that her mother had good taste. Her manners tell you that her parents were strict; her accent tells you she comes from a sophisticated, intellectual background."

"I do," she said.

"And I don't even have my own accent," William said. "I moved around so much. I used to have all kinds of different accents, trying to blend in wherever I was. But I don't have my own accent. I do not know how I, William, sound."

He swallowed loudly.

"He does not have an accent!" Luis shouted at Marina. "There are children dying inside mines, you are out on the street in a strange country with your dog, but this man is crying because he does not have an accent. I don't have an accent, I don't cry about it."

"You do have an accent, Luis," William said softly.

"West Frisian," Estelle said. "North Holland. They say *a* as *aa*, *e* as *oi*, and put a *j* in everything."

"It's who you are," William said. "A tree without roots cannot grow."

"A person is not a tree," Luis said. "A person has legs, and he can walk wherever he wants."

"*Hoi caan waljk,*" Estelle mimicked him.

"I'd love to discuss this topic with you sometime, Luis," William said. "But you do have roots, an identity. I can see your identity right through all those layers of Versace clothes."

"He tries to model himself after that horrid phone shop man," Estelle said.

"We can all see you, Luis Sol from Stompetoren," William said.

Luis tried to breathe deeply, running his hands over his face. "Why are you helping him?" he asked, turning to Marina, who was putting on her coat. "You know he doesn't belong here."

"There is no belonging," Marina said. "We are all floating in space. There is only the temporary connections we make, with a place, with another person. Short or long. Everything is always changing, and you can go in all directions. The world is big. There are endless possibilities."

She picked up her bag from the floor. William stood up from the sofa and gave her a fifty-euro note.

Estelle got up too. "My client believes he legally belongs here and this property legally belongs to him," she said to Luis. "He is working on proving it. The process will take time. Meanwhile, he is forced to tolerate your continued presence in this dwelling. He requests private use of the living room space, unless otherwise requested and agreed upon. Vice versa, he will not enter the space that is currently your bedroom without specific permission." Estelle handed Luis a paper. "Here is a schedule for use of the communal spaces: the bathroom, the kitchen, the hallway."

The Philanthropist

Weeks and months went by. Every Sunday, the same thing. It went like this: At Mr. Hond's apartment I put Luis in the stroller in the living room. Usually he fell asleep during the walk over, otherwise I would breastfeed him and rock him to sleep. Then, in the bedroom, Mr. Hond asked me to sit down by his side for a moment, and he complained of a pain in his body, the treatments that weren't working, the deterioration. Could he hold my hand for a moment? And this is the moment where the film of my memories stops and changes. The next image I can find is the light shining through the hole in the red fabric of the curtain. This ray of light was what I focused on when it happened. How long it lasted I do not know. It could be minutes, half an hour. I stared at the ray of light until the room was filled with it, so blinding that everything became white. The light blocked everything, even the sounds; only in the distance was there skin rubbing against cotton sheets, breaths, a voice requesting more and different things.

In my mind I started decorating this white-light room. Light blue curtains—I would hang them up in my mind, one hook after another. I would place a little crib in the corner and make the bed with tiny sheets, embroidered. Then I would fold the sheets in a nice way, the corner just a little bit open, inviting. On the walls I would put wallpaper in soft colors, mint green and pink—every wall I covered with it. And then in the corner a chair for me. With every detail I added to the room each week, the more real it became to me.

Afterward, I washed my hands in the bucket of green soap water I left in the kitchen. I sang the little "Mouse House" song to Luis when he woke up. Looking back, I think I believed I was wearing one of those plastic suits from the mushroom factory over my feelings, and I would be immune to what he did. I'd just take off the plastic suit when he was dead and restart my feelings again.

Back then I thought it was normal, how tired I was when I came back home in Stompetoren. I had a baby, of course I was tired. I thought it was normal that I had headaches and that it felt like the world was weighing on me. It was normal that my clothes started feeling heavy on me. When I got home to Dave's cottage on Sundays, all I wanted to do was to take my clothes off and sit under the shower. And that was how I often spent Sunday evenings, with little Luis in my arms, under the warm shower until the boiler ran out.

I remember telling myself it was all temporary. Living with Dave was temporary, it did not count. The bond he was forming with Luis was temporary, it did not count. Everything would change when Mr. Hond was dead and I got my home. Then my life could really begin, and my old self would come out again. I was planning to make birth announcements and invite everyone from Stompetoren to visit me in Amsterdam, especially my parents. I had not seen them since the hospital. When they called the house, I kept it short. David talked to them more than me. "He is trying to sit up," I would hear him say in the other room. "He eats mashed potatoes now."

Dave never started a sentence with "she," so I knew they did not ask, "How is she? Is she doing okay? Did she recover well? Is she happy, is she healthy, is she all right?"

Once Hond keels over, and they come to see me in Amsterdam, I will tell them exactly what they did wrong, I thought. But with each week that went by, Mr. Hond seemed to get better. More talkative, more energetic, more lively.

Sometimes on the train back I thought of my experience with the mouse that I raised from the dead. Now I worried if my body was truly holy. But if it was, I thought, maybe it shouldn't be, you know, used like this.

"It's your presence, it revives me," Mr. Hond said. "My lungs, they feel more open when you are here. Like I can breathe again."

Mediation

They were all together in the living room: Luis, Mrs. Adelman, Marina, William, and Estelle.

Luis was standing by his fridge. Marina was leaning against the sink. Mrs. Adelman was sitting on the sofa, squeezed in between William and Estelle.

"We have decided to cooperate only because a judge will look at whether we tried mediation if we have to go to court for an eviction," Estelle said. "But I recommend Luis hire someone who is specialized in property law instead of spaceships."

"I am not specialized in spaceships," Mrs. Adelman said, "although I do know a little bit about it. My specialty is international space law, which is a legitimate field of law and an extremely interesting one. Soon governments will be fighting over people with my expertise." She smiled and looked out the window. For a moment it was quiet. Then she opened her bag and carefully put the document Luis had found in his mother's diary on the table.

"*Donatio mortis causa,*" she announced. "A gift made in anticipation of death. Completely valid." She then took a binder full of documents from her bag and put it on the table too. "Jurisprudence. Similar cases, all promises made in anticipation of death, all decided in favor of the holder of the disputed property. Luis has a clear-cut case. But he is willing to explore solutions with Mr. Rose outside of the courtroom."

Estelle shook her head. "A binding will needs to have at least two witnesses. And all these cases you are referencing here have a dead person at the center and a transactional moment. You have neither. No death. No transaction. You don't even have witnesses. You have nothing."

"There is no dead person, but there is no living person either," Mrs. Adelman said. "And when the keys were transferred to Luis's mother, she effectively took over ownership. This was the transactional moment. If we do need to take a different legal route, the document can certainly prove she lived here in good faith."

Estelle smiled. "For adverse possession they would need to have lived here without interruption for ten years, which I can testify they did not. There was no one living here when I moved into my apartment ten years ago. Mail was always piling up in the hallway; there was no maintenance done."

"They have paid city tax for almost twenty years," Mrs. Adelman said.

"You have a very shaky case and you know it," Estelle said.

"And you don't have a birth certificate or proof of paternity yet." Mrs. Adelman smiled. "No DNA, no witness, no photo, nothing. He is staying here because he is still hoping to find something in this apartment, a nail for the DNA test, a neighbor who remembers him."

Estelle cleared her throat but said nothing.

"He was my father," William said to Mrs. Adelman. "I have the letter my mother sent from the address in one of his envelopes. I have memories of living here."

"And I think your lawyer would be able to tell you that this is very little evidence for a paternity case, especially in the case of a missing person," Mrs. Adelman said. "And if the court recognized you as his son, there is still no right to claim all of the inheritance. Other stakeholders will be considered. This is a conflict where neither party would benefit from going to court. Let's start finding a solution through empathy. Step one is establishing the problem together. We will use my five-step mediation plan, which you can read more about in my manuscript, if you are interested." On the table she placed a copy of her manuscript "Property in Space," although no one had asked for it.

"I can already tell you that the problem is that Luis is living in my apartment," William said. He looked tired, his hair was standing out on all sides, and he had not shaved in days. "The solution would be if he told the truth about the past, in detail, and then left."

"I am not interested in the past," Luis said. "I am interested in the future."

"Yes," Mrs. Adelman said. "The past, the future, the now, it must all be taken into account as we find a solution in the present. Step two is exchanging information and sharing experiences."

Estelle turned around to look at the clock. "One hour, we said."

"He took the batteries out of the clock," Luis said. "Without asking. Which is not right."

Estelle sighed. "What's right and wrong is written in the law. The rest is opinions. This whole situation is about the law. Who is the legal owner? Edward Hond, William's father."

"This situation is about analyzing with an open mind," Mrs. Adelman said. "We can go left, we can go right, nothing is set in stone. It's up to us to find a resolution."

"This situation is about how things should be," William said. "How they are meant to be."

"There is no meant to be," Marina said. "Even if there is a purpose in the universe, is there any rational reason to believe that humans would be able to grasp that purpose or fulfill a central role in it, seeing how limited our perspective is?"

"Why, again, is the housekeeper here?" Estelle asked Luis. "And why is she being philosophical? No offense."

"It is Wednesday, her workday," Luis said. "And Marina is very philosophical. She studied biology."

"Luis asked me to be here," Marina said.

"She has worked here for three years," Luis said. "She loves the apartment."

"I clean nine houses, four offices, and two nightclubs per week," Marina said. "And a hotel."

"I was awake for a long time last night," William said. "When I finally fell asleep, I had a vivid dream. I was standing in open land where no houses were built yet, no flats, no offices, no roads. It was just grassy land, endless wet, grassy land."

"A field," Luis said.

"It was this location. I could feel it. The territory where I belong. I am starting to believe my ancestors have a historic connection with this area."

"The Netherlands were underwater before this was land," Marina said. "Then it became swampland, up until the Middle Ages."

"William knows that," Estelle said. "He is a professor. And much longer ago all the tectonic plates were in completely different places. So maybe his ancestors lived on this piece of land when it was not under the sea. Who knows? It's all possible."

"Everything you say is incorrect," Marina said to Estelle. "No offense."

"The dream meant, on a symbolic level, that my soul is in the place where it should be," William continued.

"I also had a dream about that," Luis said. "I dreamed I lived here all along and he did not."

"I know Edward Hond was my father," William said. "And I am not religious, but I believe that if he was looking down on us from heaven, he would want me to have my rightful place. Not some cleaner or her son. And I believe Luis knows that, and that is why he turns so red when he talks about this apartment."

"He is not in heaven," Luis said.

"What do you mean by that?" William asked. "Do you know where he is? Is he alive?"

For a moment they looked at each other. Luis realized he had avoided making eye contact with William for a long time. It unsettled him. There was something familiar in his eyes, something soft, something hopeful but stupid. It reminded Luis of himself when he was a young and stupid child, approaching other children on the school grounds, hoping they would play with him.

He straightened his shoulders. "Of course I don't know where that man is," Luis said. "He is of course dead. I just meant, if there is a heaven, it is for a different type of people."

William raised his eyebrows. "I thought you said he was like a saint to your mother."

"My mother called everyone a saint," Luis said. "That doesn't mean anything."

"Is that so?" William shook his head. "Because some people in Stompetoren said your mother mostly insulted and offended people. That she never had a positive thing to say."

"Stompetoren?" Luis took a step toward him. "Who did you talk to in Stompetoren?"

Estelle and William looked at each other. "My client had to do his own research since you did not want to cooperate," Estelle cut in. "I advised him to make some calls."

"My father is sick." Luis's voice broke. "He did not have anything to do with this. If you called my father . . ."

"We were not able to speak with your father," Estelle said in a businesslike tone. "He is in a care home and privacy laws prevent us from contacting him."

"Mrs. Raat said that Marie Meeuwisse lived full-time in the home next door to their farm on the dike in Stompetoren," William said. "She said Marie sometimes talked about having an apartment in Amsterdam, but no one believed her. She said Marie was known as a bit erratic." He looked at Luis. "You mentioned the name Raat. I am not proud of it, but—"

"That is not relevant," Estelle interrupted William. She turned to Mrs. Adelman. "We want to make Mr. Sol an offer. That is why we are here. My client wants to offer to pay for his mother's alleged cleaning hours, on the condition that Mr. Sol leaves within two weeks. About two years of supposed weekly cleaning work, every Sunday. Fifty euros per half day, which is today's rates, not back then. And then reimbursed for her travel costs and the city taxes she paid for. We offer your client fifteen thousand euro in total. If he accepts straightaway."

"It's an extremely generous reimbursement for what she put in," William said to Luis, "considering that you lived here rent-free for eight years."

"You don't know what she put in," Luis said loudly. "She put in more than you could ever imagine. Your father was . . ." He stopped talking for a moment, the words piling up in his throat. He knew he should take a deep breath; he knew he should calm down. But his voice came back, louder, faster. "It was a promise. He promised her the apartment. You have seen it. And my mother wanted it so badly. All she wanted was to have her own place where she could make her own rules. Start her own life. Is that so much to ask? To have what others have. To live. Everybody wants that!" His heart started moving under his chest again, the rat was back.

"Let's focus on the rational side," Mrs. Adelman said. "Let's try not to get caught up in the emotional side. We are gathering information."

"Yes," William said. "And Luis was going to say something. That is the information I want to have. You said 'your father was . . .'"

"I am just saying that maybe you should know that your father was a terrible person," Luis said. The words came out fast now—when he was angry the words came easily suddenly. "And you are just like him. Ever since you came here, you act like you are better than me. Estelle acts like you are better than me. But what makes you so good? Reading a book? Studying? Nobody cares where words come from. It's not important. Nobody cares! You are just like your father. You think you are important for no reason. Old paintings, old words, stupid antiques. You don't do anything useful and then you take what you want. You just come in here—you just come in!—and take over everything. And then you throw some fancy words around and then act like it is all good and fair. You don't even care how much you scared me. You don't even care about my mother and what happened to her."

"What do you know?" William asked, his voice rising. "What happened here?"

"She cleaned!" Luis shouted. "I told you, she cleaned! It destroyed her whole life, she could not get out of bed in the morning, she changed after coming here. She never even had a chance against him." He took a step forward, he was standing in the middle of the living room now. All his words were coming from the middle of his body, they were streaming out of him as if he had broken in two.

"Take a breath, Luis," Mrs. Adelman said. "Think about what you are saying."

"I am saying William has no right," Luis said. "What does it matter if he was his son? My mother deserved it, she worked hard for it."

"I may not have cleaned for him," William said slowly, "but I have a blood connection. That is bigger than anything. I believe I have inherited his intelligence, his kindheartedness, his analytical skills. Like Luis inherited from his own parents his square build, his simple mind, his mistrust and aggression. I want my complete inheritance."

"And your father's faults? Do you also want to inherit his faults?" Luis asked, his voice sharp. "The things he did to other people? And the punishment he should get for that?"

"It's impossible to inherit crimes or punishments," Estelle said.

"The mediation has warped toward the emotional," Mrs. Adelman said. "We are supposed to consider the emotional side alongside the rational, the logical, the legal. We gather information, then seek solutions." She clapped her hands. "We have an offer from Mr. Rose to compensate Mr. Sol. Let us seek alternative solutions. Could we divide the house into two sections? How about that? Two bathrooms? Perhaps you could sit down, Luis."

Luis did not sit down. "So you only want the good things?" he asked William. "You have the right to inherit the good things, and you have the right to ignore the bad things? Your father ignored you your whole life. And still, you think he is some sort of hero? Aren't you afraid of who he really was? Do you want to inherit all of that?"

"I think you're lying," William said. "You are shouting at me and walking around like a crazy person, while I try to sit and speak calmly with you. I think you know much more than you let on. I think your mother may have hurt my father. What did you mean she had no chance against him. Did they fight? What happened to my father? What did she do?"

Luis felt a drum of rage come up from his toes to his belly, into his chest. "My mother did nothing!" he shouted, his arms spread out wide. "I wish she had done something! But she did nothing! Nothing, nothing, nothing!"

"What are you talking about?" William said, standing up from the sofa.

"We are here to find a resolution," Mrs. Adelman called out as she stood up. She waved her arms around. "Everyone calm down. Why don't we take a moment to reflect on the two-bathroom solution?"

Luis grabbed the armrest of the sofa and lifted it from the ground.

"Stop!" Estelle yelled as she tumbled from the sofa.

"This is my resolution," Luis said, dragging the sofa toward the door. "Get off my sofa, get off my carpet. Those are my rightful possessions, aren't they? I have the receipts. Let him sleep on the floor. That is the resolution."

He dragged the sofa over the threshold and through the hallway to his bedroom, not caring if he damaged his deep-pile carpet. He pushed the sofa sideways through the doorway and toppled it into his room. It smashed down on the floor between his wardrobe and his bed—it only just fit. Luis clambered over the sofa and closed the door behind him. He sat down on his bed, his heart beating loud, the blood rushing in his ears. He took deep breaths, four counts in, four counts out, until his mind calmed down a bit. When his heartbeat began banging less forcefully in his chest, he started paying attention to the voices outside his door.

"There is only so much you can do as a mediator," he heard Mrs. Adelman say in the hallway. "A problem is like a magnet. People keep returning to it, circling around it; they don't want to get away from it. They let the emotions consume them. In my practice I am always hindered by the emotions when it comes to a solution."

Then Luis heard another voice. It was Marina's. "It's much harder to let someone live in your head than in your house," she said. "They need to accept their lives are connected." She talked softly. Then she started talking about her living situation, the dog.

"Marina," Luis said through the door, "would you come in here and clean this room, please? It's not yet four o'clock."

The bedroom door could only open halfway, now that the sofa was standing next to Luis's bed. Marina had to squeeze in sideways to get into the bedroom with her vacuum.

"I have to lock my bedroom door at night, inside my own home," Luis told Marina, as she vacuumed the small areas of free carpet in the bedroom. "Can you believe it? Because I'm afraid I'll find him sleeping in my bed one day."

Marina did not answer.

Luis watched her pull the sheets from his bed and throw them in the corner. He'd seen her do that in this place a hundred times. The familiarity of these movements made him feel sentimental. Didn't she use to agree with him? He wished that she would agree with him.

"So you think I should be nice to everyone who wants to take things from me?" he asked. "Should I just say, 'Sure, take whatever you want, let's all be connected, all the people can come here and take everything'?"

"Who are all the people?" Marina said. She took clean sheets from the wardrobe.

He looked at her small, strong body, her arms reaching up.

She swept the sheet into the air like a flag and placed it over the bed.

"I have to protect myself," Luis said, standing up. "I have to create a border around myself, a border against what they want to do to me. Every person needs to protect themselves against the others. That is the first responsibility. Like you should have protected yourself from your landlord, who put all your stuff in the street."

"Sometimes, if you help the other, you don't have to protect yourself from them," Marina said. "Not always, but sometimes."

Luis turned around to the mirror. His face was red, once again, and his eyes tired. He rubbed the creases from his shirt.

"Maybe that is how it works in . . ." He could not remember for a moment where it was she was from. "We have a different life." He wasn't sure where he was going with this, but he continued. "We need to protect ourselves. We need a border to say this is mine, this is who I am, this is what I need. We need to protect that over here. It is different over there."

"It's like that where I am from," she said. "But I am not a country. I am Marina. And I don't like this 'my space, my time, my house, my money.' A sister can be rich while the brother is poor. A neighbor can be hungry while the other throws food away. I don't like it. Just for me, I have the right to say I don't like it."

"Nobody likes it," Luis said, rubbing his hands over his eyes. "It is just how it is. We cannot make it better. It is like that thing with the phones and the children."

"Everything is how we make it," Marina said. "You are just as bad as William. You don't listen to each other. You don't try to find out together what really happened and what you really feel."

She rolled the TV cart into the corner and started stacking the cardboard from the box his fridge came in.

"Should I give away my apartment?" Luis said. "What if another person comes who wants my clothes, and another person who wants my food, and another one who wants my body. We need to protect what we have. Otherwise, where does the sharing end?"

"It has not even started," she said.

"Who is sharing with you?" Luis said. "You have to work in another country to make money for your family. You don't even have a place to live, your landlord kicked you out. You make only ten euro per hour. Who helps you?"

Marina looked at him for a moment. She shook her head. "No one helps me," she said. She took her coat and her purse from the bed. "And that is really hard."

She was quiet for a moment.

"I am just trying to be who I want to be, instead of being who the world has scared me into being. That is it. I think it makes people happy when they share, and that is why I want to do it."

Luis said nothing. He thought of how he used to share food with Brigitte. She wanted to share every piece of food that she ate with him. "It's cozy," she said. His eyes filled with tears as he thought of the two of them in the restaurant on the city square on her birthday, him pulling the chair out for her, the flower brooch she had pinned on her shirt that she said made her look "restauranty." She took a bite from all the food on his plate.

With a tight feeling in his throat, Luis opened his money jar and gave Marina a twenty for her cleaning. Then he took a hundred-euro note from the jar and gave it to her as well.

Marina hesitated. Then she put the notes in her purse. "Thank you, I think," she said.

"Good luck today," Luis said.

Marina smiled briefly at him. "Okay," she said.

He felt strangely light at that moment, happy to see her smile at him. As he watched her put on her headphones, he remembered how his father would always say "good luck today" to his mother when she left for work in the mushroom factory, and later, when the roles were reversed, she said it to him when he left to look for a job. Those were simple exchanges, meaningless, but they made him sentimental now. Having someone there who wishes you good luck, who is in your corner. Who says the words "sleep tight" in the evening, who says "bless you" when you sneeze.

"Marina," Luis shouted after her when she walked down the stairs, "would you like to stay here until you have a new place?"

"What do you mean?" Marina asked. She took off her headphones.

"If you need a place to stay with your dog," Luis said, "you can stay here."

She stared at him. Then she said, "Why?"

"Then I am not alone with William," Luis said. "I feel better when you are here. It's nice to have a woman in the house. It makes everyone calm."

Marina clicked her tongue. "Sure," she said, "put it on the women."

Luis shook his head. "Don't be angry," he said. "I want to help you. It will save you money. You pay rent for your room, right? Here you don't have to pay anything. Not even groceries. You can bring your dog, we can give him a bowl of water, he can sleep on a blanket in the corner."

"Are you making a joke?" Marina asked.

"You can sleep in the bed, in my bedroom," Luis said. "I can sleep on the sofa. I work five nights a week, you work during the day. You will have privacy and can do whatever you want. You can go do all your work, all the other houses, and watch TV when you come back." He paused. "I will make sure you are fine. I will make sure it all goes really well."

The Philanthropist

Of course I knew that some things were seeping through the plastic suit. I had nightmares of my mother and my father and Jesus and all my friends standing around me, watching me, when I let these things happen in Hond's dark bedroom. Sometimes I dreamed that I was back in the hospital bed where I gave birth, and Anna Beemster pulled pages from the Bible out of me. Sometimes I would dream of cuddling with Dave, and then when he turned around, I would realize it was Mr. Hond I was holding, his sweet, sweaty smell and wrinkled skin everywhere against me.

But when I woke up, I heard the sound of my baby's breathing, so I stuffed the dreams away. The situation was temporary. It was unpleasant but better than it was for those women behind the Red Light District windows, better than it was for the women who married for money and had to spend their whole entire lives pretending to laugh at stupid jokes. This was temporary.

So I got up every Sunday to go back to his apartment once again, and take another step, and another. The number of weeks that passed were more than I ever thought they would be. Luis celebrated his first birthday. He put his hand in the candle and had to go to A&E. He took his first step. Dave found a job and got fired. The washing machine broke.

And Mr. Hond kept on living. He drank his Scotch and said, "Death never comes when you expect it, it always comes too soon or too late."

The final Sunday at Hond's apartment was like any other at first. The thing had already happened. He was sitting in the bed, reading the paper. I did not do much cleaning anymore, I made a bucket of soapy water and splashed it around a bit. I swept the crumbs and nail clippings in his bedroom into the corner where there was a hole in the floorboards. I sprayed some bleach on the toilet seat. The rest of the time I spent sitting in the living room with Luis, until Hond called me from his bedroom to say it was enough for today.

I remember I was sitting at the kitchen table that day, looking out over the garden, massaging my breast as I tried to get Luis to latch. He had started to drink less well from my right breast, and I had to keep him there for a long time so the milk got going. I put him on my chest in a different angle, not too horizontal. My arm hurt and I was tired of singing "Mouse House" over and over again.

"Marie," Hond called me from the bedroom.

His voice was raspy and too sweet, like the smell in the apartment.

"Marie," he called again.

"Wait a minute," I called. "Luis is drinking."

"Marie!"

I felt my heart thump in my throat. I put Luis in the stroller and gave him the bottle I brought just in case. He started crying.

"Marie, dear," Hond called.

I put my bra back on and walked to his bedroom. "Luis is crying," I said in the doorway. "He never cries when he gets a bottle, it means there really is something the matter. I don't know if his teeth—"

"Bring me the little one," Hond said over me. "I'll cheer him up."

When I carried Luis into the bedroom, Mr. Hond was sitting up in the bed, holding up a five-cent coin in his left hand and a 250-guilder note in his other hand.

"Which one do you want, little fellow?"

Luis stared at him. He was red-faced and teary-eyed, but he did stop crying when he saw Mr. Hond. I put him down on the floor and nudged him toward the bank note. Luis could stand now and walk while holding my hand.

"It's for your piggy bank," Mr. Hond said to Luis. "Do you have a piggy bank?"

"He isn't really talking yet," I said. "That's normal for his age, he's only one and a half. Einstein didn't talk until he was five years old, and still he became a millionaire."

"It is a gift for you," Mr. Hond said to Luis, ignoring me, "from Uncle Edward. Which one do you like most?"

I took Luis's hand, pointing it at the note that could buy us a new washing machine, but Mr. Hond shook his head.

"Let him decide," he said. "Which one, little fellow?"

Luis toddled toward Mr. Hond and grabbed the five-cent coin with his little fist.

"He knows what he's worth!" Mr. Hond shouted, his toothless mouth wide open.

Luis started licking the coin.

"Priceless," Mr. Hond said, and laughed. "I like this one! He's not pretentious, he doesn't talk. Why couldn't I have had one like this?"

I noticed his laughing wasn't turning into a coughing fit like it used to. My body went cold as I realized he hadn't had one of those coughing fits in a long time. Hadn't he been sitting more upright? Wasn't there more color in his cheeks? Was he getting chubbier? Then I noticed his cane was standing against the wall. The wooden floorboards it was standing on were a bit wet. Was that from the snow?

"You simply can't make a silk purse from a sow's ear," Mr. Hond said, still laughing. "No need to save up for university with that one."

"It's not right to talk about him like that," I said. "He just does not know the difference. He is a baby. It is good that he does not have to think about money yet."

"A child should start thinking about money as soon as possible," Mr. Hond said. "The child can stand! He is not a baby anymore. When I was his age, I was already swindling money out of everybody. Especially old guys like me. Life is to crush or to be crushed! People take what they can get, and you need to fend for yourself in this world. That's what I have been trying to teach you, little Marie. You need to stand up for yourself in this world. Not everyone is going to be as nice as me."

Uncle Luis

That evening Luis's doorbell rang. He opened the door to Marina, who walked into the hallway holding a sleeping bag, a backpack, and her little brown dog. Without saying anything, she walked past Luis and put her bag down on the bedroom floor.

Luis took his sheets from his bed and put them on the sofa, where he was going to sleep. It was getting very full in there, with the sofa, the television, and the cardboard he still hadn't thrown out. He watched Marina roll out her sleeping bag over his bed. The dog settled down on a pillow she put in the corner.

Luis sat down next to the dog and patted him on the head. "I'm Uncle Luis," he introduced himself. "What is your name?"

"Two weeks I am staying here maximum," Marina said. "And I have pepper spray."

"Shall I make you a sandwich?" Luis asked. Without waiting for a reply, he got up and went into the living room. He did not knock. It was half dark in there, and the space seemed so empty now that his sofa was gone. William was lying on an airbed that Estelle had given to him.

"Hello, Luis," William said. He got up and switched the light on. Then he looked very long and intensely at Luis, as if he was studying him.

Luis turned away from the bright blue eyes staring at him. He made a bagel with cream cheese for himself and one for Marina, taking a lot of time and making a lot of noise.

"This is for Marina," he said to William as he walked to the door. "She is staying with me now. I am helping her. She will need to use the bathroom later, so please make sure it is free. And she has pepper spray." He carried the bagels on a tray into the bedroom, where Marina was talking to her family on the phone. He placed the tray on the bed carefully, the napkin next to the plate, the knife and fork aligned on top of it.

Marina took the plate with the bagel onto her lap. She said something in Portuguese and hung up.

"My mother says hello," she said. "And the dog's name is Roman."

An hour later, Luis was standing in the doorway of his bedroom in his coat, ready to go to work. Marina and her dog were lying on the sleeping bag on the bed.

Luis had cut open the cardboard box and placed it vertically in the bedroom, so it formed a low wall between Marina's bed and his sofa. He'd offered to cut a window out of it, but she did not want that.

"Well, I'm off to work," Luis said to the cardboard.

Marina did not reply. Luis listened to the sound of Marina's breath and the branches of the tree tapping on the window. He thought of what his mother had written about the light coming in through the holes in the curtain. The memories of her story would come up unexpectedly, they jumped at him from different corners of the apartment.

"Marina, I am going to work," Luis said again.

He heard her turn on the bed, the sound of the sleeping bag brushing over her skin.

Another memory. He shivered.

"Marina," he said again, "I know you don't want to be here and you don't have so much choice. And I know you are mad. It's just that I don't want to be alone with that man. I just don't want to feel so scared anymore."

"But what do you want?" Marina's voice asked in the dark.

"I don't want him here. I don't want to explain what happened to my mother. I don't want to think about her secrets. And I don't want my house taken from me."

Marina sighed. "But what do you want, Luis? I'm not asking what you don't want. What do you want?"

"I want to be at ease," Luis said. "I want my house back." He paused for a couple of seconds. "I want to buy nice things. I want to feel free. I want to feel safe and accepted."

He was quiet for a moment.

"What do you want?" he asked.

"I want my family to be all right," Marina said.

"Yes," Luis said.

"I want to see them," she said. "I want to stop worrying about money. I want to have money. I want to have fun. I want to have a place where I can feel at home. I want to have fun! I want someone to stand up for me."

"I want to have fun too," Luis said. "And I want someone to stand up for me."

"I want someone to say thank you to me sometimes," Marina said.

"I want to have someone around," Luis said. It surprised him when he heard himself say that.

"I want to be beautiful," Marina's voice said in the dark bedroom. "I want someone to say that to me."

"You are beautiful," Luis said. "You just dress very masculine."

"I want someone to understand me completely," Marina continued. "I want to have security. I want someone to take care of me when I am ill."

Luis stood still in the doorway. From the bathroom he heard the sound of water running, William brushing his teeth. The tree branches were hanging immobile in front of the window, illuminated by the streetlamps. In the reflection in the window, he could see Marina sitting up on the bed, her arms around her knees.

"Marina," Luis said, "I want to say thank you to you."

She did not reply.

"I will take care of you when you are ill," Luis said.

Marina made a noise he wasn't sure was a laugh or a cough.

31 August
My father's home, Amsterdam

The living room is completely empty now, except for the air mattress Estelle has given me. When I am lying awake, I think about the three of us—me, Luis, Marina—how we are all trying to fall asleep in this apartment, all with our own troubles on our mind. I can't imagine Luis is sleeping well. He had dark circles under his eyes when I saw him this morning, and his behaviour seems jumpy, erratic.

And I wonder, How long can I keep this up? I am starting to feel on edge. Every night I lie awake until Luis gets home. I have developed a twitching muscle near my eye, and I've started grinding my teeth when I sleep, so much so that my jaw hurts in the morning. Sometimes I feel a sudden urge to yell, which frightens me.

Estelle has set in motion the paternity procedure. A photo of an old park bench with a plaque that indicated it was donated by my father has spurred the memory of an elderly neighbour, Mrs. Barneveld. She has reluctantly signed a witness testimony that Edward Hond lived here with a British woman during the time of my birth. She does not remember anything else. Estelle is going to the first hearing without me. I dare not leave this place, for Luis will change the locks as soon as I set foot out the door. And I have a much better chance in court as an occupant of the apartment, Estelle says. I am deeply indebted to her for her generous help. The idea that I might legally have a father soon feels very strange. What will it be like?

I notice I keep thinking about what Luis said: 'Your father was a terrible person'.

What could have happened between his mother and my father? According to Luis he gave her an entire apartment, all she had to do for it was clean a little bit. Of course there could have been more happening between them. An affair, despite the age difference? My instincts say that he would never do such a thing. An educated man who did charity, who had travelled the whole world, who was old, sick, and fragile . . . would he really seduce a seventeen-year-old? It just seems so unlikely.

When I do entertain the possibility of an affair, an unsettling idea keeps occurring to me. The document that promises Luis's mother the apartment is dated three months before Luis's birth date. Luis said his mother had been working there for some time when the document was signed. If that is all true, then could it be . . . could it be that my father had some sort of fling with his cleaning lady and she got pregnant? Did he promise her the house out of a sense of guilt or obligation? Is Luis my half brother? It could even explain why she never went here . . . the pain of missing him. And Luis's parents' dislike of talking about the apartment would be explained as well.

When I shared this idea with Estelle, she nearly choked on her Diet Coke, erupting in a chuckle. 'Couldn't be related', she grunted. 'Impossible'.

To me, everything seems possible now.

Just now, when Luis came into the kitchen to make bagels for himself and Marina, I tried to see if there is any resemblance. In every way we are opposites: He is short and broad; I am tall and slim. He is athletic; I am an intellectual. My hair is curly, and his is flat, almost reddish. His eyes are small, dark, close together. My eyes are blue and wide.

I have noticed that I look at him with softer eyes when I consider him my baby brother. I find myself being nicer to him, feeling a little bit of excitement when I hear him at my door. Yes, his interests are shallow; yes, he is predictable and primal. But there is also a refreshing lack of ego there. A modesty. The way his face changes colour as soon as he feels something is somewhat sympathetic. He is a transparent man. The gift that he wanted to give me, the bag, shows kindness. And if it's true that he does not know that he is my father's child, he is a sincere man who has been denied the truth, like me.

Am I losing it? I have already gone much further than I even anticipated. Calling those people in Stompetoren when Estelle suggested it, even though everything inside of me said it was wrong... and before that faking the fall... quitting my position at university... Where is my boundary?

I have never gone this far before in my life. Does that mean I am on the right track? Or does it mean I have lost my compass and I am doing things I will come to regret?

The Philanthropist

It ended the next Wednesday.

Dave was out on Raat's field, helping him bring in the horses before the snowstorm. I was in the kitchen, wearing all my clothes on top of one another, and they felt heavy on me. We put Luis's crib near the oven during the day, because it was the only place in the house that would properly warm up. As I looked at the first snowflakes coming down outside, forming a layer on the roof of the barn that was about to collapse, images of the past Sunday kept coming back to me. The weight Mr. Hond had gained. The shoes that were in a different place. The wet spot on the floor under his cane.

"I can't possibly go to Amsterdam now," I said out loud.

And then and there I decided we were going. I needed to know what was going on.

I picked up my sleeping baby from his crib and strapped him in the stroller, with all the blankets still wrapped around him. "We are going to the philanthropist," I whispered to Luis. "We're going to get our apartment now."

The walk to the bus stop in Stompetoren wasn't easy. The stroller kept sliding in the snow, and Luis, who was awakened by the fresh air, kept leaning to the side to put his hand in the snow. He tried holding on to bits of snow in his fist and yelled in surprise when it had melted. He'd always liked the color white. Everything that was white he had to hold on to. It was like a sickness.

Finally I just carried him, dragging the stroller behind me. The bus driver warned us that this would be the last bus for the day, it wasn't safe anymore on the road. I did not even care. I needed to confront Mr. Hond now that I dared to do it. The train ride seemed endless. The world outside the window was a white haze, it was like we weren't really going anywhere at all. I remember thinking that this unexpected storm felt like a dream and that must be why I dared to do this now, that it did not feel like the real world at all.

In Amsterdam the snow had turned to brown slush in the streets. We walked carefully over the pavement, trying not to fall, while I told Luis stories to distract him from the cold. When we came to our philanthropist's house, my fingers were so frozen it took me forever to get my key in the lock. It finally opened, and I pulled the stroller into the hallway. I told Luis to be quiet. "Wait for Mummy, she'll be right back."

A Party for Others

"This carpet isn't made for heels," Luis heard a voice behind his door say with a giggle. "It's like walking in a field."

Luis sat up on his sofa. It was Saturday, his day off. Marina was away: she cleaned offices on weekend evenings. Roman was sitting on the foot end of the bed, his ears turned toward the noise.

Now Luis heard the sound of William's voice. He got up and listened at his door. There were two people talking in his hallway. Someone laughed.

"I'm afraid the seating is a little unconventional," he heard William say behind the door, "due to some issues I am currently having with my . . . flatmate"—he coughed, Estelle laughed—"but we can sit on a blanket on the floor. It's a bit like a picnic, but since the carpet resembles a field, it's only appropriate."

Luis heard Estelle laugh loud. It was her fake laugh, the laugh she used when she had cocktails with her colleagues in the garden. Not the laugh he heard when she watched her favorite comedy on her phone in the garden and her piglike chuckles traveled up to his window.

So, they were having a date in his home. Luis thought of William, how Estelle had been so nice to him from the start. How she had put her hand on his sleeve that first day. What did she see in him? Yes, he was smart, and yes, he could be friendly. The last few days William had been weirdly friendly to Luis, helping him carry the glass table out of the living room. He even asked him how his day was when they came across each other in the hallway. Luis had no idea why he was doing it. But Luis was friendly too, and Estelle never cared for it.

The next few hours Luis spent sitting against his door, listening to the distant sounds of William and Estelle. He was asking himself if he should go out there, if he should say something, or—he did not know why he thought this—if they would come knock on his door to invite him to join. Of course he would say no if they did that. He would say that he had better things to do, that he did not want to spend time with people like them.

They did not come. Luis heard them talk and laugh. He looked about his room, the chaos it had become: the sofa, the glass table, Marina's backpack, the cardboard wall, the dog sleeping in the corner. How did this get so far? Why did this have to happen?

For a second he thought about leaving: just picking up some things, putting them in a backpack, and walking out the door, like he did in Stompetoren. But this time he did not know where to go. He thought of how he would be wandering through the city, staying in hotels, his money running out. Most apartments in Amsterdam cost more than his monthly income. Hadi said that if you wanted to buy a home in the Netherlands now, you would have to go to the countryside near Germany. What was he going to do there? For a second he thought of buying a van and living in there, so he could keep working for Bedas, but he knew it was not legal to live in a van. Back in Stompetoren there was an old guy called Sjors, Luis remembered, who lived in a van and kept getting fined for it. At one point the van was gone, and he was living in the bike parking behind the school that had walls and a roof to keep the bikes dry. He was kicked out of there too, his smelly blanket and pillows and his plastic bags thrown in a dumpster by the sanitary department.

The bikes could have a house, but Sjors could not. Luis thought of how his mother had once pointed at people giving Sjors coins and advice as he sat on the sidewalk by the supermarket. "Look, decent people," she said to Luis in a sharp voice. "Classy people. Kind people. Helping people. Giving people. Advice people. Coin people." She started raising her voice as she talked to Luis but looked at the people standing around Sjors. "Aren't they nice! Giving someone else a moment of their time! Time is money, you know. They don't have to give him a coin, but they still do. Very, very nice people. A good society. We even talk to the guy sleeping in the street, how nice are we!" She kept going on and on until everyone started staring at her, and finally a supermarket employee came up to her to say she could be fined for causing a disturbance in the street. She did these strange things sometimes, and Luis never dared to ask what was going on in her mind. What had happened for her to have those thoughts. In a way, he must have known that he wouldn't want to know it.

Estelle and William stopped talking when Luis opened the door of the living room. Estelle turned her body away from him. William, for some mysterious reason, got up and smiled at Luis. He said, "Luis, hello. We're having a little chat, Estelle and I.

I hope we weren't too loud. I know you need your rest before work. Estelle went to court for me yesterday, the start of my paternity case. I will get the result by post."

Luis nodded.

"And I was thinking, there is no reason we cannot be civilized while we go through this process," William said. "I understand you were emotional during the mediation. But I would like to express my desire to be respectful and patient with each other, and hope you would like that too."

Estelle turned back toward them. "Well said," she said to William. "The high road."

Luis looked at William. He was looking tired, dark circles under his eyes and hollow cheeks. "You are having a picnic in my living room," Luis said. "That is not the high road." He shook his head. "I am here because I need this." He pointed at the fridge. His voice quivered; he felt nervous and bold at the same time. "We need the fridge." He opened the fridge and took out the items that did not belong to him, putting them on the kitchen counter. "We," he said, unplugging it, "Marina and I." He tilted the fridge onto his back, lifting it. He could barely get it through the narrow doorway.

"Let me help you," William said. "Your hand."

"No!" Luis stepped into the hallway, grazing his hand on the doorframe. "Don't touch it. I'd like to have the fridge in the bedroom now. We do. I just need to . . . I'll carry it like this."

His arms were trembling. He hadn't exercised in almost two weeks. The morning of the day William arrived was the last time he did push-ups. In the hallway he put the fridge down on the carpet and closed the door, sucking the blood from his hand before it could drip onto the floor.

From the living room he heard nothing anymore, no talking, no laughter. He dragged the fridge farther down the hallway and plugged it in next to his bedroom door. It did not fit in his bedroom, which was full of his possessions now. The microwave was standing on the sofa, the cups and plates and cutlery were on the floor, the television in the corner. Luis sat down next to Roman, who briefly opened his eyes to put his head on Luis's leg and then went back to sleep.

Luis looked about his room. His possessions looked messy and worthless this way, even though they were all the same things that once gave him comfort and pleasure. What was it that had made him yearn for these things for so long?

The Philanthropist

I walked up Mr. Hond's stairs. Quietly. The lights were on in the hallway. In the bedroom, the bed was empty and made. The curtains were open. The curtains were never open when I came by on Sunday. In the living room there were sounds of someone walking around. The sound of paper tearing. Then the living room door opened, and I saw him. Poor, old, sick Mr. Hond. He was wearing the suit that he wore when I met him that first day. His hair was combed. He was holding a couple of envelopes in his hands. He looked healthy, standing upright.

"Hello," I said.

"Hello, Marie," he said. He did not say "dear Marie" this time. There was surprise in his voice but not as much as I expected. Like this was bound to happen at some point. It almost seemed like he was amused by it.

I put my hands on my hips and put my feet firmly on the floor, like Dave taught me to do when Raat's dogs came running at me. I said, "Not dead yet, I see?" My voice sounded more nervous than I wanted.

"Not dead yet," he said. "Actually, I've been feeling much better lately. I think it's not my time after all. Isn't that nice?"

"How long?" was all I could ask.

He smiled. "I suppose the doctors have been noticing signs of a careful recovery for a while now."

"You were never dying," I said.

"It was a pretty serious chest infection," he said. "I almost died. They all thought I would." I could see his dentures move a little bit in his mouth as he smiled. "If I didn't know any better, I would say you seem disappointed."

I said nothing.

"You should have given me a ring, Marie, if you wanted to stop by. Don't we always see each other on Sunday?"

"Now you're seeing me on a Wednesday," I said.

He looked at me, curious about what I would do next.

"I want to have what you promised us," I said, raising my voice. "If you are not dying, I want it. The apartment."

Mr. Hond shook his head. "Marie, dear," he said, "you seem a little . . . a little bit sour, maybe? You used to be a delight. That vibrant Marie, from the beginning, that innocent Marie, where is the old Marie, where did she go? I miss her."

I didn't say anything. I just stared at him. When I first met him he looked like he was in his eighties, and now, now he seemed more like seventy years old. Or younger.

"You were going to help us," I said. My heart was thumping in my throat and my temples.

"Everyone wants me to help them," he said with a shrug. He opened one of the envelopes he was holding with the Omani dagger. "Listen to this: 'To the foundation. Hello, I lost my job as a welder, it was not my fault. I worked there for twenty years, but after I missed some work, I was just thrown out with the garbage. They don't even state a reason for it. I have two children, the rent is one hundred and fifty guilders. Please help. I am trying to find new work. Thank you.'" He smiled. "What would you do, Marie?" he said.

"I would help him, he is not asking a lot," I said.

"Exactly," Mr. Hond said. He crumpled the paper and threw it in the corner. "So, you send him one hundred and fifty guilders. And then what? Then comes the next month. He knocks on your door again. Would you help him again? What he should do is sue his boss. Or even better, what he should have done is made sure that his contract provided for this. But he didn't. The world is brutal but predictable in its brutality."

"But not everyone gets the same start," I said. "It's not fair."

"Good point," Mr. Hond said. "If this man wants fairness, he should not be sending me letters with 'please' and 'thank you' asking for just one hundred and fifty. He should be banging on my door saying, '*La propriété? C'est le vol!* I demand my fair share in this world!' But the people don't have the guts to do it. They keep their heads down and say thank you and sorry and ask for a little bit of this and a tiny bit of that. And that's exactly why they don't deserve any more of it."

I looked at Mr. Hond. His eyes were strange, glowing. He looked like he had a fever.

"You're acting strange," I said. "You're speaking French."

"No, you are acting strange, my dear Marie Meeuwisse," he said. "It is a Wednesday. You have entered my apartment without my permission. I could call the police."

"It's not right, what you did," I said.

"What is right?" he asked. "Everything that happens, that you allow to happen, that is right. You make it so by accepting it."

"I did not accept it," I said, my voice soft.

"Yes," Mr. Hond said. "From the beginning you did." He walked past me into his bedroom, to his desk. The sickening sweet smell of his body seeped into my nostrils. He opened a drawer. "Now that I am recovering, I realize it is unreasonable to expect you to keep coming here. I release you from your obligation and retract my promise. But I understand some compensation would be fair. Let us say twenty-five guilders for each Sunday . . . two years . . . we'll make it three thousand guilders. How about that? That is a lot of groceries, I would say."

I looked at his crooked body, the gray strands of hair, the wrinkled hands flipping through his money, the pink lips counting each note. So used to buying what he wanted. Making things go away. My breathing was very fast and shallow. The memories of what had happened in the room started seeping in through the edges of my mind; I saw images I wanted to forget. My left hand, the hand he would wrap his fingers around when it happened, started cramping. My fingers spasmed.

I forced myself to take a deep breath. "We do not accept it. We want the apartment. Otherwise, we . . . I . . . I am going to make a case of it." My voice was so tiny I might as well have added the word "please" to my threat.

"Three thousand guilders is plenty," Mr. Hond said. He held the notes out to me. "I don't have the patience to discuss it with you. You won't do anything."

I wanted to say something. That I was not a piece of garbage you could just throw away. That I was a person.

"I am going to tell people," I said.

He laughed. "Look at yourself, Marie," he said, pointing at the mirror on the wall. "Tell me, who is going to believe you? Look in the mirror."

For reasons I still don't understand I obeyed him. I looked to the side and saw myself in the mirror. My eyes were wide, like a panicked animal's; my face was puffy from eating too much to comfort myself, it was red and patchy from being so cold; my orange-blond hair had dark roots because I did not have the energy to fix it.

"You did this," I said. "You know what you did."

He put his hand on my shoulder. "You can't hold it against me," he said. "Something came over me. Such a lovely girl, coming to my bedroom every week. The clothes you wore. You knew I was powerless. I have always been powerless in the face of beauty."

His hand slid from my shoulder to my left hand. He tried to put the money in my hand, but I did not take it. I remember I watched the money fall on the floor. And I remember him bending over to grab it. The Omani dagger was lying on the desk next to the envelopes. I do not remember taking it from the desk, but I must have. Then I remember the quiet sound of blood dripping onto the floorboards. I watched how it mixed with the snow that had come off my shoes, the drips painting red polka dots on it.

Liars

"What are you going to do, Luis?" Hadi asked. He was hanging over the counter at the Bagel Shop while Luis was clearing away the dishes.

"I need to know what his plan is," Luis said, more to himself than to Hadi.

"You know his plan," Hadi said. "He told you his plan exactly. He wants to live there. And now he is living there. He can keep this up longer than you, take that from me."

Nervously, Luis rubbed his hands over the back of his neck.

"You look bad, Luis," Hadi said. "You are pale and you look fat. I am telling you as a friend."

Luis knew it. His coat was too tight to button up. When he looked down at his clothes, he used to see the bulge of his chest muscles, but now when he looked down, he saw the bulge of his belly.

"Do not kneel when the water has risen up to your chin," Hadi said. "Do you know that saying?"

Luis did not react. He thought of William, who had been standing in front of the bathroom when Luis came out that morning. He'd said, "Oh, sorry," as if he were surprised, but Luis was sure he had been waiting for him. There was something strange in his eyes lately: he looked at Luis in the same way he used to look at his documents, with a deep frown and a hint of a smile on his lips.

"Are you listening to me?" Hadi asked. "This can't go on like this. He is not going to go away anymore. Do you know that?"

Luis knew it. But he just didn't know what to do about it. "A visitor has to go away at some point. The lawyer said he doesn't have a strong case. She said to wait."

"Stop calling him a visitor," Hadi said. "First you had an intruder. Then you had a flatmate who did not pay. Now you have a hostile takeover. What are you going to do?"

"I took all the furniture from the living room," Luis said. "All the plates and the cutlery. Even the blinds I took away. We already have the temperature low. I cut off the hot water. I play loud music. Marina is there with her dog. But he isn't moving a muscle. And if I throw him out, they will report me to the police. Estelle keeps saying she is a witness if I do something."

"Then provoke him. Get him to flip out and then report him to the police with your own witness. I don't care what you do. Just do something. Show him who he is."

"I can't provoke him," Luis said. "He is too well-behaved. He is a professor."

"Those kinds of people don't know their own boundaries," Hadi said. "If he's pushed, you'll see how well-behaved he is. All I'm saying is that you need to do something. I barely even see you, all you do is hide in your house. You don't reply to my calls. You missed Alexandra's birthday party."

"Who?" Luis said distractedly. He was putting the chairs on the tables, trying to wrap up his work as quickly as possible.

Marina was away for most of the night as well; cleaning offices. Lately Luis worried that when they were both out of the house, William would change the locks.

"Alexandra," Hadi said. "Are you leaving without mopping the floors? You know I defended you to Bedas when he said you weren't doing your work right anymore."

"I'm sorry," Luis said.

"And about Marina living with you," Hadi said. "You know that isn't right, to put her in the middle of this."

"She doesn't have another place to stay," Luis said as he started rolling down the shutters of the Bagel Store, leaving a gap open for Hadi to leave.

Hadi stepped in front of him in the street and looked at him for a moment. "That's even worse then," he said.

"I just need to close up and get back home," Luis said. He barely noticed when Hadi walked past him without saying good-bye. Quickly he locked up the store and walked through the night streets back to his home.

Since William Rose had arrived, he had slowly invaded each part of Luis's life. On the first night, he had taken over Luis's sofa. After that he had taken over the living room, Estelle, his mailbox, his bathroom, his mind. And when Luis came home from work in the early hours of that Saturday morning and he saw the light shining behind his blinds, he knew the last territorial move had been made. His bedroom.

His heart started pounding in his chest and his ears buzzed. Luis took deep breaths as he walked up the stairs. He heard the sound of a dog barking. He was trying to calm down and search for the voice in his head, his father's voice, that told him to back away from trouble, but the voice wasn't there. There was another voice now. It was Hadi's. "Show him who he is," he said.

Upstairs, Luis opened the door to his bedroom.

There he was, William, standing in the middle of Luis's disorganized room.

Marina was sitting on the bed, holding Roman, who was barking. She had tears in her eyes. "He locked Roman in the bathroom, Luis! He was so scared, I heard him barking from the street."

William was holding Luis's mother's diary open in his hands. "What is this?" he asked Luis. "What is this nonsense?" His voice was high, his hands were shaking. His normal control was gone.

Luis looked at his mother's large, square handwriting on the pages. Then he turned around and looked about his room, at his clothes that were thrown all over his bed, the blankets of the bed that were on the ground, the stacks of plates that were thrown over, the money jar that was emptied on the bed. His backpack was on the floor, the coffee tin next to it.

"That is my mother's private cleaning diary," he told William. His cheeks were hot. "I would like to have it back."

He extended his hand.

"Do you even know what it says in here?" William asked. "Did you write this? Did you write this to upset me?"

Luis laughed nervously. For the first time in a long time he was really laughing, even though there was nothing funny. "I did not write it," he said. "Why would I want to write that?"

"I don't believe my father would do any of this," William said, holding the notebook out in front of him with one hand, as if he were holding a dead rat by its tail. "He was a philanthropist, he loved beauty, he loved people. She wrote it to damage him."

"How would it damage him if she wrote it in her diary, only for herself?" Luis asked. "She did not want anyone to know; she kept it a secret all her life."

"She made it all up," William said, not listening to Luis. "And even if it did happen somehow, it was her fault. You know that? Your mother inserted herself in his life, leading him away from his work, giving him alcohol, manipulating an old, vulnerable man." He turned toward Marina. "Can you believe I even started to think Luis was my brother? That's why I came in here. I believed I might even be able to love him. I thought I already started to love him. I am sorry I locked Roman in. But I knew Luis was keeping something from me. I had to look for it. Roman kept barking and jumping at me. He was fine in the bathroom. He had water." William turned back to Luis. "Can you believe I hoped to find evidence that you were my brother? I saw the good in you, despite everything you did to me. But now I see that you are nothing like me and my father. You are like your mother. A thief."

Luis pushed away the rage that was building up in his throat. "My mother was not a thief," he said slowly. "What did she steal? She helped your father when he was sick, she did what he wanted of her, she did everything. Your father was the thief."

"Have you even read this, Luis?" William yelled. "Do you need me to read it to you?"

The Philanthropist

For a while it was just me, Mr. Hond, and the dripping sound. We both looked at the blood that was streaming from my left hand onto my fingertips and onto the wooden floorboards.

"Mama."

Behind me I heard Luis's voice. When I turned around I saw him looking at me with wide eyes, sitting in the arms of the lady from across the street, Mrs. Barneveld. She was standing in the doorway. I saw what they saw. The blood on my palm, on the floor and my shoes. Mr. Hond still on his knees, holding the money. The dagger in my hand. I let it drop to the floor.

When I think of it now, I still feel ashamed. Why had I done that? Why hadn't I hurt him, instead of myself?

Three lines I had carved in the palm of my hand, right next to one another.

"This woman is crazy," Hond said in a very calm voice to Barneveld as he got up from the floor. "She was my former cleaning lady, and she has broken into my home. I was about to call the police. I am going to have to report her."

"You call whoever you want," she said. "But I doubt you want the police in here, with all those things lying around." She pointed her garden shears at the paintings on the wall. Then she put Luis on the floor and looked at my hand.

"It's not very deep," she said. She took off her scarf and wound it around my hand. "Go to the doctor, it could get infected. And maybe you need some stitches." She said it as if she were in a situation like this every day. "Take the child and go." She grabbed Luis, who was completely quiet, and put him on my hip and folded my right arm around him. "Go on."

I started walking out of the room like a robot, feeling as if I had just woken up and was walking out of a dream, out of a nightmare, down the stairs, onto the street, into the real world. It was cold outside, and it was still snowing, but less hard. The stroller I forgot in the hallway. I held Luis tightly against me as I walked through the slippery snow to the train station.

"I'm coming."

That was all Dave said when I called from the phone booth in Central Station. He did not ask any questions, just like he did not ask any questions when I told him to pick me up from the hospital after Luis was born. The trains had all been canceled because of the snow, my trousers were soaked and dirty from falling down. I held Luis under my coat and sang "Mouse House" while we waited for his dad.

Dave came to get us, on the tractor, through the snowstorm. He drove up behind Central Station and stopped in the taxi lane. I knew how scary this had to be for him, to drive to Amsterdam for the first time, and on a day like this. He took Luis from my arms and put him on his lap, pulling me up to sit next to him. He also had a map and a baseball bat. "Just in case," he said with a shrug when he saw me looking at it. He'd also brought a coat with him that I could put on and an extra blanket for Luis.

"These Amsterdammers think I'm a snow plow or something," he said after a while, as we drove past the taxi drivers, who were honking and waving at us.

My hand was throbbing. "We've got to stop by the doctor," I said.

Dave just nodded. He did not ask anything.

I will never be able to tell him, I thought as I looked at him. So willing not to ask anything. He knew the answers would be bad. And what was I going to say? I met this old, sick, rich guy I hoped might leave his apartment to me when he died, so I tried to make him love me? And I thought he was too old to try something, and when he did try something, I was too scared to say no and I just let him do it? That it got worse every week, but I felt like I could not stop because it would all be for nothing? That I smiled and I said thank you when I left? That I had hurt myself instead of him? How could Dave ever understand it? He would react as if someone had stolen something that was his. And then he would have to do something, that was the rule. And I did not want that. And he did not want that. And that is why I said nothing, and he did not ask.

The Mirror

"'Whenever I had the chance, I shoved all the letters from the needy in the bin. Why should they get money, while I was here taking care of him? When the old man keeled over, I was going to be sitting front row.'" William read aloud from Luis's mother's diary, standing in the middle of the room. He was directing his delivery to Marina, who was sitting in the corner with her head down, holding Roman closely against her.

While he was reading, William's voice was getting louder.

Luis wanted to rip the diary from William's hands, rip his mother's words from his mouth, but he pushed the anger down. In his mind, Hadi's voice said, "Show him who he is."

"William, I think you are skipping something," Luis said calmly. "The part where your father—"

"No," William interrupted him.

"Didn't you always want to know the truth about your father?" Luis asked. "All the details?"

"Stop it," William said. "All we need to read is the part that shows you have no right to be here and neither did your mother. So fuck off." His voice was changing: it was as if some Dutch accent was making its way to the surface. So he had one after all.

"I am just curious, William," Luis said, "what you think of your father now."

"I think you should stop talking, Luis," Marina said from the corner of the room. "He is on the edge."

"Don't worry, Marina," Luis said. "William is a professor. He is always well-behaved. I am just asking him to tell us what he thinks of his family now."

William shook his head wildly. "I will go to court with this diary. Your mother admits she met a dying man and tried to get her hands on his inheritance by acting. My father saw through all of that. He retracted the promise. She never got the apartment. That's all that matters."

"All that matters?" Luis asked. "I thought where you came from makes who you are. What does that make you now, knowing that your father did those things?"

"Stop it!" William shouted again.

"The truth makes you angry," Luis said. "I understand. It made me angry too."

"I am not angry," William yelled.

"Of course," Luis said. "You are calm and I am aggressive. You are good and I am bad."

"You don't know what the fuck you are talking about," William said. "My father was an art dealer and a philanthropist. You are just a dishwasher, you don't know anything. You don't even get to say his name."

"I can't say his name?" Luis asked William. "So I can't say 'Edward Hond abused my mother'? Then what would I call him? What do you call a man who abuses young girls?" Luis heard his voice rising. His heart rate was rising.

Suddenly, William jumped at Luis, as if he wanted to grab him by the throat, but grabbing his collar instead.

"No," Marina shouted. "William!"

"You are just like her," William said slowly to Luis. "You want things that you do not deserve, without working for it. But you are too stupid to make it happen." He turned to Marina. "Don't think that his mother was some sort of victim. Listen here. She says it herself." Aggressively, he turned the pages of the notebook. "Here, she says it: 'It's no big deal. What's the difference with cleaning? What's the difference with scrubbing a stain from a towel, rubbing a sponge over a plate? . . . Who even remembers a touch? It's just a little wibble wabble. I will forget about this like I forgot the name of the New Year's Eve boy.'"

Luis looked at William's hands, clenching the diary. He was shaking. It was strange to see him so out of control. His nostrils were wide, his cheeks red, and his eyes were shooting from Luis to Marina. He had never looked so real before.

"My mother was just seventeen," Luis said calmly. "She had a baby and no money. Your father was old and rich."

William turned back around and grabbed Luis by his collar. "My father was a better person than you will ever be," he said.

"William, stop it!" Marina got up from the floor. Roman started barking.

"Marina, stay out of it," Luis said. William's hands were pressing on his throat. His voice sounded as if it came from far away. "He dumped you, William. He did not love you. Why do you defend him? Why can't you think about what he has done?"

"He never dumped me," William yelled. "He did not know—he did not know where I was . . . My mother . . ." He tripped over his own words, spit gathering in the corners of his mouth. "He loved me."

"Didn't you read what he said to my mother?" Luis said. "'I like this one,' he said to her. 'Why couldn't I have had one like this?'"

Letting out a deep howl, William tilted his head backward. Then he smashed his forehead against Luis's head.

Luis felt a sharp pain in his eye socket. Briefly, he was disoriented. Somewhere he could hear Marina scream. Roman barked.

"Get out of the way, Marina," Luis tried to say as he steadied himself against the mirror, but the words did not come out.

Then William did the same thing once again, smashing his head against Luis's.

He felt himself staggering back, trying to find something to hold on to. William's hands were hitting him now; like a child he hit Luis, the slaps raining down on his head. Luis did not want to hit back. He extended his arms to keep William away from him.

Marina was standing behind William, yelling at him to stop.

"Marina, go away," Luis said, but she did not listen.

She jumped on William's back and grabbed his arms. Black spots were swarming in Luis's vision as he saw William staggering backward to the bed. He tripped and fell sideways on the nightstand.

Marina's head hit the side of the bedpost.

Roman stopped barking.

Marina covered her face with her hands.

Behind Marina, William got up from the floor. He looked at Marina, who was sitting on the floor with her hands covering her face.

William looked as if he had just woken up. For a moment, it looked like he was going to say something. But then he limped out of the room without saying anything.

Luis heard the bathroom door open and the sound of water streaming.

He looked over his shoulder in the mirror. There was blood on his cheek.

"Are you all right?" Luis asked Marina, putting his hand on her back.

"Stop it," Marina said, her hands covering her face. "Stop, stop, stop."

"We stopped," Luis said softly. "We stopped, didn't we? William is gone."

He took a deep breath.

"We stopped, Marina," he said again, calmer now. "William has left the room. Roman is sitting here next to you. I am sitting next to you. Are you hurt?"

Marina took her hand from her face. Her nose was dark red and turning purple.

"You have a nosebleed," Luis said. He picked up the silk Armani T-shirt that he'd gotten from Hadi for his birthday off the floor and gave it to her.

She pushed it against her nose.

"It could be broken," Luis said.

"Nothing is broken," Marina said.

"Let me look at your nose," Luis said. "He really got you. I think you should call the police. You are a victim and a witness."

Marina turned her head away from him. "I think you should stop trying to use me to get him out of his house."

"I told you to get out of the way," Luis said. "I couldn't help what happened."

Marina shook her head. "You made him angry on purpose," she said. With her free hand, she pulled Roman up on the bed against her. "When you invited me here you said you wanted to help me. You said it was safe. And now I am hurt." Her voice sounded small.

"You should not have come between us," Luis said. "All we can do now is call the police."

"You invite me when there's a meeting, you ask me questions, you want my advice, you want me to sleep here. But then you say I can't get in between you two. Then you say it is not your fault."

Luis said nothing.

"I don't count," Marina said quietly.

"You do count," he said.

Marina shook her head. "You promised me you would be a good person and nothing would happen to me while I was here."

"I told you people can't be trusted," Luis said.

Marina shook her head. "So you are your own evidence."

10 September
My father's home, Amsterdam

Dad, do you ever have the feeling that everything inside you has stopped? You notice the world around you continuing, the light changes, noises come and go, your breath moves in and out, your blood pulses, your body aches, dust floats around in the space under the ceiling lamp. Time hasn't stopped, but you have. Have you ever had that?

I have that feeling now. My pen moves over the paper, writing words that seem to come from somewhere, but my feelings have stopped. Have you ever had that?

The first time I had it was when Mom left you. It is one of my first memories. I remember getting on the ferry, leaving Rotterdam for Brighton. I remember I had cried in the car. Long, deep weeps that came from the pit of my stomach, after my mother had told me how it was better not to be around you anymore. On the boat my weeping stopped. People were walking around us on the deck. My mother was pointing at the seagulls following the ferry, talking about some white hills in the distance. And I'd gone still inside.

Have you ever had that experience? That there are so many emotions rising up inside of you and you erupt like a volcano, but then it just stops? And everything moves away from you. Even your inner voice that always tells you what you like and what you don't like, what is fun and what is horrible, what you want and what you don't want, stops talking. Going flat like one of those heartbeat lines on a hospital monitor—have you had that?

Or were you really without an inner voice all along, as Luis's mother described you? Is it possible for a person to have no bad feelings at all when he does harm? A psychopath, a narcissist. Deep insecurities underlie their behaviour, Paulina said of narcissists. Were you deeply insecure? Was that why you did these things? Or was it how I think it is, that you were simply like me, a person who became paralysed and then everything just happened to you?

I lost control today. I hurt a woman. She was bleeding. Through my violent actions, she was hurt. This reads like some police report. Someone else's story. Some criminal. But it was me. William.

Dad, I want you to come back and give me an answer that makes me feel better.

It's strange to write 'Dad'. It sounds like something you say to a man you have had dinner and breakfast with; a man you have seen coming out of his bedroom in the morning with uncombed hair, in an old, faded bathrobe; a man you have seen sick, whom you have seen laughing, who has cuddled you, grabbed you, comforted you; someone whose scent you know; someone who has cleaned up your puke. That's a dad to me. I will never have a dad.

When I think of what I did today, I keep seeing it from Marina's eyes. A man, wild and angry. Yelling. Hurting her. I want to go to her and tell her that was not me. I am someone else. I am the one who studied when others were partying, the one who nodded understandingly when the faculty explained why they chose someone else for tenure once again. I was the one who was left by not one but two women for not being passionate enough, the one who helped Paulina move out her stuff after she left me.

Steering and Pushing

Marina packed her things silently. Luis was sitting on his bed, his head in his hands. The resolution that was needed—to stay calm while William went crazy—had cost him so much energy he now felt empty and sick. He looked at the clock standing on top of the sofa, half tilted.

"I don't want you to go out at five thirty in the morning," he said to Marina. "It's cold. Your work starts at seven. Where are you going to go? Just walk around?"

Marina shook her head. "And now you care again about how I am doing?" She had stuffed cotton wool in her nostril, and she started stacking up the plates that had fallen over. From the sound of the porcelain touching, he could tell her hands were still trembling. Outside it was dark. The lamppost illuminated the branches of the tree, which was now losing its leaves.

"Any other person would have done the same," Luis said. "If I give my home away, if I give my mother's reputation away, if I say yes and sorry to everything, then where is the border? There has to be a border somewhere. I had no choice." His hand reached out to Roman, who was sitting under the bed.

Marina picked up the dog before he could touch him.

"Next thing they'll be demanding the clothes off my back," Luis said. "Next thing they'll want possession of my body. They'll want to steer me like a robot."

"You are both like children," Marina said. "Maybe this is not your house. Maybe it is only half your house. You need to figure it out. How will you ever feel at ease here if you know someone else deserves it too?"

Luis closed his eyes. "He is a bad person," he said.

"You are the same."

"We are not the same," Luis said. "You heard what he said about my mother. You heard how he wants to tell everyone what is in the diary."

"You should be proud of your mother," Marina said. Her voice was shaky; the Marina who was always calm was gone now. "At least she had the guts to try something. If you were strong, if you had guts like her, you would make a room here and a room there. You put a bed here, you put a bed there. You make two kitchens, one here, one there. If you had guts, you would have calmed down the situation. You would not have shouted at me, you would have stopped and helped me and Roman."

She sniffed and her nose started bleeding again. With a hard look at Luis, she pushed the T-shirt against her nose.

Luis watched her fold her clothes and put them in the bag, her dog sitting next to her, looking at Luis as if he was waiting for something. Luis also felt like he was waiting for something, the right thing to say to her.

"Sorry," he said finally.

"I don't want your sorry," Marina said loudly. "Women always get 'sorry.' I am fed up with it." With tears in her eyes she looked up. "Maybe I am stupid. Maybe everyone is right when they say I should not trust people like I do. But if I let that go, then how am I supposed to be like? Should I be like a stone? I am not going to be that. I am not going to lose my trust. It makes me happy."

Luis thought of his mother, who had tried to be like a stone. He remembered when she had her first heart attack. She sat down on the floor of the kitchen. His father rang the ambulance. Then he sat down next to her and calmed her. He had never seen his parents like that. His father, so determined and calm. The way his mother placed her head on his father's chest and just waited there for the ambulance, while he talked to her about the neighbor's sheep having escaped. It was the first time he had seen her like that. Trusting. Not alone.

Luis thought of the first time he saw Marina, how they had set the television channels together, him holding the remote, her reading from the manual, switching between Portuguese and Dutch. How she showed him photos on her phone of her sister and her parents, how she talked about all her plans for the future, everything she wanted to do and wanted to see, what she dreamed of.

"I don't want you to become a stone," Luis said. "I don't want you to lose your trust."

"I just said I am not going to lose that," Marina said, swallowing loudly. "If you think I would let you take that, there is something you don't understand yet. I am strong. I am the strongest one here in this house. I am in the other country, I speak the other language, I clean other people's mess. And I am happy and I am strong and I am well. That's why I wanted to help you. You were struggling. You were lonely. You don't understand it at all."

She shook her head and put on her coat. Then she put her backpack on her back and picked Roman up from the floor. Luis heard the click of the leash latching on to Roman's collar.

"If things were going so well for you, you would not be here," Luis said. "You don't have anything at all." He closed his eyes, sitting still in the echo of his words. When he opened his eyes she was gone. He saw his reflection in the mirrored chest, his belly sticking out, all his possessions in a jumbled mess around him.

The Philanthropist

After that final day at Mr. Hond's apartment, I got sick. Probably it was the cold, the journey through Amsterdam in wet clothes, waiting for Dave in the piercing winds. But I felt like it was Mr. Hond who had made me sick. As if I inhaled his breath and it infected my entire body. I was nauseated and tired. While I stayed in bed, David took care of Luis. He found his little socks and his diapers in the drawer without my directions; he gave him formula milk. I remember my milk stopped flowing. What else do I remember of those days? I remember my heart pounded too hard. I could feel it move in my chest. I remember I slept. I did not know a person could sleep so much. I remember Dave coming in once in a while, persuading me to come out a little more, to take a shower, to eat something, to play with Luis for a little bit.

Then I remember the day my parents appeared on our doorstep. I could hear them from my bedroom, my mother's fake chirpy voice, the three loud air-kisses.

I walked out of my bedroom and interrupted their chitchat by shouting, "I want you out."

My mother instinctively looked over her shoulder, immediately petrified that some neighbor outside would hear it. "Sweetheart," she said to me, closing the front door.

"I was not who you wanted me to be and then you just gave up," I said.

My parents looked at each other. They said nothing.

"You did not teach me anything, you did not help me at all, but still I had to do everything right. I want you out. I mean it."

"She means it," Dave said, shrugging.

Without saying anything, my parents took their coats. In the doorway my father turned around. "We always wanted the best for you," he said.

"You need to do more than wanting," I said. "You actually need to do something. You need to explain the world to your child, you need to teach a child things. You need to let a child know what is out there. I will let Luis know exactly what is out there. I will give him life lessons, exactly how it is."

I saw Luis playing on the floor with his building blocks. He did not look up, but I knew he was listening.

"You've let me down," I said to my parents. Then I repeated it louder: "You have let me down." I kept saying it while I followed them out the front hallway and onto the driveway. "You have let me down, you have let me down." And I screamed it after them as they climbed hurriedly into their car. I kept saying it while Dave closed the gate behind them. I kept on saying it until I could no longer see their car in the distance. "You have let me down."

"Marie," Dave said, "come back into the house."

He pulled me into the hallway and tried to hug me.

"I love you," he said.

"You cannot possibly love me," I said, stamping my feet like a child. "You don't know me."

"I know you," he said, looking at me helplessly. "You are like an angel . . . but more wild."

An angel. Everyone insisted on me being an angel. Why would they love me only if I was an angel? I remember feeling so tired. I sat down on a chair in the kitchen. Behind me the old clock that Dave got from his father started chiming.

"Why do we have this stupid clock?" I asked Dave. "I don't want any clocks in the house. I hate the ticking sound."

Dave hesitated for a moment, then he pulled the clock from the wall and threw the entire thing in the trash. He looked at me very seriously. "We can do it," he said. He put his arms around me and held me close. "For Luis, okay?"

I nodded. That night I left the door to the bedroom open, and Dave came in, lying down beside me, folding his arm over me.

All the Best Wishes

There was a knock on Luis's door.

"Marina?" Luis asked, but it was William standing in the hallway, his arms dangling alongside his body, his eyes red.

"Can I see Marina?" William said almost inaudibly. "How is she?"

"She left," Luis said. "She went to the hospital." After a short pause he added, "Her nose is probably broken."

William's face turned pale as he inhaled loudly. "Broken," he echoed in a soft voice. "I did that."

Luis nodded.

"I want to apologize to her," William said. "I want to pay for . . . what she needs . . . Do you have her phone number?"

"She doesn't want your apology," Luis said. "She says women are fed up with apologies."

"Do you think she will come back today?"

"No," Luis said. "She is scared to be in a house with you now."

They were both quiet for a moment. Luis saw William glance at the blood on the floor in the bedroom and then at Luis's face.

Luis lightly touched his right eyebrow. It felt swollen and hot.

"Is she going to the police?" William asked. "I guess in the hospital they will ask how . . . And then maybe . . . I would understand it, I would . . . but it's better not . . . My job . . . in education . . . there's this requirement . . . a report around behavior . . ."

"So you are not even apologizing because you hurt her," Luis said, holding the door ajar. "You want to stop her from going to the police."

"No," William said. "Yes." He lowered his head. "I don't even know anymore . . . What kind of person am I?" He became quiet for a moment. Then he asked, "Did I do all of that?" It was a question he seemed to ask himself more than Luis. "I-I am . . ." he stammered after a long pause, "mortified . . . and so . . . It just seems . . . it just seems to me that what happened was not really how I am . . . not really representative of me . . . and . . ."

"Who else is it representative of?" Luis asked. "It was you."

"But something came over me," William said. "I could not stop it, I was powerless." The moment he said it his expression changed. "Th-those w-words," he stammered. "'Something came over me' . . . 'I was powerless' . . ."

His face became pale and he stood silent and frozen in the doorway.

"That was what my father said too," he finally said to Luis. "I said the same thing he said. Right? The same excuse he used, the thing he said in your mother's diary."

Luis nodded.

William looked like he was going to faint. He held on to the doorpost, breathing deeply. Then his eyes opened wide, in wonder, like a child seeing a bird for the first time. He said, "I am like him."

Luis nodded.

"And it's all true, what your mother said," William said.

"It is all true," Luis said. He opened the door to his bedroom wider. "Let me show you something."

He pushed his bed and sofa to the other side of the room and moved the lamp. Then he dragged the mirrored chest a little bit away from the wall. The corner of the carpet was now free. With a tearing sound, Luis pulled the beige deep-pile carpet from the floor, revealing a brown stain on the wooden floorboards.

"Blood?" William asked.

"My mother's blood," Luis said. "I tried to scrub it away, and I think she tried too, but it went all the way into the wood."

They both stared at the brown stain in the pale wooden floorboard.

"Did you mother . . ." William asked. "Did she ever . . . become happy?"

Luis shrugged. "Sometimes she would have a good time, for a while. An hour, a day. It was always like a car starting. She would do new things for a little while, getting energized, and then she would fall apart again. She was always worried about me, picking me up from school in the middle of the day, warning me about everything. When the phone rang she was startled. She had nightmares. We did not know what they were about."

"About my father," William said. He sat down on the bed. "Why didn't you talk to her anymore?"

"I wanted to live," Luis said. "She always wanted to keep me from doing things. But I needed to be out in the world."

It sounded strange now. He thought of what Marina had said: "You are a turtle . . . you hide in your house."

For a long time, William was silent. There was only the ticking of clocks, the branches against the window, and his deep breathing.

"What does Marina want?" he said finally.

"She wants you to leave," Luis said, "to leave us alone."

William nodded. He stood up, took Luis's hand and shook it.

"I trust she won't report me then," he said.

Luis looked at their hands. It was strange to feel the bony, thin fingers between his again, just like that first day. It seemed like a year ago.

"Marina can be trusted," he said. Then he added, "There are good people and bad people. And people in between. Like you. Like me. But I think Marina is a good person."

Luis watched as William stuffed his papers in his bags, gathered his clothes, packed his suitcase, and carried them down the staircase one by one.

"Where are you going?" Luis asked him when he stood in the downstairs hallway with the last one.

"I don't know," William said. "I need to think. I don't have anything to go back to in Oxford. Maybe I'll go to the Student Hotel again first . . . I don't know." He picked up his suitcase.

From outside came the sound of the first birds: the sun was rising.

"It was dark when I moved in here," Luis said. "I only had the key and one bag. Nothing else. I never felt so happy in my life."

"When I found the letter about my father, when I learned his name and this address, it was the first time in my life everything felt right," William said.

The first sunrays illuminated the poplars in the street. The brakes of the tram squealed when it stopped. Dazed people came down the stone steps of their apartments, bleeped open their cars. From Estelle's apartment there was the sound of recorded laughter from her favorite TV show.

"Well," Luis said. "All the best wishes."

He closed the door behind William and walked back up the stairs, alone.

The Philanthropist

In the days after I kicked my parents out of our home, I started living again. I got up in the morning, put Luis in a clean diaper, fed him and put him in new clothes. From there, the wheel started turning again: playing, feeding, cleaning, washing, burping, puking, cleaning, washing, sleeping, cleaning, clothing, feeding, burping, sleeping, the rounds carried on and on. Dave found a job at Boko stables. We bought a television. Spring came, summer must also have been there, then autumn. I made a casserole for Christmas. Dave bought a Christmas tree. Luis was obsessed with Christmas tree decorations, which we left up until February.

My days with Luis were full. I did not have time to think about anything. We painted the walls of his bedroom together. Luis wanted the room white—he must have been the first three-year-old in the world to choose the color white. We made a stone collection in the garden. He liked organized, calm things. I remember that when it rained one day I took Luis outside and tried to persuade him to stamp in the puddles, but he cried when his trousers got wet, and he disliked the mess the fallen leaves made in the driveway. I carried him inside and sat under the warm shower with him, staring at the moldy ceiling that Dave had promised to paint. "Where is the old Marie, where did she go?" I heard Hond say in my head during those moments, and I thought of what I had given to him and what he had taken from me.

For twelve years, I was able to push those thoughts away because there was always something that Luis did that demanded my attention. He would be crying because he ate a piece of soap, screaming because I aligned his fork in the wrong way with his plate, or rolling over the ground with all the towels wrapped around him. At school he had a phase where he refused to draw anything but circles. I fought with his teachers. Why did Luis have to draw other things? All the wibble wabble they make little kids do. Why couldn't he just be himself? If I did not like how they treated him at school, Luis was always allowed to stay home with me, and we spent the day together, playing games and watching TV. Those were really my favorite days. And at night I was so tired I just fell asleep. I'd have terrible nightmares, but I forgot about them in the morning, when the wheel started turning again.

But when Luis and Dave went to Spain for a week because his father was not well, I had time alone. Time to feel panic. All the sounds startled me: a door that closed behind me with a bang, a tap that dripped just like a clock, a man's voice coming from the road. It helped me to close my eyes and go to the "blue room" in my mind, as I called it. The gentle sway of the curtains in the wind would calm me. But at night I could not fall asleep. The images from the nightmares started to stay with me during the day. I kept wondering if Mr. Hond was dead yet. When he is dead, then no one knows, and I can let it go, I thought. When he is dead, the memories will die too.

Yesterday I opened the coffee tin and took the key to the apartment. The plan was not even to go inside or ring the doorbell. I would just sit on the bench in the park in front of the apartment, and when I saw someone else living there, I could go home.

What's Mine

In one day Luis could have restored the apartment to its old state. He could have dragged the sofa back to the living room; he could have put the fridge back where it belonged. He could have folded the carpet back over the bloodstain; he could have put the T-shirt that Marina had bled on in the washing machine. He could have picked up the diary from the floor and put it back in the backpack and put the backpack back in the closet. He could have removed Roman's pillow and his drinking bowl. He could have thrown away the comb William had forgotten in the bathroom and his tuna cans.

But all Luis had done that day was screw a bolt on the door downstairs. Then he sat down on the floor of the living room and listened to the quiet in the apartment. It was all his again, the walls, the doors, the ceilings. He had an empty feeling. His heart beat too fast. Would this feeling go away? Was it that he needed time to readjust?

He thought of calling Hadi.

He wanted to call Marina.

He even thought about calling his father's care home.

In the evening, Luis put William's air mattress, which was standing against the wall, on the floor of the living room. It was like the first night Luis spent in the apartment, lying under his coat in this empty room, no sheets, no curtains. He thought of the happiness he had felt that first day. Why had it gone away?

From the air bed, Luis looked at the living room. The stainless steel tab that could dispense boiling water if you wanted it. The oven with the steamer that he never used. The espresso machine he had bought in case Estelle ever came to visit. The marble tiles he had chosen together with Marina. What is really mine? he wondered. Why is it so hard to share? What do I owe other people?

He thought of how he had let Marina go out in the night with a nosebleed.

She had once told him that she felt like her home was in her body, but she also felt at home in the raindrops, in the trees, in the squares, in the clouds, in other people, in the entire world.

Luis looked out the uncovered windows. Dark clouds drifted by in the moonlight. He tried to feel at home in them, but it did not work.

11 September
The Student Hotel, Amsterdam

I have been back in this hotel for a day now. The room reminds me of a plastic storage box. And that is how I feel, like I have stored myself away. A pointless, unlabelled person, stored away in a generic hotel.

There's a continual stream of noise coming from the hallway, generated by British backpackers and hen parties visiting Amsterdam. When I stayed here last time, I felt strongly that I did not belong here among these people who were so unlike me. I knew who I was. So I ignored my fellow Brits in the lobby and the elevator.

But now I am not sure whether I am one of them. Maybe I am? Maybe they would not even want me.

The story that always kept me company is gone. My father was not a special, noble man. I am not part of some remarkable family. My father was a selfish man. And I am too. I am not the nice intellectual I always thought I was. The image of Marina— her hands over her face, her startled eyes—haunts me.

'Something came over me . . . I was powerless'.

My father's words rolled out of my mouth like I was his duplicate. For so long I hoped I was like him. Now I study my reflection in the mirror, hoping to see traces of my mother who, although loopy and tacky, never harmed anyone.

What would Paulina think of me now? Once, when she was a little drunk, she said my sweetest trait was my 'dutifulness'. 'You do everything by the book', she said. 'You dutifully make me breakfast in bed, you dutifully ask me about my day, you duti-fully go down on me, you dutifully buy me flowers, you dutifully read my papers'.

'That sounds horrible', I told her. 'Someone who consciously fulfils their duty—is that who you want to sleep with?'

'It's sweet', she said with her prolonged drunk s. 'It's like you are never going to do me harm, I know that. You are too dutiful for it'.

My thoughts spin in circles through my head. All my life I had been called a bookish nerd; now I was someone who fought. Estelle keeps calling me about the paternity court case and I can't bring myself to pick up.

Inheritance

The days after William left, Luis slept on William's air bed in the living room. He slept badly. Every sound woke him up. A banging noise coming from above. Could William be on the roof? The sound of water running. Was there someone in his apartment? A scraping noise from downstairs. Had the old Mr. Hond come back, putting his key in the door?

Luis felt like his mother, sitting up straight when the phone rang, her face turning pale. Was it possible to inherit someone's feelings? Someone's fears? When he got up in the morning it was as if gravity was pulling at him. He showered, he ate, he worked. He tried to clean a little bit. He hung up the clock in the living room. But he felt like he was waiting for something.

Maybe it was Marina. On Wednesday he looked out the window to see if she would come walking down the street, even though he knew she would not show up.

On Thursday Luis dragged the fridge back into the kitchen. He cleaned it from top to bottom, adding the groceries in the right compartments. The shiny door of the new fridge reflected the morning light on the trees outside, just like in the TV commercial. Luis also brought the TV back into the living room and put the carpet down over the bloodstain.

Then he sat in the bedroom watching the branches ticking on the window, until he went to work, where he did his job, and he walked back again, looking at the clouds that were yellow little trails in the moonlight. Does Marina feel at home in that cloud? he wondered. How is she doing? Does she have a nice place to live?

When Luis walked back up the stairs to his apartment, he felt his feet getting heavy. What was it that he had loved so much about living here? Was it really worth how he treated Marina and lying to William?

At the top of the stairs he picked his mother's diary up from the floor, where it had remained since the fight. He sat down on the stairs and started reading it again, slower this time.

The Philanthropist

And now I sit here, in Mr. Hond's apartment. Twelve years since that Wednesday when I left.

There is no one here.

Everything is clean.

For hours I sat on the bench in front of number 354 yesterday, just looking up. No one went in or out of the apartment. When it got dark no light switched on inside. And when I walked up to the door I noticed the letter box was completely full. Envelopes and papers were sticking out. One of them had "Last Warning" written on it. I smoked a cigarette on the doorstep, like I had done for years, and then I opened the door with my key, like I had done for years.

I did not walk up the stairs straightaway like I used to, but I stayed in the hallway, to listen. There was no sound coming from upstairs, no footsteps, no coughing, no voice. I saw the walls were bare, only a few empty hooks as reminders of all the paintings that had hung on these walls. The stairs were dusty. There were dead flies on the steps. The sweet smell that I knew had mixed with the rotten smell of stagnant water.

Upstairs, in the apartment, there was no one. The sculptures and the paintings were gone. In the bedroom the desk was still there. Some newspapers lying around, ten years old. A pen, a notebook. A glass with purple stains from evaporated red wine.

The bed was still there.

The red curtains.

I put all the envelopes in an old coffee tin that I found in the kitchen. Almost automatically, I started tidying up. The old newspapers, the dead flies. The dust. I washed the glasses and plates that were lying around. It got dark. The last tram went by, I heard its squealing brakes in the street. I was aware I was missing the last train. I felt the strange need to stay, to clean everything, like I used to do every week, but this time really clean it. For me. And all through last night I have done that. I did not sleep. The floor, the tiles, the stairs, the windowsills, the windows, the bath, the walls—everything I have scrubbed clean. All the furniture is gone now; all the light bulbs except one I have thrown out.

Now I am sitting here on the floor, with the first light coming in through the window. It smells like bleach in here now.

All my memories are written down now, just how it was.

It was all my fault, of course, I know that. I should not have done all those things. I should not have gone to Amsterdam, I should not have gone up to Mr. Hond's apartment, I should not have tried to get my hands on his money, I should not even have been there at all. I should not have been pregnant in the first place, I should never have chased boys and got drunk, I should have done only hand and mouth things like Maureen and Anna. I should not have been so curious.

But what should I have done? Should I have been how my mother wanted? Sit down, be quiet, read books. Pretend that I did not have a body that shook and twisted and convulsed and bled and yearned and wanted to kiss and finger and lick? Why did I feel like I let others down more than myself when I was pregnant? Why did I feel so ashamed for what Mr. Hond had done with my body? Why is one thing you do with your body seen as so wrong and another thing seen as so good? I did not like it when my grandmother washed my body with the rough washing cloth, but I was taught to endure it. I did not like it when I had to sit my body still in the cold church for hours on the hard bench, to hear I was a sinner, but I was told that was good. I did not like to keep my voice down, I did not like to stop crying after I fell, but I had learned to push my feelings away in my body because my parents wanted me to. That was something to be proud of.

I am thinking of that time I raised a mouse from the dead and wondered if I was holy. Not as in pure, a virgin, but in the way the pastor described the relics in the church. "They are more than just things," he said. "They are something to worship, to always take care off." What if I had kept on believing I was holy? What if I had dared to look at my pregnancy, really think about it, without being so ashamed? What if I had gone to see Dave and told him about the pregnancy, and we talked and we listened, so we could have decided together? What if I had never learned to press my feelings away? How would it have gone with Mr. Hond?

The questions are spinning in my head as I sit here. I feel like I have clarity here, in this room. It's like the old Marie is still in this place somewhere. The sun is making long shadows on the floor. Luis would like it. He loves watching the shadow lines that the sun makes. Last week I found him in the living room, sitting on the floor in deep concentration. When Dave asked him what he was doing, Luis said, "Waiting for that shadow to touch the corner of the shelf." I watched how Dave sat down next to him, with his hand lightly on his arm; how they watched the shadow together and how they cheered when it got there. I remember how I wished I could tell them everything. Even Luis. I wanted them to sit with me and keep their hands on my arms while I talked, and then we'd wait together until everything moved into the right place inside me again. Can I clean this up alone, inside myself? Can I find the old Marie again? Does a secret ever really die? Or does it just grow into different shapes, into other people, polluting them?

The Apparition

Luis closed the diary. He thought of how he had found the apartment that first night. All the rooms were empty, except for the bedroom. She had hung up light blue curtains, the railing clumsily attached with nails to the wall. There was a crib in the corner, an Ikea chandelier hanging from its own wires, and a rocking chair next to the door.

The room had looked sort of good if you squinted your eyes. It reminded him of the selfies he saw Estelle take in her garden sometimes. She would organize all the flowerpots around her, hold a glass of wine, turn her body in a sideways angle, and wink at the hand holding her phone. Frowning, she would then look at the result on her phone, only to start over again, rearranging the flowerpots and pulling at her dress. The result had to look like something she already had in her head. Was that what his mother was doing when she was here? Creating the life the real Marie should have had in that room, hoping that she would then become her?

Was that what he himself was doing in this house, with all his stuff?

He thought of how his mother had changed over the years. She got bigger, at least doubled in size. As a child he liked how soft she was, cuddly, like a pillow. As a teenager he was embarrassed by her size, and as a twenty-year-old he was angry at her, because he thought she was doing it on purpose to get sick and keep him there with her bad health.

He thought of how he never held it against his father that he destroyed his own body, but with his mother he did. And that he never had felt like he needed to take care of his father, but he did for her. He had always known that if his mother hadn't gotten pregnant, she would have finished school, she would have moved away, she would have gotten a good job, she would not have stayed with his father. And he felt guilty about that. Now he knew that if he hadn't been conceived, she would not have gone to Amsterdam that day, she would not have met Mr. Hond, she would not have spent her life fighting gravity.

It was then when Luis heard the sound. It sounded like someone breathing close to him, on the stairs. He turned around. At the top of the stairs he saw his mother, or a vision of his mother—because it couldn't be her, he knew it couldn't be—standing there, looking at him, her hands across her stomach. She wore the blue silk nightgown she wore on the day he left. Her chest was rising and falling with her heavy smoker's breath that had gotten worse and worse in the last years. Luis sat paralyzed. Cold sweat formed on his back. His mother looked at him, the gown too short on her large body, her knees round and saggy under the seam.

Luis could not take his eyes off the vision. She couldn't really be here, she couldn't, she was dead and she was buried, but still she stood there, and Luis felt at the same time the strong, familiar feeling of her body and the frightening impossibility of this happening.

If I look away and look back, she will be gone, Luis thought. He forced his eyes away and stared at the front door for what seemed like minutes. But when he looked back the vision hadn't changed. It felt as though there was even a warmth coming from her body, like the steam that used to rise up from the muck heap in winter. He got up and walked up the stairs toward her. When he got close, he looked at his mother's face: the soft hanging cheeks, the deep frown in the forehead, the small, soft eyes that had a little twinkle still.

He did not say anything, he just looked at her. He saw her faults and her traits and her mistakes and her memories and her jokes and her movements, which were lodged in the cells of her body and also in his.

"I'm sorry I left you," Luis said to the vision.

His mother seemed to sigh. A bored, annoyed sigh.

Why would her vision be different from who she was? She was not some ghost in a movie who came back in an illuminated dress to say she was sorry and that he had the right to live in his own way. She was not going to say, "I forgive you," and then grow angel wings to fly away. She was dead and her body was burned at the crematorium across from the Egmond Tropical Swim Paradise. She was not angelic; she never had been. "You can't squeeze juice out of a dry orange," his mother used to say.

He accepted it. She would never say sorry to him, and he would never say sorry to her. There was no conclusion for them. They were just two people who had tried.

Luis remembered a moment—he was small then—when his mother took him to the Modern Art Museum in Alkmaar. She had seen a poster announcing the Mondriaan exhibition. It was a very normal memory, a mother and a child, on a bike and in a bus, going to a museum, but he knew for his mother it was hard. She did not like to go out; she did not like museums. But they went and they looked at Mondriaan's lines and colors, then went home together on the bus and the bike with a brochure in a linen bag. At home they had looked at the brochure with his father. He and his mother had cut out the nicest image, while his father made a picture frame for it. He remembered the radio was on.

Luis reached out his hand to touch his mother's arm. He felt only the wood of the stairs under his hand. She was gone.

Vondelpark

L uis was walking outside. The Vondelpark was a sea of grass, interrupted by small ponds and playgrounds. The trees lining the walkways were turning red and orange. On the benches couples sat kissing, smoking weed, listening to music. Children were chasing each other in the playgrounds; parents were watching them with tired eyes. Every jogger and cyclist passing Luis by left a trail of sounds, words, or music. It was as if the world had been gift-wrapped and put in pink ribbons and given to him all over again.

"Yes, the idea is to share it," Luis said in his phone to Jet Adelman, the lawyer. The moment he'd made the decision he'd called her. "We will just try it."

"We will just try it is not a legal strategy," his lawyer replied. "What if you disagree on something like the use of the bathroom or having guests, and it becomes a source of conflict? Sharing starts with boundaries."

"Then we will make boundaries," Luis said cheerfully. "We already have a conflict anyway. I just realized the conflict will never go away, even when he goes away. It has already happened. Our lives are connected. We just need to make the best of it."

"It's important to think it through," the lawyer said. "There are many consequences of sharing. Do you split the bills when he showers longer? What if you want him out? What if his old mother gets sick and she has to move in with him?"

"His mother is dead," Luis said.

"Well," the lawyer. "That is one thing at least."

Luis laughed. Nothing could change his mind. "My mother wrote in her diary about making your feelings holy. And my feeling is that I don't want to send William away. I want to share it. Sometimes you have to do more than you planned."

"Mr. Rose has a stronger case when he lives there," the lawyer said. "The law looks at occupancy. If he does still want to claim the inheritance, he might win and, as an occupant, kick you out. So, you know, you can be nice, but that will not make the world nice to you."

"That's what I said to Marina," Luis said. "And I was right. But I was unhappy. And she was wrong, but she is happy. She is not afraid of anything. That's why I was so happy when I first moved to Amsterdam. I had lost everything and wasn't afraid of anything. Then I became scared again, scared to lose my house, scared that the neighbors wouldn't like me. I don't want to be scared."

"Our entire society is based on the rules that you are now ignoring," the lawyer said. "All real estate is assigned to someone. There is not supposed to be ownerless real estate. Do you want to let that old missing man continue to be the legal owner?"

"Yes," Luis said.

His lawyer was quiet for a moment. Then she said, "I have to admit, from a personal standpoint, it's an interesting experiment. It's always thrilling to see someone go against a system despite all better judgment."

"Yes," Luis said. "Thank you."

She promised to put a sharing agreement on paper for him.

Luis hung up. The wind was soft on his skin. It had been a long time since he felt the wind. He even felt it on his earlobes and eyelids. He looked up. The branches of the trees formed a roof over his head. For a second, it felt like the whole world was the home of Luis Sol. He spread out his arms. Then someone told him he was not allowed to stand there because it was a bike zone.

Extraterrestrial

William was standing in his pajamas in the doorway of his tiny room in the Student Hotel. He was wearing a strange cap and a hotel robe.

"The receptionist told me my brother was at the front desk," William said to Luis.

"That's what I told her," Luis said. "Brother, sort of brother. Acquaintance, flatmate. What does it matter? Can we talk?"

It took a while until William reacted. Then he nodded, turned around, and walked into the room, where he lay down on the bed.

Luis followed him in. He looked about the gray-and-green hotel room. It all looked like it was made of plastic. Around the hotel bed there were empty cans, folders, and many crumpled sheets of paper with William's handwriting on it.

Every place this man enters starts to look the same after a few hours, Luis thought. For a moment, doubt about the apartment-sharing plan entered his mind. But then he saw how William was lying on the edge of the bed, his legs under the blanket, and a feeling of warmth came over him.

"So, I have an idea. We will share the apartment," Luis said.

William said nothing. He stared at Luis.

"I take one room, you take the other room," Luis said. "We share it."

"Share it," William echoed.

"Yes," Luis said. "Just share. Like children sharing a toy in a playground."

"Children fight over toys," William said, closing his eyes. "Why are you here, Luis? You are rid of me, you have won."

"I did not get rid of you," Luis said. "You were still in my head."

A rattling sound came from the hallway, followed by a loud bang and cheering.

"Backpackers," William said. "They are racing down the hallway on the hotel cart. They gave me this." He pointed at the cap he was wearing that said POUR DECISIONS with a bottle next to it.

Luis watched William pull the blanket up to his chin. The way his hair was sticking out from under the cap made him look like a fifty-year-old child.

"I don't understand what is happening, Luis. Why are you here? I want you to forget about me. Forget all of it."

"I want to explain it all," Luis said. "Marina and my mother helped me understand." He opened the curtains and the window of the hotel room. Cold air and bright sunlight streamed in. He caught a glimpse of himself in the mirror. His eye was still purple where William hit him.

"From when I was thirteen years old, my mother went on trips to Amsterdam to the apartment," Luis said. "She told us she got the apartment from a distant, rich uncle called Edward. She did not want to explain it. I did not know my mother's parents, so I did not know how many uncles and aunts she had. Every time I asked a question about it I made her upset. I learned not to do it. She would leave in the morning and come back at night. When she came back she always seemed different. Her voice was louder. She had all these plans, she made us throw things out and buy things, she would change her hair and talk a lot about the future and how everything would be different. I did not like it. But I learned that after a few days or a few weeks, she would go quiet again, take her long showers, forget about all the plans, become depressed."

"Please," William interrupted Luis. "I left. Isn't that enough?"

"You will understand if you listen," Luis said. "Let me continue. I was just a child, so I did not think too much about it. I did not know what was going on, I just did not want her to be upset, so I never brought it up. When I got older and went to high school for the first time, she said I should be very careful around others, because they would damage me and I was not strong enough. She said people damaged each other, and once you get damaged you never become whole again. These were the life lessons a mother needed to teach."

He thought of how terrified he was on that first day, seeing the older kids in the hallways.

"And she was right. People weren't nice to me. I was laughed at because I could not read so fast. A teacher once said I had a turtle brain. When you had to make a team of two, I had to team up with the teacher."

A faint smile appeared on William's lips. Luis smiled too.

"My mother was right, but she was also wrong. She did not even see the good things anymore. My father, who really loved her. She did not believe him, I think."

Luis looked at William, who had his eyes closed under the ridiculous cap.

"When I pretended to be sick, my mother kept me home from school. When I said I was nervous, she kept me home. I failed the first year of high school and then the second year two times. I used to be happy when I could stay home, because I was shy. I was not good with words. My face turns red sometimes, maybe you have seen it. It was only later I realized it was not good for me. I did not have a lot of friends. When I went out I was worried about leaving my mother alone. I turned fifteen, seventeen, twenty. All the kids from school had jobs. Some even went to university. I was waiting, but I did not know for what."

"Is Marina's nose getting better?" William interrupted him.

"It wasn't broken," Luis said. "But I will get to that. I just need to tell you this. When my mother had a second heart attack she almost seemed happy. I remember she was lying in the hospital bed, holding my hand. The doctor said I would need to help her a lot. And all I thought was: I will never get out now. My mother did not see that she was the bad thing that was happening to me. That night I took the key to the apartment from the coffee tin and left. I did not say goodbye, I did not kiss her. I did not give her a kiss goodbye at all."

Luis thought of his father's eyes watching him from the shed as he opened the gate. That was how he left: the coffee tin in his backpack, his father's eyes on his back, the memory of his mother's arms under his hands as he moved her out of the way.

"Then I came to my apartment," Luis continued telling William. "Our apartment. Late in the evening. I put the key in the lock and it opened. It was empty, it smelled of bleach. I bought an inflatable mattress. A chair. A table. I kept thinking someone might come. My mother. That rich uncle. But no one came. The bills that came in I paid. I took a new phone number. The apartment I sanded and painted, filled it with all these new things. A blank slate. And then you came, and all you wanted was to talk about the past."

William pulled the blanket over his face. He still hadn't said anything.

"I kept telling Marina what you did to me was not right," Luis said. "But I realized today we were not right. Both of us have been like children. The children of our parents. You wanted to use your history like a blanket to comfort yourself, so you don't have to be your own person. I did not even want to talk about my parents. But what if we can do better than our parents?"

William did not reply.

"I'm talking a lot," Luis said. "Normally I don't talk so much. But what I learned is that a secret never dies. It just goes on and on and pollutes everything. We need to clean it up. We need to look at the reality and listen to our feelings. And my feeling is that I can make some room for you. That is why I let you in that first night, that is why I let you stay. I can share the apartment. We both have the right. Not in the way of what is right with the law, or in the way of what is right with what was promised or what is right with what my mother had to give, but what is right with the future. Do you understand? I am willing to share it. It's small, but who says it's too small? Maybe it's just good enough."

Luis smiled. "Maybe people will say it is strange to share it," he said. "But I now think it's strange I refused to think of it. We kept talking about who your father wanted to have this house. But what does it matter what he wanted? He did not even love us. He did not love you. He did not love your mother, he kicked her out. He abused my mother, he lied to her. Why do we care what he wanted or think about what all the documents say is right? We should care about what we want and think about what we feel is right. It's like that expansion you keep talking about, from that Needsy fellow. Why not accept that we are stuck together even though we don't like it? I think that I can be happier if I don't have to be scared of you. And you can be happier if you know that you did not take my entire life from me."

"And Marina? The police?"

"That wasn't true," Luis said. "Her nose was hurt, not broken. And Marina did not want to go to the police."

Now William looked straight at Luis for the first time. "You lied to me," he said.

"Yes," Luis said. "It was wrong. And you lied to me and pretended you fell down the stairs, and you broke into my room, and you hit me like a lunatic. But now we forgive each other."

William was quiet for a while. Then he said, "Still, I did it. That her nose wasn't broken does not make it good." His lip was trembling. He looked like he was going to cry.

"Did you eat anything since coming here?" Luis asked.

"I mostly wrote letters to myself," William said in a toneless voice.

"Do you need to see a doctor?" Luis asked. "You are very pale."

"I need to accept the unresolved absurdity of life," William said with his eyes closed. "That is what Paulina would have said."

"Who is Paulina?" Luis asked.

"Paulina is my ex-girlfriend," William said. "I had had the letter from my mother for quite a while already, but when Paulina left me I decided to come to Amsterdam. She said I was completely lost. And I hoped to find something in Amsterdam to prove to myself that I wasn't. But now I know it's true. Everything I have ever believed is gone. My origin is tainted. It's an existential crisis."

"You are not an extraterrestrial," Luis said. "You are a human. And humans make mistakes."

"What?" William said. "Oh." He put his hands over his face and made a sound. Luis wasn't sure if he was laughing or crying. "It's all very kind of you, Luis . . . but . . ."

"But what?" Luis said.

"How could I be comfortable there? After my father . . . what he did in that house . . . And I even resemble him."

"You can live there as you," Luis said. "You are someone without your father. You did all those things, with the words. The university. You wear a hat. That is you. If he never gave you anything, then why do you need to let him take something from you?"

"I don't know," William said.

"Let's forget about him completely," Luis said. "The mistake my mother made was to believe him. He told her that the world was unequal, that everyone was just here to help themselves and you had to be tough and hard. And my mother believed it most of the time. She never looked at my father, who stayed with her for no reason other than love. He was all those nice things your father said don't exist. She herself was all those nice things your father said don't exist. She took me to museums, you know, when she hated going into town. People do nice things for each other all the time. Even the animals, Marina says. We don't have to be like your father. We can say to hell with him. We, William and Luis, are our own people."

William smiled a faint smile. "To hell with him," he echoed softly.

16 September
My home, Amsterdam

Short flashes of Amsterdam shot by through the window as Luis sat next to me in the metro, taking me south back to the apartment. He was talking nonstop about tiles, kitchenettes, extra bathrooms, minifreezers. It was an unexpected change— this morning I woke up in the Student Hotel with my identity smashed to pieces, and I had planned to spend my day as I had spent my last days: diving deep into self-pity.

Every time the metro went through an underground section, I saw my reflection in the window. My tiredness had caused a certain dissociation, and I could see myself as if I were looking at someone else. I saw a tall, skinny man on a blue plastic metro chair, a man with tired eyes, a pretentious scarf, and a white baseball cap, who was sitting next to a broad-shouldered man in a white Armani sweater with a gold chain and a black eye.

What a combination.

My baseball cap said ARMANI. *Luis had given it to me because he said the* POUR DECISIONS *cap looked ridiculous. I sort of felt the same about the Armani, but he had looked so pleased when I put it on.*

'Now', he had said, 'we really are like brothers'.

Luis, we are not brothers, we are opposites, I immediately thought, but I did not say it. My previous conviction that we were completely different people had disappeared. I knew less about myself than I ever did before. In that moment in the metro, I felt like I could become anything. A fisherman. A tango dancer. A psychic.

All my life I had spent in academia, tracing the roots of words and finding their origins. Trying to make everything connect and make sense. I forgot that words in the end were just the tools of stupid humans and their stupid needs. Guttural noises that turned into front mouth sounds, evolved just to be able to say, 'Give me that stick, I want to hit someone over the head with it'.

What am I trying to say? I am realising I used to be so confident that there was something underneath everything, some beautiful belonging, some reason that would make everything make sense. But it is not true. Creation just moves forward, like a little river finding its way. Just like Luis's lawyer said at the mediation: 'We can go left, we can go right, nothing is set in stone'.

For me, it looks like I am going to live my life as a failed academic who was born for no reason, lived in random places, then ended up with a flatmate in Amsterdam who does two hundred sit-ups a day.

Who is going to love me now? I thought, and I must have asked this out loud, because Luis, the simplistic Luis, said, 'I will love you. Hadi is a little difficult, but I am sure he will like you'.

'Not you!' I wanted to scream, but instead I started laughing. Luis started laughing too.

And I don't know exactly what it was that was funny, but it was all so silly to me that I could not stop laughing. The lady across from us in the metro glanced at me, a little smile playing over her face. The two boys behind us started laughing too. I don't know if they understood what was funny, but they laughed, and there was a relief in it. We all felt it. Maybe it was something about us, all going somewhere, all trying to do something, and, in the meantime, being so ridiculous. Or maybe we just laughed for the fun of it. It does not matter. Luis and I stayed in this strange, jolly mood as we exited the metro. He kept on talking about tiles we could buy, marble tiles, and how we could tile the entire apartment, making little kitchens and living in the clouds and the trees. I just laughed, I could not stop anymore.

At the apartment Luis made me a sandwich. He let me have his bedroom, and he rolled his television in there, placing it across from the bed. Together we sat on his bed and watched a documentary about the Mars landing on this giant television. We quietly sat there as a little cart roamed a planet so much worse than ours, trying to figure out what is going on there and if we can live there, so we can continue to mess it up over here. It was beautiful.

Now I am sitting in Luis's bed, in his bedroom. My bedroom, as he puts it. He just went to work. And I . . . I feel happy. I am aware some relief around the Marina situation must be part of my euphoria, and sleep deprivation has affected me too, but I feel like a portal has opened to another world where I simply don't care about things that used to bother me. Who am I? Who are you? What is mine? What is yours? Who cares? I don't want any more worries. At the moment I should want to lay my head down and be happy. I just simply can't recall why I should not just be happy like this.

Tiles and Mirrors

Luis woke up on the air bed in the living room, which was now his bedroom. His only room. It was light outside, the sun shone into the living room, which meant it was after twelve o'clock. Luis sat up in the bed. It had been a long time since he'd slept so well. He thought of the day before, how he had brought William back to the apartment, put him in bed; how he had wished him good night before going to work.

"I've put clean sheets on the bed," Luis had said, as he watched as William got under the covers, wearing Luis's white Armani sweater. His shoulders looked even skinnier when he was wearing Luis's clothes. A warm feeling had gone through Luis's body as he watched William in his bed. He thought of the first night he'd had this man in his apartment. That strange, tall man, walking over his clean carpet with his long dripping coat.

William took the blankets and pulled them higher up to his chin. "You've got a good bed," he had said to Luis.

"Yes," Luis had said. "You can have it."

William stuck out his left arm from under the blanket and switched off the light by the bed. He had done it without looking where the switch was, as if he did that every day, every night.

It had been very strange to see William's outline in the bed, in the Armani sweater, as if Luis were looking at a very long, skinny version of himself in his bed. It was like a dream where you look in the mirror and you've turned into someone else.

Luis got up from the air bed in the living room and splashed water on his face over the sink. He felt clear and rested. Today he could start planning a small kitchen in the bedroom, with a little fridge and a kettle and an electric hob, so he and William each had their own space to cook, and they only had to share the bathroom. He could install it for William; he had seen a kitchenette in the Bruijn Keukens brochure a while back, glossy white with a black granite counter. He could make two sinks in the bathroom, one for each. The bill they would split; even though it would be mostly work on William's side of the apartment, they would split it.

William would have to get used to taking his shoes off in the apartment, but Luis would adjust too, he would not go into William's room if there was no answer to his knock, he would make shelves in there for his books and documents. And if William insisted on having no carpet in his room, maybe they could agree on marble tiles for the floor. The only thing Luis refused to have were those bare floorboards William liked so much. But they would discuss it, they would find a way.

Luis walked into the hallway and knocked on the door of his bedroom. William's bedroom, he corrected himself in his mind. "I'm sorry," he said to the door. "I want to ask you something. Do you prefer tiles or carpet?"

There was no reply.

"We can tile the floor," Luis said through the door. "I saw a little kitchenette for you, with a marble worktop. Maybe if we also do marble on the floor . . ."

No reply. Maybe William was still sleeping. He seemed a bit exhausted.

"William," Luis said, knocking again. "Are you awake?"

No reply.

"William," Luis said to door. "Are you sleeping? I want to ask you about floors."

He softly opened the door. The bed was empty and unmade, there was no one in the room. Luis found a note on the bed, addressed to him.

"I have a father," it began.

I have a father.

I woke up very early in the morning to a text message from Estelle giving me the news. She had received the court's decision in the post a few days before, and she had already set in motion the estate claim. 'I have been trying to call you to tell you: you are officially the son of Edward Hond', she wrote, 'with congratulations from the judge'.

I told Estelle I was upstairs and asked if I could stop by her place. Luis had given me a copy of the key the night before, so I could now leave and enter the apartment when I wished.

Estelle gave me the letter from the court and immediately started mapping out the steps I should take to claim the apartment.

But all I could do was stare at the letter from the judge. It was as if someone had handed me a note that said: 'You exist'. I thought of myself as a child at school, when the teacher was making rounds in the classroom, asking everyone 'What does your father do?'

'I don't have a father', I had said in a voice without sound.

'Everyone has a father', the teacher had explained to the class. 'But some children do not know who their father is. And that is fine'.

But it was not fine. The silence in the classroom made it clear it was not fine to not know who your father is. Even Martin Simons sat up a little bit more straight after my confession, while he had just told the class his father was nothing, he was on disability benefits.

But now I knew who my father was. Edward Hond. The judge had said the evidence was 'sufficient'.

Estelle finally saw my shaking hands holding the letter and stopped her legal rambling.

'You must feel so proud', she said. 'Or relieved? Actually, I have no idea what you feel'.

And in that moment, I decided to tell Estelle the entire truth. Sitting at her living room table, with my head down, I told her everything. The diary I found, the words Luis's mother had written about my father, his awful deeds, how I attacked Luis, how Marina's head had hit the bedpost, her crying, the tainted legacy, Luis's epiphany and his proposal to share—all of it.

Estelle's first response to my story was to ask if I could please take Luis's coloured ceiling lights down, seeing that I was in the front room now.

With pain in my stomach, I realised she must not have understood the importance of what I was telling her and told the story once again: the diary, the sexual abuse of Luis's mother and all the embarrassing details, the way I had lashed out at Luis, Marina's jumping on my back and scratching me, the fall, her bleeding nose, my now distorted sense of identity.

Estelle's response surprised me. She asked if I got a hepatitis B shot.

'Hepatitis?' I asked.

'Or A or C or whatever it is called', she said. 'I heard of a policeman getting hepatitis from a homeless man'.

When I said I was extremely ashamed of what my father had done and felt emotionally torn now that he was finally confirmed to be my father, confused about what I should do about Luis and the apartment, Estelle finally seemed to get it. She told me very firmly to take a step back and look at the bigger picture. 'You found out that Luis had been lying, hiding the fact that he knew she never owned the apartment. You find all kinds of things his mother has written about your father while he claimed he never heard of the man? Isn't it natural for you to lose your composure at some point?' She shook her head. 'And what Luis's mother says your father did? It's really horrible, of course, you know. On the other hand, men do those things all the time. They think it's mutual, they think the other one is enjoying it. Men think they are so attractive all the time, even when they are much older and fatter, they think they are attractive still. Girls need to keep that in mind. Especially when they throw themselves at someone, like Luis's mother did. What else was he supposed to think? Are we supposed to blame your father for believing he could be loved still? Do you blame him for that?'

'Well', I said. I shook my head. It wasn't sure what to say to that. 'I don't know if it was about love', I said finally. 'And she was very young'.

'First of all, we only have her account', Estelle said. 'It was different times then. Second, she was pregnant, so she knew what men were like. All women know what men are like'. She was quiet for a moment. 'Of course, they surprise us sometimes. But then you look back, and you think, you know, Why did I even get in that situation? I should not have been there in the first place'. Estelle looked out the window and crossed her arms over her body. 'Of course, if you have to be somewhere for work, it's difficult. Sometimes you can avoid it with jokes, or you make sure someone else is in the room with you . . . You start wearing really boring

clothes, but then you are told you are not presenting yourself well. And then you realise you can also get harassed when you wear a really big winter coat, you know, that night when you were wearing layers of scarves and sweaters and suddenly you find yourself dealing with this guy at a bus stop . . . You just realise you can't fight it. All you can do is use it to your advantage, walk the line, get out of there when it gets dangerous. And then at home, you can rest. You can put on a onesie and take off your makeup. That's how it is'. Estelle was quiet for several minutes. Then she shook her head firmly. 'It is not your problem anyway. You are the rightful owner of the apartment, and this needs to be legally settled. And I think the court will decide in your favour'.

'Luis wants to share it and ignore the legal side', I said in a weak voice. 'He wants to invent a new way of living'. As I said it, I heard how ridiculous it sounded.

'Of course he wants to share it now', Estelle said. 'It's either half for him or nothing. Do you really want to rob yourself of your own life? You know sharing is not going to work. What if you want to start a family? What if you want to move somewhere else? Have you thought of that? In our society, the home is the sanctuary. The place where you are safe. You must fight to have that place, not give it way'.

I hadn't thought of that. I had tried very hard not to think about anything ever since the past night, which was my first glimpse of happiness in a long time.

'Was there anything in that diary about the inheritance?' Estelle asked.

*I nodded. 'There is a mention that he retracted the promise',
I said.*

*'That's great', Estelle said. 'That means she could not have
seen herself as the owner, and she was not there in good faith. So,
the next step is to declare your father missing and set in motion a
suspicion of death trial as next of kin. Then you can claim your
inheritance. The court will decide in your favour'.*

'But is it right . . .' I started.

*'That's what the law is for', Estelle said. 'To decide what is
right. If I have to check a contract for a company that makes land
mines, I cannot start wondering if it's right. If it is all right by
the law, then I trust it is all right, that is my point of reference.
We can't start thinking about every little thing as individuals.
We would not be able to leave the house anymore. We would not
be able to do anything in this society'.*

I nodded. The situation made me nauseated.

*'You can forget about it now', Estelle said. 'Luis's idea to just
keep it all in your father's name and carry on is simply ridiculous. I hope you understand that. We have enough to make
our case'.*

*And I did. For a moment, it sounded good, but it's not the
way things work. I hope Luis will understand somehow, when he
finds my note. I am writing this at Estelle's place, I am staying
here until Luis leaves for work tonight. It feels terrible to let him
down, even though Estelle says I should not call it that. When
Luis was still hostile it was easier to stand up for my inheritance,
but it's hard to do it to someone who calls me 'my brother'. Yesterday I found myself smiling as I heard Luis whistle along to 'Last*

Christmas' as he got ready for work. It's strange, how the body reacts to what it perceives as joy and safety.

Esperar

Dear Luis,

I have a father. My paternity case is finalised. I just heard the news from Estelle. The judge has agreed Edward Hond is my father. Estelle has immediately set in motion a suspicion of death trial. When my father is declared deceased, I can claim my child's portion under inheritance law. Meaning: this apartment. As your lawyer will inform you, it is your right to file a counterclaim. Then the law can decide for us what is just, instead of just doing what we want without it being properly arranged. Your plan was kind, and I will always remember it. But I have decided it is not just. It is better to communicate through our lawyers from now on. I shall make an effort not to be in your way.

With sadness,
William

This was the letter Luis had found when he opened the door to William's bedroom.

The court case was going to take place on January 12, at the Amsterdam District Court on the Parnassusweg. Mrs. Adelman had explained it all to Luis on the phone when he called her. William had his paternity approved, his father had been declared deceased, and he was claiming his inheritance. The entire estate of E. Hond—which was only the apartment because the rest was missing—would be transferred to William, unless someone filed a counterclaim.

Mrs. Adelman filed this claim for Luis. She encouraged him to stay in the apartment and not interact with William Rose.

This was easy for Luis because he never saw him. Sometimes he would hear very quietly a door open in the morning when he was still in bed and footsteps going down the stairs. Sometimes when he came back from work late at night he found a light shining from underneath William's bedroom door.

"I could have told you," Hadi said to Luis. "The plan was ridiculous. Don't complain about it because it is all your own fault from the start."

Luis did not complain. He was feeling strangely neutral about it. He had done what he wanted to do, to offer to share it. And he still wanted to share it. But if William did not want to, there was nothing to be done. "The most important thing is that I feel good about what I do," Luis said to Hadi. "Marina has taught me that."

"When you become homeless you might find that is not the most important," Hadi said. "But I am glad you feel good."

And it was true. Sometimes when he walked home from work and made fresh footsteps in the snow that fell in the night, he surprised himself by smiling, or when he was in the shower, a song came up from his throat. One night, when he encountered William on the staircase as he went up, Luis found himself cheerfully saying, "Oh, hello, William," before he realized it. William said nothing in response, just rushed quickly past him down the steps.

During the days before the court case, Mrs. Adelman made Luis sign papers and she left him voice mail messages like: "Good news, we have filed our reply. We are going for adverse possession, under the act of good faith." Weeks later there was another voice mail: "Good news, we have registered our witnesses."

When Luis went to his lawyer's office to discuss the case, she was more fired up than he was. "You still stand a chance. Your mother kept her side of the promise, she should get something in return," she said while walking circles around her little glass table. "This case is important: it's not simply about the validity of a deathbed promise, but it's about the injustice of inheritance. The endless passing on of wealth to family members. The root of inequality. It blocks the human development to make each generation strong enough to stand on its own, and the inequality it creates instills a fear of others in those who have more. And this works against the human desire to share with those who have less."

The case had even inspired her to start working on a new chapter of her unpublished "Property in Space" manuscript. It was called "Inheritance: The Root of Inequality."

"I feel optimistic," Mrs. Adelman said.

She did not look optimistic, but she did look energetic. She was waving her hands as she talked, pointing at papers and raising her voice. She had found Mrs. Barneveld willing to sign a witness statement, and she had convinced her to come to the court to testify. She collected all the evidence of Luis's city tax payments over the years and uploaded the relevant pages of his mother's cleaning diary to their file.

She also sent Luis invoice after invoice, and Luis's extra shifts at the Bagel Shop were barely enough to keep up with it. Looking at his possessions gave him an empty, nauseated feeling, the same feeling he had when he'd looked down at the dark stain in the wooden floorboards in the bedroom, before he put the carpet down. This was a period of waiting.

Esperar, Marina's voice whispered inside Luis's head. She once told him it meant "hoping" and "waiting" at the same time. It was strange that more than anything else, Marina was on his mind. He had spent some time looking for her. Hadi knew where she used to live with her friend, but there were three Polish men living there now. They did not know Marina, and they did not know where she had gone.

The Court Case

On the day of the court case, Luis put on Hadi's white linen suit. He trimmed his beard. The case was at nine o'clock, and it was still dark when he walked out his front door. It was cold too, as it was winter now. The wind blew straight through that linen suit. The poplar tree in front of the house had lost its leaves.

His lawyer was already waiting for Luis when he got off the tram in front of the courthouse. He looked at lady justice standing there, a blindfold over her eyes, a scale in her hand. "Sure, put it on the women," he heard Marina say in his head.

"You look terrible," Mrs. Adelman said, as they walked to the courthouse. She looked tidy, almost like a real lawyer, with sleek hair and a jacket. It was just the starry space pin on her chest that made her stand out. "I told you to wear a proper suit, the judge looks at that. White linen is for the beach club."

They both emptied their pockets at the entrance of the courthouse and walked through the body scanner. When Luis saw himself in the mirrored elevator doors, his reflection shocked him. He looked just like he used to when he lived in Stompetoren. The hair, the beard, the wrinkled clothes. "You simply can't make a silk purse out of a sow's ear," Mr. Hond had said. It was true. At least he got to pretend for a while.

"Marina wanted me to ask you to stop calling," Mrs. Adelman said.

"Marina? Is she all right?"

"She is doing great," Mrs. Adelman said. "She wants to go back to Brazil to finish her master's in biology. She is going to set up a community near Minas Gerais."

"Brazil?" Luis asked.

"Yes," Mrs. Adelman said. "Could you stop calling her?"

"Yes," Luis said. He wanted to add, "Tell her I am sorry," but he remembered she was fed up with apologies. "Please tell her," he said to Mrs. Adelman, "Luis will stop calling and he says thank you to her."

At that moment Luis saw William and Estelle at the end of the hallway, entering another elevator. Mrs. Adelman patted him on the shoulder. "Don't worry about them. We're going for the win."

"I don't want to win," Luis said. "I told him I think we both deserve half of the apartment."

"Today is not about deserving," she said impatiently. "Today is about inheritance law."

When Luis and Mrs. Adelman came out of the elevator, William and Estelle were already seated on the plastic chairs in the waiting area. Luis and Mrs. Adelman sat down on the opposite end of the room. Now and then a new case name was called out. Across from Luis sat two elderly women with stacks of papers on their laps. They looked nervous too. He wondered what kind of problem they could be having. "Conflicts, conflicts, conflicts," he remembered his lawyer had said during their first meeting.

"How do you do?" Mrs. Adelman said to Estelle and William when *Sol v. Rose* was called and all four of them entered through the high doors of the courtroom. The room reminded Luis of church: the high ceilings, the benches, the elevated chairs for the judges, the holy atmosphere. When his Dutch grandmother had died his mother had taken him to the ceremony in the church in Alkmaar. The pastor had praised her in a solemn voice. Luis's mother blew her nose loudly every time he said things like "kind" or "good heart."

Everyone stood up when the judge came in. She was seated on a high wooden stage in front of the courtroom. She had a friendly smile and dark circles under her eyes. The black gown with the white scarf looked similar to what Estelle and Mrs. Adelman had put on. It all looked like it was the start of a play, a comical play, Luis thought as he sat down next to his lawyer on one side of the room.

William and Estelle were sitting on the other side of the aisle, whispering to each other, while the judge summarized the case in a dry voice. Both lawyers made their opening statements. Luis looked at William while Estelle talked. William kept his eyes focused on the folders on his lap, the same folders full of documents that he had dragged into Luis's apartment on the first day. Folders full of clues and details vaguely related to his father.

He hangs on to those yellow folders like they're a life raft, Luis thought.

"The judge is asking you a question." Mrs. Adelman squeezed Luis's leg.

Luis looked up.

"Your mother, Marie Meeuwisse, worked for Mr. Hond, about three to four hours each week, over the course of twenty-eight months, between 1984 and 1986. We have a witness . . ." She looked through the papers. ". . . a Mrs. Barneveld, who has confirmed in writing she saw a woman named Marie visit the apartment regularly. We also have a key to the apartment with your mother's name on it and the words 'in gratitude.' We have been presented with a document signed by Edward Hond, promising her the apartment after his death, dated 1984. Finally, we have a diary, in which your mother describes her encounters with the deceased. The ink has been dated back to 1998, when your mother would have been thirty-one. You can confirm with one hundred percent certainty this is indeed your mother's diary that has been submitted, written by her and no one else?"

"Yes," Luis said. He added, "No one else uses the words 'wibble wabble.'"

"We hold that the apartment was a gift, made in contemplation of death," Mrs. Adelman explained. "We hold that he never officially retracted the promise. They simply had an argument. He did not ask for the key back, nor did he make another will. The services he required were delivered, as you may have read. Mrs. Meeuwisse paid a high prize for delivering these services, as you may also have read."

"The court cannot take the nature of these services into account in a civil case," the judge said. "Those details would belong in a criminal trial."

"It's not a detail," Luis said. "She tried to tell herself it was a detail. But if sharing an apartment is already so difficult, how difficult is it to share a body? How much is that worth?"

Luis turned to William, who was still bent over his papers. "You know me now. You know what happened to my mother. She paid the price, and I know you now. I know you deserved better than what you got. I don't like living there on my own anymore now, knowing what happened to you. Your father was as cruel to you as he was to my mother. It's not right for me to have it and for you to have nothing. Can you be at ease there if I get kicked out?"

William did not look up at Luis.

The judge sat back in her chair and shook her head impatiently. "Mr. Sol, we are here because you want to order the court to transfer the property to your name," the judge said. "I am trying to give you the opportunity to provide evidence that this would indeed be rightful. And now you are stating that it would not be rightful if the estate became your possession?"

"What my client is trying to say," Mrs. Adelman said, squeezing Luis's leg very hard, "is not that he believes his own claim is not rightful. It was more of a general political remark on the nature of possession. I believe Mr. Sol is simply expressing the view that whatever is decided, there will always be an injustice somewhere, historically. Most land was divided before there even were laws, by conquest. This property has been passed on through generations, creating a land where all land is taken, unequally and unlawfully divided, and equality is simply impossible. Therefore, my client is saying nothing is rightful, not even the promise made by the deceased was rightful, if looking at it from that angle. Nothing is rightful. What would be rightful is if everyone had access to a home, a home they could not be evicted from. If everyone—"

"Mrs. Adelman," the judge interrupted her with a sigh, "as you know, and as you should have told your client, we are here to follow the law, not to challenge it. And I want to hear from your client, not from you, the answer to this question. Do you think your mother believed, when she took over the bills and visited the apartment, that Mr. Hond had wanted her to live there?"

Luis cleared his throat. With a calm voice he said, "My mother had learned by then that Mr. Hond liked to promise things so people would do what he wanted. She learned that he did not care what would happen to her. Or him." He nodded at William. "I think he did not care at all what would happen to the apartment after he was gone."

At that moment exactly the door of the courtroom opened slowly. A beam of light fell on the courtroom floor. The judge looked up. Luis, Estelle, William, and Mrs. Adelman turned around in their seats, looking at the open door. It seemed that in that moment, everyone present expected to see Mr. Hond come in through the door, his skin tanned and wrinkled, perhaps wearing a straw hat. Old and crooked, but still strong, with piercing eyes.

For a moment, Luis actually really saw him, but it was just a figment of his imagination, like his mother's appearance at the top of the stairs had been a figment of his imagination. Mr. Hond wasn't there; he just existed in their minds now, and he would never come back to explain what he had done and why he created such a mess.

The doorway remained empty, and they all remained quiet and waiting, as if some kind of spell would be broken if someone said something. Then the usher poked his head around the door and said, "A lady has presented herself, but she is late. She is a witness in *Sol v. Rose*."

In the illuminated doorway Mrs. Barneveld appeared. Her grocery bag was hanging from her arm as always, with the garden shears poking out the top. "Dreadfully sorry," she said as she walked up to the judge's table. "They tried to keep me from bringing this into the building." She took her garden shears from her grocery bag.

"This is our witness," Mrs. Adelman said, "Mrs. Barneveld."

Mrs. Barneveld sat down in the seat behind Luis. And when it was her turn, Luis watched her climb up to the witness box. The court usher had given her a chair. Her eyes were shiny, and her movements were abrupt, emotional.

"Before we do the cross-examination," she asked the judge after her witness statement was read, "can I just say something else?"

"The witness is not allowed to comment on the case," the judge said. "Any additions to the witness statement must be lodged before trial and exchanged between parties. It is allowed to provide new evidence during trial only if it just became available."

Mrs. Barneveld nodded. "Yes, yes, there are a lot of procedures. Not unlike church, I think . . . walking back and forth, standing up, sitting down, don't question it . . ." She touched her hair and nodded at the court reporter. "You can write 'The witness has new evidence.'"

Mrs. Barneveld's Statement

"I have lived on Rooseveltlaan for so long . . . I remember when it was still called the Zuider Amstellaan. I remember when the Germans marched down our street. I watched the whole war with my little eyes, the Jewish neighbors disappearing, my mother walking around in the neighbor's fur coat after she was deported. The weight my mother lost in the winter, how she sent us out to ask the neighbors for food. My father risking his life to get us potatoes, but still smoking his cigarettes even though it cost us food stamps. I remember when the Canadian liberators came in on their tanks, one gave me a bar of chocolate in exchange for a kiss. That was my first kiss. I was ten. And I remember how the girls who had been dating the German soldiers were dragged out of their houses and people yelled and cheered while shaving their heads. My little eyes saw all of it.

"And I have learned three things.

"First of all, never rat anybody out. Their business is their business, I haven't seen a thing.

"Second, the worst people take the most action. And unless nice people also put in an effort and take risks to make it better, the worst people will win. Doing nothing is never good.

"And the third thing I learned was that there is nothing bigger than us, no God and no purpose, none of it. It is just a mess, and we need to make the best of it.

"So I try to live my life by what I have learned. I saw them come and go on Rooseveltlaan. That Edward Hond, he moved there just after the war, I think. Old money type. Always traveling to faraway places, always talking about how he had a chalet here and a house there, art dealings and charity dinners and so on. I did not pay much attention to him. I became the head of the ladies' department at a clothing store. Later, I also started the Park Committee while I was caring for my ailing mother, since I was the only one of my siblings without children. Maybe that's why I did not care for that period so much, the sixties and the seventies. All that wild stuff, the disco. I was just trying to keep my head up and my spine straight. Maybe I've been a little bit jealous of all that frivolous stuff they had and I did not. Well, I had nature. I've always had nature. Nature is honest, it is not hypocritical. A spider makes a web, a fly lands in it, struggles, and gets eaten. Everything is true to its nature, it grows and it dies."

The judge cleared her throat. "We don't have the entire day, Mrs. Barneveld. Could you tell us when you saw Marie Meeuwisse for the first time?"

Mrs. Barneveld smiled. "I will get to it. Thank you for your patience. Being on the Park Committee was important to me, is what I am trying to say. And that is why I did not like her."

She nodded at William.

"Not Marie, but Edward Hond's first woman. William's mother."

The sound of William moving his chair back echoed through the courtroom. "You knew her?" he asked. "You said you didn't remember anything about her."

Mrs. Barneveld nodded. "But I did. She was Edward Hond's young British girlfriend. Well, younger than him at least. Some horrid flower name, like Sunny Daisy or something. A nurse, apparently. A creature of the sixties, always talking of colors and vibrations. She only believed in good things. She insisted on joining the Park Committee, although she could not speak any Dutch and had no knowledge of plants. She promised her husband would make a large donation to the park, which allowed her to get away with all kinds of terrible ideas. 'Why not grow dahlias here?' she said. 'I sense the color pink could be strong in this corner.'

"'Those flowers don't grow here,' I tried to explain to her. Too much shade, the wrong soil, the wrong plants came before it. You have to start your garden from reality, not from a dream. But that was exactly what she did. With Edward too.

"The little flower patch became important to her. She was there every day, overwatering it, putting on too much manure. I even saw her singing to the soil as she poked the ground with her fingers, urging her dahlias to come up. My perception was that she was trying to find every excuse not to be in the apartment with the old Hond. The rows she had with him were well-known in the neighborhood. The way she screamed '*Ed-ward, Ed-ward*' when he had locked her out of the apartment again, everyone within a kilometer would hear that."

Mrs. Barneveld adjusted her hat.

"In any case, the dahlias wouldn't grow. She became pregnant and stopped coming. I was relieved for that. She then had a baby, a little boy. Willempje." She pointed at William. "That's what we called you then, Willempje." She shook her head. "He was a scared child. Always crying, whining. Taking after his mother. She was not looking so happy either. But I did not stick my nose in her business. We would nod at each other in the supermarket, that was it. After a few years, I ran into her by the flower patch. She was frantically digging up the dahlia tubers, the bulbs.

"I said to her, 'They were ruined by winter, sweetheart. You should have gotten them out before the frost. But they will never grow here anyway. Sometimes you try as hard as you possibly can, but that is no guarantee that it will succeed. Sometimes it just won't grow.'

"When she looked up I saw that her eyes were red from crying. She looked thin, tired. Something about her was different.

"'None of it is your fault,' I said firmly to her. 'He is an unpleasant man.'

"She broke down completely. She started talking about her relationship, Hond's unpredictable behavior, his charity that was not so charitable, the antique trade, the outbursts he had when she asked questions.

"'And to William he is not . . .' she whispered.

"'Kind?' I asked.

"I remember she just shook her head quietly. 'I worry that if he grows up with a father like that, he will become like him,' she said.

"And we had a conversation, it was a very fast conversation. Could she get to her passport? How much money did she have?

Was there a day when he was away when she could leave? Could she pack and hide a bag?

"She left just a week later. I was relieved." Mrs. Barneveld sighed. "I thought, well, that was that. Everything carried on as usual in our neighborhood. People came and went. Hond disappeared for a few years and came back. Went to Cyprus during the Turkish invasion, I believe, and he told some neighbors his lung disease was caused by inhaling smoke when the northern shore was bombed." She shook her head. "Then the second girl came along." She pointed at Luis. "His mother. It was 1984, I think. She was very naive. A child, really. I tried to stop her from going to his apartment with him, but she would not have any of it. Every Sunday she came to his apartment, and she stayed there for hours. It concerned me, especially when I saw that belly growing. When the baby was born, I was relieved, because she had been visiting Hond for only five months. It couldn't be his." Her voice went soft. "I stopped paying attention, until I saw her sitting on the park bench one day with the baby, breastfeeding him. There was something defeated in the way she held her shoulders, the way she held her head. And then I remembered that woman, how she had sat on the same bench, the same defeated look. So, against my principles, I started to do a little digging into Edward Hond's background, just to be prepared."

Mrs. Barneveld took the garden shears from the bag and placed them on the bench in front of her.

"The snowstorm was in the middle of the week. That's why I was surprised to see her. She always came on a Sunday. I was in the park, fetching my garden shears. I had forgotten them, and I remembered them when it started snowing. Those things rust very easily. And that's when I saw her walk down the street. Her jacket and her hair were covered in snow, and she was holding the child and dragging along the stroller. Why would anyone take a child outside in this weather? I wondered. I watched her go up the steps of number 354, and when I came closer, I saw she'd forgotten to close the front door. She had parked the stroller at the bottom of the stairs, with the boy strapped inside. A few minutes went by as I stood there, in the snowstorm, looking at the child in the stroller in the hallway. I wasn't sure what to do. Of course I wanted to stay out of it, but I worried about the little boy sitting there unattended, at the top of those stone steps. Then I heard loud voices coming from the second floor.

"'I release you from your obligation and retract my promise,' I heard him say. His voice was loud and harsh. 'Who is going to believe you?' Then I heard screaming. I took the boy from the stroller, ran upstairs, and saw that room. She was just . . . she was standing in the middle of the room, her hand covered in blood, her eyes completely wild. He was as cold as a crocodile. Asked me to call the police. I tended to her first, making sure she got out with the little one, then I turned to him. I remember I looked at him for a long time.

"'What did you do to her?' I asked.

"'Don't be ridiculous,' Hond said.

"He sounded arrogant, but I could tell he was scared. I wasn't like those naive girls he could bully with his low voice.

"'Go take care of that park of yours,' he said.

"'I will,' I said. 'I do it every day.' I took the garden shears out from under my coat. 'Have you ever used one of these? They are very sharp. I can cut through very thick branches. You'd be amazed to see how easy they fall off.'

"To demonstrate, I took a painting from the wall—a black canvas, I believe—put it between the blades of the shears, and snapped it in two.

"Hond said nothing. He did not threaten to call the police, and I knew he wouldn't.

"'All those beautiful artworks and antiques you have,' I said. 'It's hard to sell those in a respectable way, isn't it, if they weren't acquired in a respectable way. One might even start a foundation and take donations, instead of payments for the art.'

"He muttered something, that I did not know what I was talking about.

"'I called Tax and Customs some time ago,' I told him. 'They asked me to name you. There's a committee in The Hague that has a long list of artworks that changed ownership during the war. And that's only in the Netherlands. In Russia they are doing the same thing. In Spain. In Greece. Of course, I don't like to rat people out. That is my rule. But if I ever see another woman or girl leaving your home, I might break my rule.'" Mrs. Barneveld shook her head. "He left soon after, like a dog in the night, the wheels of his suitcase rattling over the stones. Coward, he was. For a long time I wondered if I did the right thing. And I think I did not. I think I should have reported him."

Suddenly the noise of a chair being pushed back sounded through the courtroom.

"This is not fair," William said, standing up. "My father is not here to defend himself."

"It's not relevant to the case," Estelle said to him.

"Sit down, please," the judge said. "This witness statement is relevant. Mrs. Barneveld, you state that you heard Edward Hond say he retracted his promise?"

"Yes," Mrs. Barneveld said.

"And you state that he wasn't dying when you confronted him in 1986?"

"Oh no," Mrs. Barneveld said. "To the contrary. He seemed to be getting younger, if anything. He simply left. The apartment was empty for a year, then another year. Sometimes I would see a light switch on in there, and someone seemed to be inside for an hour. I thought maybe some rich person had bought it as a pied-à-terre. They do that. All the bills seemed to be paid."

She nodded at Luis. "Then, about eight years ago, Luis arrived. I recognized him straightaway: the square face, the eyes too close to each other, the red cheeks. He walked a bit like her, too fast, too close to the wall. He stuck his key in the lock, and a little later I saw a light in the apartment upstairs. He always greeted me nicely, never littered in the park. At least something turned out right, I thought. It seemed like a good ending, until he arrived." She pointed at William. "That dog is back, was my first thought when I saw him. He looked just like him, the same way his head cocked slightly to the side when he walks, the arms dangling alongside the body. But I knew it could not be him. Edward Hond, I mean. It was thirty years ago!"

"I look like him?" William asked in a voice that sounded like a child's.

"You look just like him," Mrs. Barneveld said. "And I soon realized you were Willempje. But I never wanted to tell you anything about your father because you spoke so highly of him. A philanthropist, an intellectual. Why would I destroy that? My role was played out, I thought, it was in the past. You tell them either everything or nothing at all. But when I saw Marina sitting on the bench in the park with her nosebleed that early morning, I realized nothing was in the past. It is like the garden. You need to know what has grown there before you can plant something new. Old roots need to be unearthed, the soil needs to be weeded and plowed, otherwise you don't know what will grow." She leaned over toward the court reporter. "Write down that I think they should inherit the apartment together. And then they should sell it together. Go someplace else."

The judge took off her glasses. She rubbed her eyes and then said, "Thank you for your statement, Mrs. Barneveld," with a sigh. She put her glasses back on. "We will now take a break. I want to convey to the plaintiff that the gift of the apartment was made on a condition: a weekly visit until death. Since Edward Hond left, this condition could not have been met. Also, I would like to convey that the apartment was not taken over in 'good faith' if the mother of the plaintiff knew the promise was retracted. For adverse possession to apply, the apartment has to be inhabited in good faith for ten years. Or in bad faith for twenty years. These terms have not been met. I strongly advise both parties to discuss an alternative solution or settlement before we proceed with this case."

"Can we please have a glass of water here?" Estelle's voice cut through the courtroom. "My client is not feeling well."

All heads turned toward William, who was sitting in his chair with his head leaned back, looking very pale. His hands had finally let go of the yellow folders, Luis noticed.

Estelle placed a glass of water in his hand and started talking to him in a low voice. "It's a good thing, what Barneveld said. You are winning the case."

"I don't think we should go for a settlement," Mrs. Adelman said to Luis. "We will get them in the next case. They have to bring eviction procedures against you. That means there will be another judge looking at the case. This time we will emphasize the adverse possession route. You have lived there for nearly ten years, you've paid taxes, you've refurbished the place. You have rights. They know that."

"Another case?" Luis asked.

"They can't just throw you out. Could buy you another six to ten months. And it is very interesting for me to pursue this case."

"I don't want that," Luis said. "I am the one who is in the middle of it; for you it is just interesting." Then he asked, even though he already knew the answer, "Did we lose?"

"Yes," the lawyer said. "Not officially yet. But, yes, we probably lost. The judge was just letting us know we were going to lose, urging us to settle with them during the break. My advice is not to settle. We can take it to the High Council, of course; it could be interesting. I mean fascinating. Important."

"No," Luis said. He walked up to William, who was sitting in one of the plastic chairs. He still looked very pale.

"Congratulations," Luis said.

William did not look up.

"I will need some time to get out of the apartment," Luis said. "And I want money for all the improvements I made."

William did not respond, but Estelle stood up and extended her hand. "Very clever, Luis," she said, nodding. "No more court cases, no more legal hassle. An amicable solution. William will very generously give you one month and two thousand euro."

"I asked William," Luis said.

"William is my client and he agrees," Estelle said.

William did not look up, but he nodded. "I want this to be done."

"Would you like to sign straightaway?" Estelle took a document from her bag. "I already prepared something."

"Luis," Mrs. Adelman said, putting her hand on his shoulder, "I strongly advise you to at least let me negotiate for you. It will buy you time and I can negotiate a payment for you. My invoice will be at least two thousand euro."

"If we let the court decide, the judge will make you pay for legal fees too," Estelle said to Luis, writing some things down on the contract. "This is the best solution for you. You refrain from taking this to the High Council, you refrain from trying to claim any further rights to the apartment or the estate. You will leave in a month."

Luis nodded. He signed the paper and watched William put down his signature too, the same loopy *a* as his father's.

Luis Returns

At the station Luis looked up at the signs above the platforms: DEN HELDER, NIJMEGEN, ROTTERDAM, BRUSSELS, HAMBURG, PARIS.

He thought of what Marina had said. "The world is big. There are endless possibilities."

Thirty minutes later Luis sat in the train to Alkmaar. Outside the window Amsterdam's skyline was disappearing in the distance.

Most of his possessions he had given to Hadi; the rest he had sold.

He had been staying on Hadi's sofa for the past few weeks.

"You can stay longer if you want," Hadi had said. "I told you."

"I know," Luis said.

"I mean it," Hadi said. "You can stay. We'll find you another place. Somewhere close by."

"How can I afford it?" Luis said. The money he made at the Bagel Shop was enough to pay for just a room in Amsterdam. It seemed like a better idea to do what Mrs. Barneveld had said. A new start. Go somewhere else.

The nursing home in Stompetoren was on the corner of the village square. Luis remembered it from when he was young, the elderly sitting in rows on chairs in the garden. Some of them were knitting, some of them were falling asleep, some of them waved to the children coming out of school.

On his father's floor the walls were painted yellow. There was yellow tarpaulins on the floor. The familiar small, dark eyes stared at him from the white bed.

"What do you want?" his father said when he saw Luis standing on the threshold.

Luis said nothing. He looked at his father. A nurse came in and took his father out of the bed and put him in a wheelchair, just like Luis had done for him for so many years.

"Can he drink here?" Luis asked the nurse.

"He gets two beers every day," he said. "But he has lost interest in alcohol. They forget about it, after a while."

"I get one cigarette," his father said. "Which I did not get yet, by the way."

"You did get it, Dave," the nurse said. "You did get it."

His father turned his wheelchair to the window, looking out. "Shitty weather," he said, "as usual."

"Yes," Luis said.

In the hallway the nurse walked up to him. "He doesn't recognize you, but he remembers you," he said. "He talks about you. That his son is a big shot in Amsterdam. That you made your own way, that you escaped Stompetoren."

"Yeah," Luis said.

He waited by the bus stop. The bus to his old home on the dike took fifteen minutes. When he passed Raat's house, he saw the roof of his childhood cottage sticking out above the hedges.

The cottage looked the same as it did before, except that the door and windowpanes had been repainted in a darker blue. The roof of the old barn had collapsed completely.

From the road, Luis looked at the people sitting inside his old home.

There was a yellow light coming from a shaded lamp on the kitchen table. A woman stood with her back to the window, washing her hands. Another woman was closing the curtains in the TV room, where the light flickered as it had always done. He wondered who they were. He wondered what it looked like on the inside now, what his bedroom looked like.

Do I belong here? Luis wondered. The flat horizon—a long line interrupted only now and then by a tree or a farm—that line was etched in his memory.

"Luis?"

Behind Luis stood Louise-Lotte Raat in a big winter coat and slippers. Her silhouette was just like her mother's now. "I thought it was you! Did you come back to see your old place once more?"

Luis nodded.

"You look good," Louise-Lotte said. "We never saw you anymore after you moved out. I often wondered, How is Luis doing? Not everyone stays, of course. And I was happy for you that you left, into the big wide world. Your parents were very proud."

"Proud?"

"Well . . ." Louise-Lotte turned a little red in the light of the streetlamp. "Your mother did not talk much, of course. But your father told everyone you were a real Sol. 'They explore the world,' he said. He was really proud. And in a way, it was good for him that he had to step up and care for your mother. He had to get his act together. And he did, to a certain extent."

"He got his act together," Luis echoed.

"Yes," Louise-Lotte said. "To a certain extent. And your mother let him. They seemed truly happy, those final years. I was so pleased she found a friend in Anna after you left."

"Anna Beemster?"

"I think they really reconnected in your mother's last years, you know, both having that experience of the kids leaving the nest," Louise-Lotte said, making his mother's life sound totally normal and ordinary. "Anna even spoke at her cremation service."

"I wasn't there," Luis said softly.

Louise-Lotte said nothing for a moment. Then she said, "Well, you were there for all that time before. And we saw that."

Luis nodded at his old home. "Do you know the people who live there now?"

"No," Louise-Lotte said. "They haven't actually introduced themselves."

Together they stared at the two silhouettes in the living room.

"I was just saying to Ma the other day, I don't know what to think of them. How did they even get it? Dave was in no state to sell it."

The wind picked up; the smell of a burning muck heap was blown toward them. Luis pulled at his collar. The two women in his old home sat down at the dinner table. A child's bike was leaning against the wall. For a second he pictured himself ringing the doorbell, asking to have a look around his childhood home.

He thought of what Marina had said: "There is no belonging . . . There is only temporary connections we make, with a place, with another person. Short or long. Everything is always changing, and you can go in all directions."

5 April
My home, Amsterdam

And now I have the apartment, it is mine.

Strangely, I don't feel anything. The change inside of me that I always hoped for did not happen. I am still myself, and I am still alone. The apartment is now empty. Luis has taken all his hideous furniture, the carpet, and the curtains. Even though it looks better than before, I still need to make improvements, make it my home, but there is no energy left in me as of late.

When I first started fighting to get my property, I felt so strong, so determined. I was William, the son of the philanthropist Edward Hond, a man who belonged here, a man who would not move an inch. Now I am still William, the son of Edward Hond, but I do not like what that means.

Having to accept my father was a different man from who I wanted him to be was a great disappointment, which I feel is partially to blame for my state. I believed I could find my worth in his worth, and I made such a strong connection between the two of us that I now feel his bad actions are connected to me too.

Maybe they are. If I accept his gains, like his apartment, should I also accept his debt?

Estelle has moved away. She helped me take down Luis's tacky ambient colour lamps that shone on the trees and the marble name plate on the door. Then she repainted the shared hallway and sold her apartment. She wanted something bigger for herself, she said. The home is the sanctuary, after all. The new owners of her apartment have stopped by. I found out Estelle had told them a very quiet Oxford professor lived in the upstairs apartment, William Hond, who may even be a baron.

Of course I told them the truth: I lost my job and am currently doing online tutoring. I go by William Rose still. That is who I am. There is no title, no story, no shoulders of past generations to stand on, no expansion. Most days I feel like nothing more than a body with a lot of thoughts.

Yesterday I was standing in the living room, looking up at the sky. It was clear night, and I could see all the little stars above us. More than ever, I felt like a wandering, meaningless entity on a wandering planet in an immeasurable universe, as Paulina always warned me I was. It's the truth, the closest I can get to the truth. But it is a slippery existence when one doesn't have any stories to live in.

I often think of Luis. How is he feeling, what is he doing, where is he now? I think of the evening we spent together, watching the documentary. The way we laughed, how comfortably we sat together. It is funny, but I realise I'd grown used to his presence. Somehow, to have my opposite so close to me, made me feel stronger about who I am. Now I sit in the one room, I sit in the other room.

Of course, it is still important that I have succeeded. I have to remind myself I am in my rightful home and it is just. But sometimes it strikes me as odd, how much this apartment was in the centre of my mind before, how far I went to protect my possession of it.

Other times, I wake up at night and I am scared. I have this strange feeling that Luis is near, that he is sitting in the garden shed below, waiting for me to leave the apartment. Sometimes I think I hear him throwing pebbles against the window, but it is just the sound of the branches from the poplar tree against the glass.

Sometimes I find myself thinking of what Luis said that night when he got me out of the hotel. 'You wanted to use your history like a blanket to comfort yourself, so you don't have to be your own person . . . But what if we can do better than our parents?'

I wonder how it would be if I had given Luis more money. Maybe helped him a little bit. I wonder how it would be if I tried to do a little bit of good, to balance out the injustices my father has done. And then I tell myself that for every place and every possession you can go back and find some injustice in how it came to belong to someone. Is it up to me to change that?